About the authors

Shreya and Siddhartha are the co-authors of *My Fantastic Failures.* The siblings are also the co-founders of their international fashion brands August and AIGHT which they retail online and at their flagship store Pret Castle.

Shreya is an IT professional with a decade of experience working in India, Australia and New Zealand. Presently she is busy expanding their business and devoting time to writing. When she finds time, she spends it in the scenic settings of nature. She loves eating finger chips on a beach. A hungry reader, she reads everything, even the fine print on the bill boards. An animal lover, she takes great satisfaction in working for animals. She lives in Auckland, New Zealand. A face that smiles in passport photos too is married to her soulmate Sapan.

Siddhartha is the Director at August Fashions and Pret Castle. Alumnus of NIFT, he holds a patent in green fashion. His work was invited by London Science Museum and has been considered one of the top nine fashion innovations across the globe. Recently a NASA scientist presented his work in a Silicon Valley conference. Sid has showcased August and AIGHT at India Fashion Week and Paris Ethical Fashion Week. His work is covered by Discovery 'Tree Hugger', FTV and leading forums in India and internationally. Beyond work, he plays guitar and keyboard. He is also an enthusiast lover of plants and animals. If you see money plants hanging out of a bulb or plants growing in coffee mugs, you can look for Sid around. The animal lover in him is available 24x7 for any animal in need. He lives in Greater Noida, India.

My Fantastic Failures

College courage. Dreams.
Entrepreneurship ...and a Relationship.

Shreya Upadhyaya

Siddhartha Upadhyaya

Srishti
PUBLISHERS & DISTRIBUTORS

Srishti Publishers & Distributors
N-16, C. R. Park
New Delhi 110 019
editorial@srishtipublishers.com

First published by
Srishti Publishers & Distributors in 2015

10 9 8 7 6 5 4 3 2 1

This is a work of fiction. Names, characters, places and incidents either are products of the author's imagination or are used fictitiously. Any resemblance to actual events, locales or persons, living or dead, is entirely coincidental.

Typeset by Eshu Graphic

Printed and bound in India

Dedicated to our parents

Dr J.S. Upadhyaya • Santosh Upadhyaya

They never cease to inspire. We hope someday we can also be kind, inspiring, humble and helpful like them and spread goodness around.

Acknowledgements

Thank you dear readers for giving us an opportunity to share our story with you. We are humbled. Many thanks to Srishti Publishers for giving us an opportunity to reach you all.

Heartfelt gratitude to our parents Dr J.S. Upadhyaya and Santosh Upadhyaya for making our lives worthwhile by being perfect parents, trainers and mentors. We are thankful to God for blessing us with this wonderful set of parents. It has been an honour to belong to them. We take pride to be known as their children.

We are forever thankful to Sapan. He is my husband and an elder brother to Sid. A very dear person in our lives, pillar of support and someone we fall back upon in times of crises. Also, thanks to him for his wonderful suggestions.

Always supportive family – Yogesh Sharma, Somlata Upadhyaya, Madhubala Upadhyaya, Ratnakar Swain, Rajalaxmi Swain, Madhusmitha Swain and all other dear family members.

Difficult to imagine life without you guys, who in your splendid individual ways have been very supportive always – B.D. Bhojwani, Sanjeev Jain, Rajeev Jain, Sandeep Tiwari, Devender Negi, Alok Priyadarshi, Sanjay Bhardwaj, Anuj Kumar, Virendra Singh Guddu, Rajendra Pal and Brijpal Singh.

Friends, who are like extended family – Puneet Pathak, Samit Kumar, Alok Kumar, Abhinav Gahlaut, Ravi Kumar, Manish Anand, Amit Kumar 'Bhoorang', Rahul Singh, Somanshu Kalra, Kavita Raheja, Anjali Sharma, Raman Khosla, Charu Khosla, Aarti Arora and Rajesh Arora.

Thanks to the students of IIT Roorkee, Saharanpur campus we continue to share our lives with. We respect your presence in our life and see you as a gift we have received from our father.

Thanks to the almighty for transforming our dream into reality. It feels like just yesterday that we were looking for a brand name. Merely a figment of imagination once, the name fought with other possible names to exist today. The name is 'Pret Castle'.

Thanks to our mentors, Paulo Coelho, Harivansh Rai Bachchan, Giorgio Armani, Dhirubhai Ambani and Richard Branson who shared their inspirational lives with their great work thus giving us an opportunity to get inspired. But how is it possible to have such mentors? We read books and made them a part of their life.

Your mentors can not reach you and make you part of their life; but you can have as many mentors and make all of them a part of your life.

Sid and I, individually also would like to express our heartfelt gratitude to each one of you without whom this book would not have been possible. Our sincere thanks to all you wonderful people.

Shreya –

- Akanksha Tyagi, Moitrayee Bhaduri, Sujoy Neogi for accepting to be the first readers of the manuscript and giving their valuable suggestions. My memories of Akanskha reading books dates twenty-one years back, when we were in class six. So when she said she liked the manuscript, Sid and I worked with double the speed to finalise it. Jeevan Gaikwad and Moitrayee Bhaduri – I was inspired by you both to write a book.

- Conway ma'am and Poonam ma'am for having faith in me since childhood. Rami aunty for constantly denying any help to me in writing my moral science answers in class one. She made life easy for her daughter by writing her answers but did larger benefit to me by setting me on a quest to write the best answers myself and discover my love for writing.

Siddhartha –

- Aneesh Mittal for fighting my high court case. Somlata Upadhyaya, my aunt to show me the way to take the case forward.
- NIFT for giving me a direction in life. All my friends and classmates from NIFT.
- A special thanks to those who said 'no' to me and made my life difficult over and over again. You have been a real source of inspiration.

And most importantly, we are grateful for all the failures that happened in our life. We are glad to share them with you for they became the reason that we could achieve our dreams. Thus the name.

Welcome to *My Fantastic Failures.*

About the Book

Do you know what does flying straight mean? It means if there is injustice – seek justice, if there is a dream – chase it, if there is a failure – step over it.

Who flew straight?

Well, many do and Sid too has flown straight all his life. He flew straight through the fashion world too. (Don't read it otherwise!)

This journey started when Sid went to study fashion technology at India's premier fashion college in Bangalore in 2004. Exceptionally intelligent and blessed with creativity, he came across as a humble boy who was in general respectful to all. This son of an IIT professor possessed infectious passion to inspire anyone to dream like him. "He will excel in whatever he decides to do", "He is a visionary", "It is rare to find people with his caliber and passion for work" – were few things that people had to say about him.

Sounded simple and obvious that Sid could easily achieve whatever he wanted. But it wasn't that simple. Not if you are Sid because he knew just two things – fight for his right and dare to dream. Fearless, he would look at anyone in the eye and state the facts. This definitely does not make life easy for anyone.

The same applied to Sid. He filed a court case against his college for unfairness meted out to him by a teacher. Under threats from the college, completing his studies appeared to be a distant dream. Later, he also turned down the job offered at campus to chase his dreams. In the quest to chase his dreams, he faced numerous rejections and criticism from the fashion fraternity and braved doubting eyes of the society. Amidst this, he constantly faced the pressure of expectations for he was born and brought up in an IIT campus. To top it all, one day, one of his father's friends even regretted naming his son on Sid's name.

Did he make it, though? Yes, he did. So don't read this book to find out if he made it. Instead read it to know how he made it.

In January 2008, Sid's elder sister Shreya returned from Sydney. She had been there for two years on an assignment with an IT company. Sid was in his fourth year of college in Bangalore. After college, he was to go overseas to work for an apparel company.

All hunky dory, right? But neither of the two was happy with what they were doing. And it was because what they were doing was nowhere close to what they had thought for themselves.

It is then that these two siblings, both in their early 20s, entered an interesting pact which could let them safeguard each other's dream in face of failures and challenges.

The pact was that Shreya would 'invest' in Sid until Sid was able to realise his dreams. The day Sid fulfilled his dream, he would invest in Shreya. The word 'invest' may sound vague or small, but it depends on what meaning it holds for one. For them, it meant the investment of time, efforts, patience, determination and so on.

This story of ordinary siblings with extraordinary determination is based on real life events. It has the potential to charge you up and infuse courage in you to live your dreams.

Set in the backdrop of college life, this inspiring, dramatic, daring and yet humour filled story has the 'what next element' to keep you hooked. It comes across as a powerful and fast-paced story that can instantly strike a chord with everyone. It also brings out a beautiful relationship of a brother and sister and how far they went to finally fail the failure.

Preface

"Not to give you a job. Not to give you an internship. But I am here to give you a dream," Sid was talking to the students of a college where he was invited to deliver a guest lecture.

He continued to talk. "When you aspire a career in the fashion industry, do not be carried away with the glamour. There is a lot of hard work behind what you see on the ramp. And not everything is a ramp walk. Look beyond. You have creative minds. You have the potential to create employment. Instead of finding a job, identify your talent and think of how you can create jobs."

As Sid progressed breaking several myths of the fashion industry, he reached the most important slide of his presentation. He made an offer, one he was capable to make that day after years of rejection, criticism and hard work.

He offered to dream together. "You design a collection on paper and send it to me. My team will evaluate your designs. Those who get selected will be asked to develop a collection. I will give you the retail space, free of any cost. Sell your garments under your name."

Offering a retail space free of cost and allowing the designers to sell under their own name meant removing the biggest obstacle in the progress of any designer. Sid understood it because these were the two foremost challenges he had faced when he was trying to establish himself in the industry.

His ideas were welcomed. There was an energetic uproar and he was surrounded by students who wouldn't let him leave after the presentation.

I watched him live his dream. Apart from encouraging entrepreneurship, Sid's dream was to remain connected with schools and colleges. He believes fresh minds are the most creative. Experienced people are learned and unlearning takes time, and not everyone is ready to unlearn.

In the meantime, an old man came to me and said, "Thanks ma'am for coming to our college. No one till date has spoken to our students with this vision. My experience says you both will go a long way. What Sid talks about is much ahead of his age."

Saying this, the man walked away. He had, however, reminded me of the journey Sid had undertaken six years back in 2008.

It was the year when Sid passed out of college and I was asked this question by almost everyone – my friends, Sid's friends, family friends and acquaintances.

The question was – *"What is Sid doing?"*

My answer was – "Sid is working to create jobs for others. He will set up a business. He has developed a technology to promote green fashion. He has got a patent, will find his brand..."

But even before I really started to explain, there was a strange restlessness on their faces. Their mind forced them to validate an assumption they had already confirmed to themselves. The assumption was – Sid chose business because he didn't get a job in the campus placements. And while they rehearsed a polished question to put across to me, they made me feel like a sister who had built up a jazzy answer to cover her brother's incapability of finding a job.

All in all, I failed to give a desirable answer. But to come to think of it, was there any other way I could have explained the situation?

The answer is, no. In India we are expected to pass out of college with a job in hand, work diligently and then get married in a few years. Take a bank loan to buy one house and one car and extend the family. For those in the IT industry, one extra point is to go onsite. Buy a second, third and may be few more houses with wise intentions to return to live in them one day. Though with changing time, the new generation dares to break this web of expectations, but a majority still continue to live by them.

So for the obvious reasons, after cutting me short, the second question I was asked was–"*What else is he doing?*"

It was a polished and rehearsed question when all they wanted to say was – "brand, patent, green fashion – all this is fine but where is he working? How much does he earn?"

I sincerely tried again to explain that not everyone is alike. Not everyone prefers a job. Just like being in a job is important, it is significant that some become entrepreneurs too. If everyone started doing jobs then who would create opportunities for those who wish and need to be in jobs? The high paying jobs in IT and retail were also created by the business started by such entrepreneurs. The business that has grown to employ thousands was once a start-up. So, if not respect the entrepreneurs equally, at least give some respect and acknowledge their efforts and courage. Can't we do even this wee bit for the entrepreneurs who have started small today to eventually become big tomorrow?

I explained not to prove a point and justify or protect Sid's image, I spoke so that maybe I could see a few more who would dare to break the rules and become job creators. Or at least become supporters.

Talking of supporters, Sid was lucky. Our parents supported Sid and it was enough for Sid to keep going. He refused to give up and this is how he won.

He dared to dream. He dreamed and he achieved. Each time he achieved, he set his target ahead and did not stop. He doesn't think he has achieved anything great and I wish he continues to think so because this is what keeps him going. We cease to grow the day we think we are big enough.

[illegible] by them.

So if the [illegible] sorting the short, the second [illegible].

He had [illegible] to [illegible] — [illegible]. This much [illegible]?

[illegible] and acknowledge their efforts and [illegible] important?

I explained to [illegible]

[illegible] was enough [illegible] He refused to give up and [illegible] on.

He had [illegible] and did not stop. [illegible]

1

Reunion in Bangalore, 2008

What it takes to be born and brought up in an IIT campus

"What have you been doing?" I asked Sid who was in his fourth year of Apparel Technology at NAFT (National Academy of Fashion Technology) Bangalore. NAFT is one of the top-most colleges of fashion in India.

"Green and ethical fashion is what I have been working on," Sid replied smiling.

In his second year of college, Sid had developed a technology named DPOL (Direct Panel on Loom). DPOL made eco-friendly clothes and had some interesting features.

I decided to talk about it later as there was something more pressing for me to know.

"And... what about the court case?"

"Going on, but I have almost won it. Some final hearings are due."

It was a year ago that he had filed a case against his college. The problem was not the college but a teacher who did wrong with Sid's academic result.

"Okay good, but was there a need to fight for it and go to court?"

He smiled back and I knew he was saving his answer for a later time. Who would know this better than me! I respected it and decided to wait for the time when he would like to share the story with me.

This was a quick conversation between me and Sid as we briskly made our way out of the Bangalore airport. It was 9:00 pm and my flight from New Delhi had arrived on time. Sid had come to receive me at the airport.

We were meeting after almost two years. Completing my MBA from Christ College Bangalore in year 2006, I had joined one of the fastest growing Indian Information Technology multinational companies, Satyamine Consultancy Services. Within three months, I had moved to work for one of its clients in Sydney, Australia.

I had returned to India after two years now. I stayed at home for a month and then travelled to Bangalore to join the Satyamine, Bangalore office.

"You look famished. Are you not eating?" I changed the topic pulling his leg.

Sid is three years younger to me and we have always been like friends. Destiny also had a role to play in keeping us together. A month after I joined MBA in Bangalore, Sid was also selected for his graduate programme in the Bangalore branch of his college.

"You see, I am busy in setting up the business," he smiled and replied.

He smiled because there was a reason behind it. The reason was the choice he had made.

It was not at all natural or obvious to think that Sid would be setting up his own business. In fact, the surroundings in which we were raised was capable enough to turn hostile towards you and deem you as a failure in life, if given even a weakest signal of you dreaming to set up your own business. Well, I am talking about what it takes to be born and brought up in an IIT campus. To be precise, we were born and brought up in the IIT Roorkee, Saharanpur campus.

Generally, kids living in normal circumstances face expectations from their parents and surroundings when they reach class ten or twelve. And I am talking of the 1990s. This is the time of board exams or IIT JEE or medical entrance exams. That's the normal kind of pressure I had seen my school friends undergo too. But kids living in the campus were a rare species and their condition hasn't changed much even today. We face competition right from the moment we go to kindergarten. If the schools are not enough, parents put kids through numerous competitions which they organize in the ladies club, hobby club or staff club.

'Why only us?'

This question bothered me for years until I discovered a very valid reason behind it. For organizing an event, what is the foremost thing you need? Well, the most important thing is to find and fund a venue. But the luxury of living in the campus was such that the aunties had a variety of venues at their disposal. Available free of cost, they used the auditorium, guest house or the large sprawling lawns to organize competitions for kids.

For them it served the purpose of entertainment. But my point is that why did they have to entertain themselves at the cost of our happiness. I mean, they could have used the beautiful facility to jolly well organize picnics and food festivals. But no, organizing food festivals would have required them to cook. So the easiest was to organize post event dinners and lunches from the university mess and use the large army of kids for entertainment. So sometimes we walked the stage in disguise of beggars, vegetable vendor, Superman, Dracula, etc., in a fancy dress competition and sometimes we raced with a lemon in our spoons, making every possible attempt to reach the finish line at first to claim a Bournvita quiz book as the first prize and get in another trap where parents expected us to participate in quiz competitions a few months later.

All through our childhood we were trained to sleep by first looking at the light in the study rooms of other kids. This meant you couldn't be the first one to switch off the lights of your study room and go to sleep. And if you really wanted to delight your parents, you had to be awake till those two particular kids turned off the lights. They were

Mohit and Mehul. Mohit was a year elder to me and Mehul. They both were the biggest enemies of every kid in the campus. Given a chance, the other twenty of us would have beaten them up for they were the only reason of unhappiness in our lives. They scored a ninety-six percentile and yet their family would be the disaster struck family. And when they were not happy even at a 96 percentile, how our parents treated us was obvious.

I cursed Mohit and Mehul all my life but when wisdom prevailed, I realised another reason for our sufferings. Designed by Swedish people, our houses no doubt were beautiful and a favourite topic of study for the architecture students, but I hated them because the study rooms faced the road and were visible to everyone. These rooms were the guest rooms by design, but most parents in the campus had converted them into study rooms.

It got worse during the time of our results. In every single household, parents chanted the names of Mohit and Mehul to humiliate their kids. You know why? Because no matter how much you'd study, you'd score less than Mohit and Mehul.

On exam results days, it was not Brakha Dutt or Rajdeep Sardesai who gave away the breaking news; it was the household maids who turned into the most sought-out reporters. They were all uneducated, but they knew the marks of every single kid of campus on their fingertips.

The maids hated Mohit and Mehul because their mother was a miser. She would not give tea, biscuits and other perks to the maids but the maids still didn't hesitate to display their love and admiration for Mohit and Mehul during our results as reporting the marks of the two boys earned them uninterrupted supply of tea and biscuits from our mothers.

Apart from the marks, for an extra biscuit from our mothers, they also reported about what Mohit, Mehul ate, what time they woke up, where did they sit and study, what guide books they referred to, what programmes they watched on TV, the position of their beds and the like.

Needless to say, we hated the maids. But their reporting sometime helped us too. Especially when our friends were not allowed to come for the park meetings.

There is a famous story featuring Minkoo bhaiya. In the evenings at six, post result days, we gathered in our campus park to share our sorry state, discuss the brutalities inflicted on us and to hatch a plan to boycott the Mohit-Mehul brothers. Two such meetings went by, but Minkoo bhaiya didn't show up. Some said he was running a high fever and some said they saw a red mark on his face. We were worried but no one dared to go to his home for various reasons – his parents were strict, our results were just out and they could ask us our marks and spoil our mood with acidic comments.

We decided to wait for the maids to break the news. In the meantime the speculation was rife that Minkoo bhaiya's absence was yet again due to his performance in the maths exams. Despite making sincere efforts, year after year, he scored miserably in maths and the irony was that his father was the professor of mathematics. So obviously, the result days were the toughest for him.

My ears that were on high alert caught the news. I heard the maid tell my mother that the previous night when Minkoo bhaiya's father asked him to be like Mohit and Mehul, a usually quiet Minkoo bhaiya could not control it any longer and asked his father: 'Did I ever ask you to be Dhirubhai Ambani and make me a proud son?' He earned a tight thrashing for it.

Living under such circumstances, who could be spared from getting affected? Our parents were also very obviously concerned and felt answerable and responsible to the belief system and lifestyle they had. But we were still fortunate for a reason. Our parents had succumbed to the social pressure, however they harboured a secret desire for me and Sid. So while they liked talking to us about getting selected in IIT, they also wanted us to become able to create jobs and not just settle by taking one for ourselves. And to make us able, they conditioned us to dream big. The outcome of this is what we became – didn't make it to IIT, but turned restless and ridiculously ambitious.

"Yes, I see that you continue to remain original. You fear no Mohit or Mehul and you will definitely create jobs!" I laughed.

As we spoke, we made our way outside the airport and I couldn't stop appreciating the beautiful Bangalore airport built by GMR.

"This new airport looks good. But isn't it very far from the city?" We were now standing at the departure area waiting for the bus service bound for HSR layout.

"Yes it is, but one good thing is the excellent bus service. Ah, see here it is!"

"So you were telling me about DPOL," I asked after having settled down in the bus.

" Yes with DPOL, one can produce ready to stitch shaped woven garment components. This increases fabric efficiency by 15%-22% and reduces lead time by 50%. In simple words, DPOL can reduce the wastage of cloth. That's how clothes produced from DPOL are eco-friendly."

"This is wonderful. And who gave the name DPOL?"

"One of my professors has been appreciative of my work. He suggested that I call it DPOL."

"Ok, good. So is DPOL popular only in your college or do people outside also know about it?"

"I have shared my work with a few professors in the United States and they have given a good feedback on it. I have also published papers on it in ethical fashion forums on the internet and last month I was invited to chair the Textile convention – Bangalore Chapter."

"Wow! I didn't know you have progressed so well on this," I said beaming with happiness. "So you are using threads on the loom as a starting point to create a DPOL fabric. Right?" I asked. I inferred it from the full form of DPOL – *direct panel on loom*.

"Yes."

"And the outcome of this process is a DPOL fabric?" I said taking the conversation further. He answers only what is asked.

"Yes, a marked up fabric. 'Marked up' makes it a DPOL fabric," he said.

"Okay and then this fabric can be cut on mark-ups?"

"Yes," he said looking out of the bus window. "This is our stop."

We had been so engrossed in our conversation that we didn't realise that two hours had gone by.

I looked around the house to make room for my bags. We lived in one of the oldest houses of the HSR Layout, which was only a kilometre away from Sid's college. This independent faded cream coloured ground floor house with no construction on the first floor was pretty big, but it still was a little small for us. And the reason was that at any point of time, there lived no less than six students in this house.

There were three rooms to house two students in each room, one attached bathroom with a toilet, one tiny toilet, a kitchen, living area, a store area and a narrow backyard. There was a big porch in front of the house and a staircase leading to the terrace. The best part was that the landlord visited only once in six months. With these ideal conditions, this oldest house had actually transformed into the youngest and most happening house of HSR layout.

The house always buzzed with parties, guitar practices and pranks. The house was also an emotional support to many. To local students it was a guest house if their parents didn't allow them to enter their homes after a late night party. For others who were going through a breakup, it was a place to find a shoulder to cry and nurse their wounds. Open at all times, the house was kind of a 24x7 helpline.

The design of the house was interesting too – credit to its owner, an old man who followed Vaastu. All the three rooms of the house were adjacent to each other, like the compartments of a train. Each room was painted in different colours – fluorescent green, dirty pink and the most normally coloured room was Sid's room. It was the corner most and like all other rooms, had two sets of mattresses with no bed, one table, and one chair. The only thing that was different here was a computer with a TV tuner card. So Sid's room automatically became the entertainment room.

"You guys haven't still set up the kitchen?" I asked Sid while eating a masala dosa. Sid had packed dinner for us from Food Days, an eating joint near his college.

"Not possible to have a kitchen in this house. You know it."

I had stayed in this house for four months before leaving for Sydney. I remembered the challenges I had faced in setting up the kitchen. Those who believed in sneaking in and eating up food outnumbered those who cooked.

After having done with the dinner, unpacking my bags, taking a shower and meeting up with everyone, finally Sid and I settled in our room.

"Show me the DPOL sample products," I said.

Sid had made space for my clothes in his cupboard by moving a black polythene bag to the top most section of the cupboard. He mentioned it contained DPOL fabric, which he had planned to show me the next day.

He took out a black and white dress from the bag.

"Gorgeous it is!" I said feeling the texture of the dress with my fingers.

He smiled with innocence in his eyes. It reminded me of our school days when he used to show me his sketches and paintings and would wait for my reaction. Sid had been immensely creative since childhood.

"Have you documented DPOL anywhere? I mean you have progressed so far. There should be a record of the things."

"Yes, I have documented it. Check http://august.synthasite.com/ when you get time."

"Great, I will. And what's the next step?" I said.

"I have done my part, now you are here. I was waiting for you. Tell me what next."

I didn't expect this coming my way so early. "Hmm... okay, let me first read more about DPOL and understand what you have done so far, then we will decide the way forward."

It was 12:30 am and we were still nowhere close to sleep. I was not able to sleep because of jet lag, and Sid was used to sleeping late.

"Tell me what else is happening," I said.

Catching up after two years, we had so much to discuss. And it is now when he unfolded on the court case.

The court case – When I braved my college

12:30 am – 4 am, February 2008

"There is this Computer Science teacher. Her name is Mugdha Singh. She was teaching me in the third year of college. After the class, she asked the students to ask questions. I had a doubt so I raised my hand and asked her the full form of 'JVM'. She did not answer my question and I could see she had felt offended."

"Why offended?"

"Maybe because I was a good student and was the topper of all branches of our college and she thought I was asking the question to pull her leg."

"How can a teacher think like that?"

"She was a young teacher and inexperienced too. She often fumbled while teaching. But that's fine. We all start somewhere someday. I always cooperated and even helped her at times."

"Then why did you ask her the question?"

"It wasn't planned. I saw JVM flashing on my computer as I compiled my programme, so I asked her instantly. But she took it wrong way."

"Wrong way?" I asked.

"Yes, in the following exams, she marked me with an F grade."

"You mean almost fail?"

"Not almost... It is fail!"

"Did you not ask her the reason?" I was sitting upright in anger now.

"Yes, I did. She said that I didn't answer the questions the way she wanted and without giving me a chance to speak, she left the class. I went to those who had received good grades. They were surprised that I had got an F and wondered why she had graded me so. But I knew why she had done it."

"So you accepted the F?"

"No. A few days later, I went to her and said that I wanted to see my copy and get it re-evaluated. She got infuriated and turned down my request. She also said that the copies had been destroyed. It was the rule of the college to destroy the copies after the exam."

"What did you do then?" I asked.

"I discussed it with dad and he said that in IIT, they show the copies to the students. My college was a central government body too, so they should have also shown me my copy and technically they could have never destroyed it. Dad suggested that I file an RTI (Right to Information). The college would have to honour that in any case."

"So did you file the RTI?"

"Yes, I did. Delhi and Karnataka were the only two governments who had passed RTI act way back in 1997. I was fortunate to be in Karnataka. Dad told me the process. I had to fill a form and drop it in a post box. It was that simple! And that's how I filed my first RTI."

"What happened after that?"

"The director called me and showed me the copy. I brought the issue to his notice. He accepted the teacher's mistake but he said he would not be able to do anything about it as he could not go against a teacher."

"It means your teacher was lying about the copies being burnt!" I said, "Well, anyway, did RTI help?"

"It did. The next day I received a call from the teacher Mugdha Singh. She said that she would increase fourteen marks in my copy but I would have to withdraw the RTI application."

"What did you do then?"

"I didn't accept and declined to withdraw the RTI. She in fact infuriated me by the way she spoke to me. She sounded as though she was doing me a favour by making this offer."

"Didn't you ask her where did she bring the copies from that she said were burnt a week back?"

"Yes, I asked her how she had managed to revive my copy from the ashes. She hung up on me."

"What happened next?"

"She must have complained to the director because the next day when I saw the director in the college corridor, he didn't appear the usual happy at the sight of me. And by afternoon I came to know that a panel had been set up to investigate the case. The coming months saw many meetings where I was ordered to be present to hear the proceedings of the panel."

"Sounds fair... they finally were making an endeavour to re-evaluate your copy."

"It was nothing like it sounds. It was their way to threaten me. This panel of four teachers warned me that if I did not withdraw my RTI application, they would not let me finish college. By hook or crook, they wanted me to settle with the fourteen marks increase."

"Unbelievable! But I must say you were brave to face this."

"I had no option. I had to be strong. But there were times when I broke down, though I didn't show it. In fact, I had no one to discuss what I was facing. When I tried to share it with my friends, they could not relate to it."

"I can understand, but what did you do then?" I asked

"I continued attending the proceedings of the panel. But soon I got an idea. No one believed the language they used while talking to me so I decided to record the sessions. I used the same pen drive that you gave me. I knew it could do small recordings. I started carrying the pen drive at all times in my pocket. I made sure that I wore shirts and trousers which had pockets. This is how I recorded the proceedings of the panel discussions. Each evening I downloaded the recordings on to my computer and created a folder of the audio files. I also maintained a backup. And on weekends, I listened to the recordings to create a case file for myself."

"What was your plan?"

"I had no plans. I just wanted to keep a proof of what was being done to me. But in a few days, I realised the continued harassment, listening to the recordings and preparing the case created a negative energy around me. It affected my DPOL work. It took a toll on my health too. I started experiencing panic rush. My ears turned red and hot and I felt uncomfortable. Dreams haunted me where I saw myself standing in the panel discussion and being threatened by the panel that they would not let me finish my degree. I decided to tell mom and dad about it during my Diwali holidays.

On the first day of the holidays, I broke down at midnight. I walked into mom and dad's room. Tears rolled down my eyes for the first time for this case. I woke them up and narrated the complete situation and asked them to help me file a case in the high court. Within a month of that, I filed a case in the Delhi High Court."

"I can understand. We get emotional when we come near our

parents. And it was important that you cried. And I must tell you that you did absolutely the right thing by filing the court case. But tell me, how was this received in your college?" I asked.

"The news that I had filed the case was widespread among the college students and they were all supportive of me. On the other hand, the director and the panel increased the harassment. Now it was not just the RTI; they wanted me to withdraw the case too. The teachers gave me average grades. They didn't let me top and didn't fail me either. The worst was to come. In May 2007, my summer internship started with India's largest branded fabric and fashion retailers. Their facility was located in the outskirts of Bangalore. I had to start early morning to travel fifty kilometres one way and change three buses and walk quite a lot to reach the place. Knowingly, the panel started calling me early morning every day for the day-long meetings. This meant I either missed the internship or the panel meeting. I raised this concern in the meeting, but the panel paid no heed to it. As a result, when I missed the internship, the panel warned me that if I did not go for the internship, they will flunk me. They knew it was practically impossible to attend the meetings until the afternoon and then go for the internship. They were doing all of it deliberately."

"Awful! But finally, did they fail you?" I asked.

"No, they were just building pressure on me. They could not fail me for the fear of the court case and did let me go for my internship after a few days by limiting the meetings to twice in a week. My internship got over, and I entered the fourth year of college. But the harassment continued. The teachers also continued to give me average marks, no matter how well I performed. But yes, there were a few teachers who understood the wrong being done to me. But no one supported me in front of the director. They said that the institution is always bigger than the individual. With passing days, the director got worse. He increased the pressure on me to withdraw the case. One day I succumbed to it and called up dad and said that I felt like killing myself."

"I can't believe you even thought of that. What did dad say to you?"

I wanted to know how my very practical father had handled the situation.

"As always, he was not surprised at all and asked me where I was at that moment. I told him I was standing outside the director's cabin."

"What happened then?" I asked.

"Dad said that he would not stop me. This was my decision. But first I must finish the reason behind my decision. Dad replied with the same demeanour and poise which he maintains in all situations. Instead of dad, I was surprised now. I was disturbed so I had blurted out that I felt like killing myself, but I didn't mean it. But dad hadn't taken it lightly."

I knew how my father would have replied. It reminded me of a day when I had asked him what he would do if he came to know that I had fallen for bad company in my college and had started smoking and drinking. To this he had laughed and replied, "Why would I do anything? It is your body. You have to take care of it. Parents can't be with children all the time. We took care of you when you were small. We have done our best to imbibe the wisdom in you which will make you decide right and wrong for yourself. And I believe whatever you decide will be best for you."

At the end of the discussion also, he didn't display the remotest of curiosity to find out whether I had started smoking or drinking and why I had asked him the question.

"What happened next?" I asked Sid.

"Dad asked me to stay where I was and to wait for his call. I waited outside the director's cabin. After a few minutes, I heard the director close his cabin from inside and within minutes dad called me. He assured me that the director would not trouble me again."

"But what could he have done sitting a thousand kilometres away?" I was laughing.

"He called up the director and told him about my call and also told him what he as a father had suggested to me about killing the reason before killing myself. When the director asked him about my whereabouts, dad told him that I was waiting right outside his office. And I understood that's why the director had locked his door just before dad called me."

"So did things change?" My heart was jumping with excitement to know if that one phone call had changed anything.

"Oh yes, definitely. That day onwards, the director wasn't hostile and managed a smile on his face when he saw me," Sid laughed. " He also assured me that the issue would be sorted soon but he never told me how he was thinking about resolving it and I too didn't ask."

"Unnecessarily he supported your teacher in her wrong doings and got stuck in this issue."

"Yes, he was a good man otherwise. And you know, one day a funny thing happened. He called me to his office. My hands were full, so I put down a few things on his table. He carefully looked at the things and pointed to a pen drive and asked me, 'I hope you are not recording our conversation. I have called you only for a general discussion about your technology' ," Sid laughed.

"And what is the status now?" I asked.

"The case is on. Whenever there are hearings, the panel teachers go to Delhi. I am aware of which day which teacher will be absent. The students are told that the teachers have gone to Delhi to attend meetings in the Delhi branch of our college. However, the truth is something else."

Sid winked and smiled. I was glad he was smiling through his struggle.

"Where does the case appear to be moving?" I asked.

"In my favour. My friends already say that I have won," Sid was happy as he said this. "The teachers and attendants who supported me secretly are now standing up for me. And the management also appears to have acknowledged their defeat. They now fear I might go to the media and make their wrongs public."

"Attending the hearings in Delhi does not disturb your classes?"

"My lawyers say the recordings and scripts I prepared are very helpful and they can manage without me. I will have to go for the final hearing," Sid said.

"Hmm...I admire your courage and determination to fight for your right so early in life. No one wants to mess up with college. But were you not afraid before filing the case?" I asked.

"If I had not fought for my right, I would have lost myself. And I didn't want to lose myself. The fear of losing myself was too tall in front of the fear of failure."

It was 4:00 am when we finally decided to sleep.

Patent – Sounds cool, eh?

"So how does your day look like?" I asked Sid. At 11:00 am, I was still lying in bed.

We could not sleep even after our discussion the previous night. Sid spent the night nursing me. I was dehydrated by vomiting due to change in drinking water. Terrible weakness and cold shivers made me miserable. I could not go to office. But one good thing was that we had one more day to catch up.

"I'll be home mostly. No college these days. My final year graduation project is going on."

"For internships, don't you get companies in your college?"

"Yes, we do get and mostly everyone is doing internships in companies. I too got it with a company but I didn't opt for it. I am doing the cost benefit analysis study of DPOL as my project."

"This is nice! But given that you don't have a good equation with your director, how did he allow it?"

"True! In fact he was very strict on approving the internship synopsis for even those who were doing it with companies. Almost every other student had to redo them. I was sure he would trash my idea but still I decided to give it a try."

"And?" I asked. Could not wait for the pause he took for the smile.

"And I was surprised that he instantly approved my synopsis. Not only this, he said that he was confident that I would do a great project."

"Hmm... was it because of dad's call?"

"Could be, but he had been appreciative of DPOL in the past as well. It's just that the Mugdha Singh case had spoiled matters."

"Hmmm... I am glad at least he approved your synopsis," I said. "And how is it like now... are you working by yourself? You don't have to go anywhere? I mean you at home at this hour?"

"I am not alone. There are three of us – Rahul Patna, Kumar Rahul and me. We meet every day in college. The college has given us one room. We meet and decide our day's work and divide the responsibilities. So it's all good." He gestured the good going with a thumbs up.

"Sounds good but how do you guys divide the work? No battles there?" I asked recalling my MBA days when we did projects.

"We divide the responsibilities based on our interests. Rahul Patna is very agile. Being a sportsman, he can't sit still, so he does the running for operations work. Kumar Rahul is good in analytics and I manage the overall project. So we have no fights." Sid seemed infused with passion.

Awake now, I too pulled out my laptop, placed it on my pillow and decided to learn about DPOL from www.august.synthasite.com, the website, which Sid had mentioned to me last night.

"Un hun... patent – sounds cool! You really have got it, right?" I asked him laughingly.

On the website it was mentioned that DPOL holds a provisional patent. Sid had mentioned the patent but I had a reason behind my doubt.

Sid had been notorious since childhood. And a few years back he had proved that he had not changed. He had given me his resume to edit. I realised he had given me my resume and not his. When I told him that by mistake he had given my resume to me, he said, it was his resume. When I said, it can't be as it had my accolades mentioned on it. He said that whether I had done them or he had done, it was the same thing. I asked him if he had written that he had completed an MBA too. To this he said that he had not included it yet as he was still doing his graduation but he felt like he had done his MBA as well.

"The patent is for real. Trust me," he laughed out loud and said.

"Does that mean you have grown up in the two years I had been away?" I took a dig at him again. "Good, good... tell me more about it." I felt proud.

"Work on DPOL started in my sophomore... that's in 2006 in my second year college. In 2007 I filed the patent and got the provisional patent by end of 2007. As a final step, we need to now file for the final patent after December 2008. There has to be a gap of one year between the provisional and final patent."

"This is great! By the way, who wrote your patent?"

"The provisional I wrote myself, but for the final we may need to talk to the patent writers," he replied.

I knew he could do things like trying to fix a fused bulb or attempting to generate energy by floating a web of plastic balls in a bath tub, but patent-writing was a specialised skill. I scrolled down to read further.

"Still in college and you are already holding a patent of a technology you developed, have chaired a textile convention, have been published on international green fashion forums and have developed a sample DPOL product," I said counting on my fingers. "You are doing very good, boy!"

"Hmm... but have not been able to get any funding for DPOL. I have made business plans and submitted them to many VCs (venture capitalists) but no funding so far," he said.

"Don't worry, it will happen," I said and noted a few names of the VCs from Sid and read about them on the internet.

The next thing I remembered was waking up when the sun had set. I had dozed off after the heavy dose of medication.

"Want to come out for a walk?" Sid asked.

"Yes, why not."

"I want to take you to the aquarium shop. I want to get an aquarium for us but was waiting for you to approve of it," he said.

On our way to the aquarium shop, I asked him, "What were you doing for so long on the computer?"

"I am trying to write the final patent."

"But you said it is the professional writer who will write our final patent?"

"Yes, they do but I heard they charge a lot so I may have to write it myself."

"I know you can do it, but it may get rejected or it may take time for approval if you write it," I said.

"Hmm... I have also researched on patent writers in Bangalore. But no harm to begin writing it. Will hand over my work to the writer once we find one," he said.

'To begin' is the most important thing. Start with the things that are in your hand. This unlocks what is ahead.

We returned home with an aquarium. Very carefully Sid placed it on the only table in our room. We got two white angel fish and two orange gold fish. They are a safe combination but the seller asked us to observe their behaviour for a few days.

Naming the fish, introducing them to the members of the house and attending to the suggestions to decorate the aquarium with glass pebbles and plants took a few hours. Finally, the euphoria of the new aquarium settled down. We called the patent writers and finalised to meet a lady lawyer.

She was a middle-aged lady. She ushered us into her office, which must have been the porch of the house previously. Very enterprising, I thought.

Asking us to wait for ten minutes, she went to join the evening pooja in her house.

"Who wrote the provisional patent for you?" She asked after quickly reading the summary of the provisional patent.

Sid smiled and she knew the answer.

"You wrote that?" Clearly surprised, she asked to confirm. "Has it been approved?"

"Yes it has been approved and it has almost been a year since."

She again flipped through our loosely stapled six pages. Then looking closely at a round blue ink stamp she said, "Yes, it shows here that you are going to complete one year this December."

"Yes," Sid said.

She was impressed. She picked up a fluorescent highlighter and carefully marked the six pages.

A discussion followed. She tried to understand DPOL. And it didn't take long that she surprised Sid. She mentioned a Japanese designer who had a patent close to Sid's concept. She was a lawyer, who had nothing to do with designing, but she was well informed.

Impressed by her, Sid explained the DPOL in detail. She leaned back on her chair to observe the enthusiasm with which Sid explained using diagrams. When Sid stopped, she said, "No one can do this better than you, Sid. You must write the final patent yourself."

Sid and I quickly exchanged a glance and then looked at her.

"No, I am serious. Not only will you do justice to this patent, but will also save a lot of money."

She explained the standard process to write and file the patent.

"Can you do it?" I asked Sid. She also looked at him expecting a promising nod.

"Okay... yes, I will write it."

I still wanted to know how much money we were going to save. I asked, "I am just asking... generally what are the charges to get a patent written?"

"Starts at eighty thousand rupees and can go up to three to five lakhs"

"Okay." I said hiding my surprise. It was way more than what I had expected. For a moment I contemplated on becoming a patent writer myself.

The coming days saw Sid work on his internship with the two Rahuls. Apart from proving the economic viability of DPOL, they were also making the second sample of DPOL. This time it was a light pink and wine coloured silk jacket with a Chinese dragon on it. The evenings were spent writing the patent and publishing his work in relevant forums.

When the first sample was made, I wasn't around so it was exciting to see the second sample being made in front of me.

Not only did my job and Sid's to-do list kept us busy, the house in which we lived was also buzzing with activity. We were living in the most happening house of HSR layout.

A day at the most happening house of the HSR layout

It was 5:00 pm, I was reading *Losing my Virginity* by Richard Branson while Sid was working on his laptop.

I had returned from Sydney but still worked for the ANZ region. I started my day early and returned home by 4:30 in the evening.

"Where is everyone?" I asked.

It wasn't a usual day because every day by five in the evening, our house was exploding with music, laughter, dance and utter chaos. By this time everyone returned from college. And no one returned alone. They brought their friends and friends in turn brought their friends.

"Harsh is sleeping and Rajat has gone to Ankur's place," Sid replied.

Harsh and Rajat were Sid's classmates. The three had rented this house in the second year of their college after changing many houses in their first year. Harsh and Rajat lived in the room next to us. A bathroom in between separated our rooms with doors opening into both rooms.

"Where are Aditya and Anupam?"

They lived in the room next to Harsh and Rajat's room. This third room of the house was like a guest room which saw a change in occupants every three to four months. These days, it was Aditya and Anupam, two second year college students living in this room.

"They will be late... preparing for an upcoming college fest."

"Kritika also didn't come today. Where is she?" I asked.

"Don't know," Sid replied.

It would be unfair to count Kritika as a visitor because she was a close friend of Sid, Rajat and Harsh and our home was like a second home to her. Tall, fair, slender, and blessed with sharp features and high cheek bones like a model, she was the most beautiful girl of the college. She was the Miss India contestant from Bangalore. And for obvious reasons this heartthrob of college had an unparallel fan following. Juniors and seniors would die for her as would her classmates. Highly creative, she was also the best design student of the college. With her intellect, she proved wrong the notion that beautiful girls have less brains

Now the million dollar question is that despite having such a big fan following and loads of lucrative evening party options, what brought her to our crazy home? Sid, Harsh and Rajat were not even her classmates. She was in design and they were in technology. Still more than her house, she was found at our home doing her assignments. What could be the reason? Well, the answer was Sid. If whole of the college was crazy for her, she was crazy for Sid.

To be precise, she was not found in our house, she was found in our room. When Sid worked on his laptop, she sat next to him doing her work with colours and chart papers spread all over the place. The number of hours they spent together gradually had started showing in their interests too. Sid who was an apparel technologist saw himself design, which he had unconsciously picked up over the past four years from Kritika. On the other hand, Kritika praised and followed ethical fashion.

They were always found together but still their relationship was an enigma. Some suspected they were 'girlfriend-boyfriend', some said they were just friends and gelled well because they both were kids at heart, and some said they were two intelligent people who loved each other's company when they worked because they both were extremely passionate about their work. This relationship was an enigma to me too but I never felt the need to know the actual status, so I never enquired and lived with suspense until the day Kritika herself decided to talk to me about it.

It was just a week after I had returned from Sydney and one afternoon, out of the blue, she blurted out to me that she loved Sid. Taking a deep breath and absorbing what she had just told me, I asked her, if Sid shared the same feeling. She replied that she didn't know. I changed the question and this time asked, if Sid knew she loved her. She looked confused and said, "I think so." The answers could have been 'yes' or 'no,' but 'I think so' left me perplexed. I asked her to tell me the entire story.

She told me that a few days back, she had sent an SMS to Sid telling him how she felt about him, but Rajat had read it. She explained that when the message beeped, Sid was sitting in Rajat and Harsh's room and Sid's mobile was in Rajat's hand. Sid asked Rajat to read the message to him. Rajat said that it was Kritika's message but expecting nothing of this sort, Sid asked him to read it to him nonetheless. Sid didn't respond and Kritika never asked him about it. They continued to live as they were.

I spoke to Sid about the whole thing in front of Kritika. And as expected, he told me that he could not even think about anything of the sort at the moment. He said he had achieved nothing. And he couldn't ask her to wait because he knew it was going to take time to be successful in the path he had chosen for himself. He closed the discussion saying, *why should she suffer because of me.*

Kritika got up and left. However, the next evening, things were the same as earlier.

"Did she call you?" I again asked Sid about Kritika.

"No..." Sid replied. "But I am hoping she'll be here soon."

Sid was right. At 5:30, Kritika appeared. She looked completely lost and tired with a pencil in her hair and both hands holding bags with fabrics popping out. There was another red bag with small mirrors, which she wore across her shoulder. It too had beads hanging out till her toes. She had very effectively used every part of her body to carry things. Walking into the room, she literally crashed, offloading all her bags.

"Where are you coming from? Are you okay?" I asked her as she entered our room.

The doors of our house were always open, especially in the evening, for everyone to just walk in. Sid also looked on, waiting for her to reply.

"I am coming from the Majestic market," she said grabbing a bottle of water from the table. "Bangalore summers are no longer pleasant."

Clearing off the water she had poured on her t-shirt, she settled to pull stuff from her bag. "I am tired looking for the matching beads," she said placing a bead on a same coloured beige fabric.

"But this matches!" I said looking at the fabric and the bead. They matched exactly.

"No! They do not match. Less of gloss on the bead would have given the tone. I mean the colour is same but the tone isn't."

"For that you have to understand that they both are different materials so you can't match them a hundred percent. The bead is smooth and the fabric is embossed. A little rough texture to the bead can help though," I said casually.

Kritika stood up and ran out. She left me wondering if I had said something, which I shouldn't have.

"Where did you go?" I asked her when she returned after a few minutes.

"It is tiled floor here."

"So?"

"I wanted a rough surface." She said and handed me a bead. "See this. I rubbed this on the road. With a rough texture, the bead now matches the fabric exactly." She said with excitement.

"Thank you so much. You don't know what this means to me... I should have come here an hour earlier... I was unnecessarily worried..." she went on endlessly.

Surprised, I looked at Sid for help to stop Kritika's overwhelming outpour. But he paid no heed and continued to work on his laptop. Getting no response from him, I asked Kritika, "It's okay. But why do you bother so much? It almost looked the same earlier."

"No no... it wasn't the same." She went on explaining and pulled out peach coloured ribbons from her bag.

Seeing neither of us give up on questions and answers, Sid looked back at me and said. "Let her be. She won't listen to you. It is for her final jury. So everything she'd want has to be purrrfect!"

Kritika didn't respond as she probably hadn't even heard what Sid had said. Lost in her thoughts, she was already twisting the ribbon to make roses.

"Final jury?" I asked Sid as I placed my book aside and picked up a white ribbon to help Kritika make roses.

"A fashion show where all the design students will present their collection."

"Okay, so all this will be on stage?"

"Yes... on the runway."

"From that far, who'll be able to see the texture of the beads? I said.

"A designer would. She would," Sid replied.

"And if you put fewer beads, God forbid the beads go completely unnoticed?" I was curious.

"There are rehearsals that happen. So everything will happen as a designer wishes."

Fascinated at the mention of the fashion show I asked Sid, "Have you attended any fashion show till date?"

"No, I will attend when I walk the stage." There was an aplomb and sincerity in his voice.

It is free to dream and feel good about it. After all, it is those who dream, who achieve it.

I noted his intentions but still felt he was kidding.

He added, "But yes, I have seen many ramp walks. Be it any function in our college, they do ramp walks. For outsiders, you can call it a fashion show."

"Can I get to see a fashion show?"

"Why not? And this reminds me..." He pulled out an envelope from his book and extended it towards me."

As I read the invite, he said. "This year our graduation day is being celebrated in a big auditorium of the city. Until now it had always been conducted in the college campus, but this time they want to do it on a large scale."

He continued, "There will be a fashion show. Kritika's class will present their work. For the final jury, the college hires professionals. So you can call it a real fashion show, not like those that happen year round in the college campus. Also, the best designs and projects will be given awards."

"Sounds like one eventful evening," I said feeling lucky holding the invite in my hand.

"Yes it is! Do you know of this new actress who made her debut in Shahrukh Khan's movie? She is the daughter of the famous Indian Badminton player. I am forgetting her name..." He asked me, trying hard to remember the name.

"Devika Kuriakone?"

"Yes, she has also once walked the ramp in our college in the past. So we get the honour to have the best models for our show."

"Wow!" I said excited at the idea of attending the first fashion show of my life. And then I wondered what Sid would do on the day of the final jury. "Tell me one thing. Kritika is a fashion designer so she will present her work in the fashion show. But what will a fashion technologist like you do?"

"We will present the findings of our projects. For example, Rahul Patna, Kumar Rahul and I will present the cost benefit analysis of DPOL. In all, it is going to be an interesting evening where all the final year design and technology students will present what they have learnt in four years of college."

"You can get an award too?" I asked excitedly.

"After the case?" he laughed, "Not a chance!"

In the meantime, Harsh entered our room. He was whistling and getting ready to go out. "What's up, guys?" he said and picked up the deodorant that I had bought just the previous evening. Without my permission, he sprayed it all over himself. I coughed out the vapours floating in the room.

Rajat shouted from another room, "So much happiness! Where are you going?"

"I am going for a Jagjit Singh concert," Harsh replied taking a break from whistling.

But there was no rest to his hands. Now he was setting his hair with gel.

"You don't have money to pay rent. Will cry at the month end but you have money to buy the ticket," Rajat laughed.

"Don't spoil my mood and tell me if I can wear your shoes for the concert?" Harsh said. A gentle admonish 'dont spoil my mood' transformed into plead. Only Harsh could manage this diversity of emotions in a single breath.

"Okay, go!"Rajat said.

"You agreed?" Harsh was surprised.

He was surprised not because Rajat gave him the shoes. In fact, the shoes that Rajat owned were worn by Harsh most of the time. For formality Harsh would ask for permission and Rajat would play around and then say yes.

"Ahaan... agreed without any argument. You're in a good mood... come on tell me what is your plan for the evening?" Harsh asked.

"Nothing like what you are thinking. Come on, go now..." Rajat said lying on the bed...that is the mattresses.

"You can't get off this easily," Harsh said and pounced on the bed to lie down next to Rajat. Am I getting a surprise? Are you also coming to the Jagjit Singh concert?"

"I go to pubs. As if you don't know. I will be going to college for dinner."

"Ooooo college..." Harsh teased Rajat on top of his voice and then echoed the golden advice for his juniors in the adjacent room.

"Anupam, Aditya, did you hear where your Rajat sir spends his evenings these days? So now it is official that it's not the pubs but our college that is the best place to spend your evenings." Still lying down on the bed with Rajat on his side, Harsh fixed his eyes on the door waiting for either of the juniors to walk into his room.

None came but Aditya replied, "Harsh Sir, it's not about college, it's about Rajat sir. He doesn't need to go fishing for a good company. Our Tom Cruise is in demand anywhere he goes."

After a while, Harsh left for the concert. Bathed in my deodorant and dressed in Rajat's shirt and shoes that fitted him just well, he looked handsome. If Rajat was Tom Cruise, Harsh was Tom Hanks.

Rajat also left after some time. Ankur, who stayed nearby picked him.

After sometime, Sid, Kritika and I also left to buy more fish for our aquarium. After buying the fish which the seller packed for us in polythene filled with water, we went to the college cafeteria for dinner.

The college had the girl's hostel within the premises but boy's hostel was outside the campus. So at 9:30 pm the college doors were closed for the boys. And this also meant that the dinner was over by 9:00 pm. We finished our dinner just in time.

Rajat and Ankur, who were hanging around in the corridor between the girl's hostel and cafeteria, joined us. We dropped Kritika at her place. By third year of college, girls were also allowed to relinquish their hostels. Kritika lived near our house with her friends.

"What's happening here?" Sid asked a group of boys standing outside our house. They were Sid's classmates along with two new faces I didn't recognise.

"We are waiting for Harsh," someone from the group replied. They were clearly very angry. They were waiting for Harsh to come and wanted him to throw Binu out of our house.

Binu had come to stay in our living room just a day before. He was from the Delhi branch of their college and had come to Bangalore for a project in an apparel company. He was looking for a place to stay for just ten days. The helpful Harsh extended the much needed help and allowed him to stay with us. Simple, isn't it?

But it turned out to be a serious issue. Binu was not as simple and boring as his name. We came to know that Himanshu, who was Sid's classmate was dumped by his girlfriend for Binu. That is why Himanshu had come with his friends to beat up Harsh. His point was that how dare Harsh give Binu shelter after knowing that his girlfriend had left him for Binu!

"It's not Harsh's fault. You are unnecessarily venting the anger of your breakup on Harsh. Instead, you must sort it out with Binu and your girlfriend," Sid tried to pacify them.

"I don't know... Give me Harsh," he roared like a roadside rowdy.

As Sid made another attempt to pacify him, I remembered the previous night, when Harsh was happy about having Binu for ten days with the idea of individual rent contribution coming down, giving him a way to accommodate his and his girlfriend's tickets to another upcoming concert.

I prayed Harsh should not return anytime soon. Just then, something unexpected happened. Not Harsh but Binu walked towards us with Himanshu's girlfriend. Himanshu mellowed down.

With a straight face, completely ignoring us all, hand in hand, they both walked into our house. For a second it felt it was their house and we were the outsiders. I looked at Himanshu, but he didn't say a word and left with his friends.

It was 11:30 pm and Harsh wasn't back yet. With lights off, lying on his bed, Rajat was on phone. Who he spoke with and what he said was a mystery. He managed these calls with lip movements. At the sound of something falling, I went to the third room to find that Girish had come over. Girish had previously occupied the room that Adıtya and Anupam now lived in.

Girish was a soft-spoken boy. I thought he would stay for longer, changing the reputation of the short stays in the third room. But he left soon. The reason was his desire to do anything for his girlfriend. One day, his girlfriend Nannu fancied seeing him dance like Salman Khan. It so happened that when he was dancing the signature step of Salman Khan with the towel between his legs, everyone present in the house peeped through the loosely closed door. As a result, the coming days saw Girish mocked in the house. It was in good spirit but the shy boy felt embarrassed and one day, not able to take it anymore, he left the house.

Today, he had come to look for a visiting card. Aditya and Anupam were helping him in the search though it was very unlikely to find it in a house filled with crafts and artwork. However, turning over the mattress upside down, they were finally able to find the card.

It was 12:30 am but Harsh wasn't back yet. I feared if Himanshu had beaten up Harsh on his way back from the concert. I was awake waiting for him for a long time but gave up when I could not keep my eyes open any longer.

The next morning, I was getting ready and wondering whether Harsh had returned. Minutes later, a loud fart confirmed Harsh was back. Sometimes someone else's fart can also bring relief to you!

2

Graduation day – May 2008

The day I had been waiting for had finally arrived. It was Sid's graduation day. I returned from office an hour earlier. There was a line of bikes parked outside our house. As I approached the door, the fragrance of mixed perfumes filled my nose. I stepped into the house, teeming with curiosity.

The chaos was similar to a wedding house. Not less than fifteen over-spirited girls and boys were getting ready with the enthusiasm of brides and grooms. While girls helped each other with makeup, the boys were busy as well. If one was shaving, another was applying gel to his hair to make it stand. In one corner, someone had literally poured the perfume bottle on his shirt, while another sulked collecting the pieces of a broken perfume bottle. Making my way through this, I reached my room.

"When do we leave?" I asked Sid, happy and excited. He was dressed in formals and had just finished cleaning the side soles of his shoes with an old toothbrush. He was very particular about his shoes and maintained them sparkling new.

"We will leave at six," Sid said and opened the flap of his laptop.

"Great. I'll take fifteen minutes to get ready," I said as I pulled out my dress for the evening from the cupboard.

"No problem. Take your time," Sid said.

His gaze fixed on the laptop screen, he was thinking hard.

"What are you thinking?" I asked.

"About the patent," he said.

"Must be very difficult... Isn't it? That's why they charge so much to write them." I was still scouting for reasons to suspend the thought of me entering the field of writing patents.

"Difficult? Yes! A little. You have to think from each scenario. And no scenario at any point must coincide with the patent that has been acquired by someone earlier else the patent is not granted."

Sid's phone rang as he was speaking.

"Ok, come over and then we will discuss," he said and disconnected the call.

"Is anyone coming?" I asked.

"Yes, Rahul Patna is coming over. He said we may get an award today evening," Sid said. He looked happy but didn't seem convinced by what he had heard.

"What makes him think that?" I asked as my heart yearned for even a frail reason to support my optimism. That's me, always looking out for reasons to validate my decisions and desires.

"I don't know. You ask him when he comes."

After sometime, Rahul Patna walked into the room. Within two minutes, Kumar Rahul joined us too.

Rahul Patna was surrounded by Kumar Rahul, Sid, me and a few others who were waiting for the update he had got from college.

"Ok, enough of the drama! Now will you tell us how do you know we are getting the award?" Kumar Rahul asked.

Rahul Patna laughed but didn't give any details.

"He is lying," Sid dismissed him and stepped back to find a chair to sit on. Kumar Rahul also prepared to leave.

Seeing the excitement fading, Rahul Patna said, "Hey, don't leave. Listen up. I didn't see any list, but I think there are eighty percent chances are that we are getting it because I saw a lot of trophies in the Director's room."

"This is not valid logic," Kumar Rahul said.

"I know, but look at it this way. The technology projects have been done in groups of two-three members. Like the three of us, right?"

"Yes," Kumar Rahul said.

"If our project does get the award, we'll get three trophies. That is why there are many trophies there," he explained.

"You are mad." Kumar Rahul laughed.

With the bright green expanse of garden around it, the auditorium stood in the middle decorated with lights. It was buzzing with the energy. Girls and boys, dressed in their best made their way up and down the auditorium stairs escorting the guests. It was the day for the final year students. So when the seniors came as guests with their friends and family, it was the juniors who ran around to manage the event. The guests were welcomed at the reception with a bouquet of flowers. The veranda outside the hall was also decorated with diyas and colourful rangolis.

When we entered the hall, the song 'Khandissa' was being played in the background. It was dark inside. We slowly made way to our seats. I sat next to Sid. But even after ten minutes of sitting, I could not settle down. We had to either get up or squeeze ourselves to give way to those walking past our seats. It was mostly the design students. They were either looking for safety pins or requesting the technology boys to give their ties to make some adjustments to the dresses that were to be on the ramp in a few minutes.

Finally the buzz settled with a whisper that the chief guest had arrived. Everyone took their seats. The stage was shining bright. Lighting the lamp, the chief guest inaugurated the event. In no time, the soothing background music broke into loud upbeat music and the first set of models took over the ramp.

I witnessed one of my dreams come true. I could not believe

models were walking just a stone's throw from me. Perplexed and overwhelmed, I ended up watching the first fifteen minutes of the show from behind my camera. I didn't want to miss any moment.

Each design student presented a collection of six dresses. After a brief about the theme and inspiration, the models walked the ramp in sync with the music. The stage exploded with creativity. Not just the clothes but the shoes, accessories, makeup, body paint – everything was designed to present the collection in uniformity. At the end of each collection, the models presented the designer to the audience by walking alongside the designer on the ramp.

"Why don't you enjoy the show? I will get the photographs for you. See so many professional photographers are taking pictures," Sid said and I realised he was right.

After Sid, it was my camera that asked me to stop. Its memory was full. Frantically, I deleted some pictures and then sulked as I was unable to take pictures of the butterfly collection on the stage.

"Don't worry, you will soon see a bigger show. I will walk the ramp for you." Very seriously, Sid consoled me.

It was the second time he had expressed his desire to be on the ramp and although I was busy cleaning up my camera, I took note of what he had said because he rarely expressed his desires.

"It's Kritika next," Sid said in excitement and sat upright on the chair.

With my camera ready after deleting some photographs, I too took my best position to capture the pictures. I already loved her collection but it looked much prettier on the stage. It was soothing with colours like beige and maroon. Her wearable and very stylish collection that models wore with high boots and accessorised hair was the best collection of the evening. And her hard work to match the beads with the fabric was worth it and worked as icing on the cake that set her work apart from others.

"She will win the best designer award," I said.

"Looks like," Sid replied with eyes fixed on the stage as Kritika took a bow and the audience applauded and cheered for her.

Two more collections were showcased after Kritika's and the fashion show was over. Within minutes, the auditorium was transformed into a conference hall. A new set of lights brightly lit up the stage. A projector was set up and a podium and few tables and chairs were placed.

"What next?" I asked.

"You have seen what fashion designers do. Now see what fashion technologists do," Sid smiled.

Mr. Brandon, their faculty assumed a position on the podium and gave a brief description of the projects that were undertaken by the technology students.

Small groups of students took turns to present their projects. They had achieved significant savings for the companies they worked with but the applause after the presentations was nowhere close to the applause for the fashion show. Some of the guests had even started leaving. A few more presentations followed and the events of the evening came to an end.

The chief guest was escorted to the stage for the speech. As he spoke the stage behind him was prepared for the award ceremony. After the speech, the organizers asked all the final year design and technology students to come up on the stage.

"Shall I also come to the front? I asked Sid, "Will take your pictures."

"I am not getting any award. You stay here, else your seat will be gone."

After the speech and the photo session, the award ceremony started. Kritika didn't win the best designer award. There were few more awards for the design students but she didn't get any.

With a smile that she forced on her face, she clapped for others all through but when the last award also didn't come to her, her smile vanished. She looked up to see Sid and they both exchanged a quick glance. I was sure Sid would pull her through this.

After the design awards, it was time for the technology awards. Sid clapped as his classmates won the awards but he appeared lost. I knew what he was thinking.

No, he wasn't waiting for his name to be called. Instead, he was glad that he had finally passed out of the college with a degree.

The students stood in a semicircle on the stage. When their names were called, they walked to the chief guest to collect their award. Amidst this sound of claps and announcement, I suddenly saw Rahul Patna step out of his place. It seemed as though someone had pushed him. He instantly turned back in doubt to look at Kumar Rahul and Sid. In the meantime, Kumar Rahul too stepped out and then both the Rahuls pulled Sid towards the stage. The three of them walked the stage hand in hand.

Seeing them do the small jig and walk the ramp, I ran with my camera to take the most important and most unexpected pictures of the evening. Thankfully, I managed a few.

They had won the Best Innovation award for their project on Cost Benefit Analysis of DPOL.

"This is for you." Sid said handing over the trophy to me. His eyes were moist and voice was shaking.

I choked with emotions. But before Sid and I could share the moment, Rahul Patna and Kumar Rahul joined us.

"What was the confusion? Why didn't you guys move?" I asked clearing my throat and absorbing back the tears that were brimming.

"I wasn't listening," Sid said.

"I was listening, but I didn't hear our names," Kumar Rahul said.

Finally, Rahul Patna explained. "Not our fault. They first said the name of the project. It struck me it was our project so I stepped out. But I was confused when I turned back to see you both standing there blank. With no hope from you both, I waited for our names to be called out. When the names were said, Kumar Rahul managed some expressions but Sid was still standing lost and it is then that we both pulled Sid to take the walk on the ramp."

3

After Graduation Day

The Pact

"What are you doing these days?" I asked Sid as I sipped my Bournvita.

I managed to make Bournvita milk and Maggi on a small cylinder, which I had found a few days back underneath an inverted carton box in our kitchen.

"I have almost completed writing the patent. This week I will dispatch it."

"Okay and what plans for Bangladesh?" I asked. He was campus placed with three of his classmates in an apparel company in Bangladesh.

"I don't know," he said and picked up his Bournvita mug. "Why did you make it so hot?" He complained burning his tongue.

Honestly, hot milk wasn't my revenge on him for making me wait by delaying a decision on Bangladesh.

I had been asking him about Bangladesh for two months now. I didn't like the state of limbo and it concerned me. His going to Bangladesh meant I would also relocate to Delhi. I wanted to relocate to Delhi but I was happy to stay in Bangalore if he was staying in Bangalore. But he was just not making any decision.

However, I had thought about it and I clearly wanted him to stay back and pursue DPOL and set up his business. I felt, if he took up the job, his condition would be exactly like that dog who chases a car but doesn't know why he is doing so.

There were times when I was desperate to express my views but I had to be careful with my words because he listened to me. I wanted him to take a decision himself, free of any influence because becoming an entrepreneur was a big step. It could not be forced.

But now with just three weeks for him to leave for Bangladesh, I again struck the conversation, hoping he would have a plan.

And he finally spoke. "If I go, I will not be able to pursue DPOL," then he took a pause and a deep breath and said, "I think I don't want to go."

He said and looked at me for my reaction. I deliberately didn't react or say anything. I wanted him to elaborate about what was going on in his mind.

He added, "You are working after your studies. I should work too. If I don't work I will feel guilty."

It was time for me to speak up. "If the earning part deters you, I think you must talk to Dad." I knew he had spoken to him last night. Dad had called me after speaking to him, but I wanted to hear his version.

"I spoke to him yesterday," he said.

"Is it? What did dad say?" I asked pretending I didn't know anything.

"Dad said I am free to do whatever I wish but I must do it wholeheartedly, give it hundred percent sincerity and keep patience. He believes I have all the ingredients to achieve success in what I choose to do."

"See, now you have dad's official nod too."

"Yes," he smiled, "But dad said one more thing."

"And what's that?"

"He said that my both kids complement each other and if they both are together, they will achieve whatever they want."

"Of course, I am not going anywhere now. I am with you. Let's do it together. And we have spoken about it already, haven't we?"

"Yes, I know, but I still have a guilt that I should take up a job and earn," Sid said.

"I repeat... don't (pause) worry (pause) about (pause) earning (pause)," I said very clearly.

"Hmm..." he forced a smile on his face.

To free him of the guilt, I said, "Dad says we complement each other, right? So let's make it official with a pact."

"What pact?"

"I invest in you for you to chase your dream. When you have achieved your dreams, you invest in me for me to chase my dreams. How does that sound?"

He thought for a moment and said, "Sounds like an idea!"

Sid was amazed at the idea.

I added. "Since I am already earning and you are working on your dreams, let us continue this. So this day onwards, you are my investment."

"Okay. Anyway if we don't do it with this support from family then who else will," he said as he raised his hand to give me a high five.

"Yes exactly, and you know, it is the best investment I have made in my life."

"How is that?"

"People in a job can at best buy a Honda Civic or Accord. I mean EMI free. And that's what I will also own in few years. But when you have become a big businessman, I will get BMWs and Mercedes. We limit our desires when we work for someone, but in business, the sky is the limit."

Sid laughed, "You are so creative in your ideas."

"Oh you know... I so love it when I am praised for my wisdom. So here is another pearl of wisdom for you. *One can never sell his/her job to another person and earn money but a businessman always has the option to sell his/her business and make money."*

So finally, Sid didn't go to Bangladesh.

Panipat – The Dhaba cum Pub sorts Life

"You have only two DPOL sample dresses. The black and white western dress and the dragon jacket. Now make an entire collection," I said to Sid.

"Production run is quantity. Factories and export houses talk of producing in numbers. We have covered almost all the set ups in Bangalore but no one is ready to produce less than a hundred pieces."

"Hmm... but to start the business, we need a DPOL collection," Further contemplating on the options, I asked, "Where, besides Bangalore do you think we can develop the collection?"

"Panipat," he was prompt with the answer. I knew he must have already thought of Panipat, but must have been delaying it for some reason in his head.

Panipat reminded me of a dad's friend.

"You can talk to Dad. One of his friends is posted in the Haryana Pollution Board these days. Maybe he can help find a unit to develop your DPOL collection."

Encouraging him to take quick action, I reminded him of his impending Delhi visit. "And anyway, you have to go to Delhi to meet your lawyer regarding the case."

"Yes, a good idea. What would I do without you!" he exclaimed with happiness.

Grabbing his phone he went out of the room to speak to Dad. Things happened at lightning speed. Dad spoke with his friend, who within hours identified a unit where Sid could do his work.

To accommodate his Panipat work, Sid re-planned his travel. He decided to leave for home as soon as he could, stay there for a few days and then go to Panipat for a few weeks, come back home for another few days, meet the lawyer in Delhi and then return to Bangalore.

"Where is Sid?" I asked mom. It was the third day of his stay at home.

"He left for Panipat this morning." Mom complained, "What is the need to rush? He has just finished the studies. He could have stayed with us for a few more days. From the day he arrived here, he didn't even sit and talk with us. He was just running around to arrange things and then within two days he's left for Panipat."

I listened to her but I had no words to pacify a disappointed mother because I thought about Sid. He often asked me. 'Is it too late to start?' A boy in his early twenties talking about being late in starting his business amazed me. The least I could do was to support him in what he was doing.

"So all set for the production?" I called up Sid.

"Seems they said yes to uncle fearing to deny a pollution board official, but now they are saying they cannot accommodate my work."

"You want me to talk to uncle?"

"No, let it be. I will figure something out. There are a few other units nearby."

A few hours later, Sid found a unit where he could do his work. Not only was this unit better than the previous one, he also found a friend in the senior supervisor, Vivek.

When things do not work out the way we plan, we must not lose hope. Instead, we must keep working towards them. Something better is bound to happen.

He spent the whole day at the unit with no proper food. It was a tiring schedule. I wanted to help him but I could not go as I didn't have any leaves. I could not even talk to him during the day. I couldn't hear him at all because of the poor phone signal and the sound of machines in the background. The only respite was that he wasn't alone. Vivek was with him. And I spoke to him after 11 pm when he returned to his guest house.

"Where are you?" I asked him. It was the routine late night call to check if all was well.

"I am not home yet. It is raining heavily and the roads are flooded with muddy water. I took a rickshaw to home, but it has broken down."

He was talking loudly and I could hear the heavy pour of rain.

"Are you very far from home?" I asked loud enough, which made Sameer walk into my room to check if all was fine. Sameer was the new boy who had come to live with us in the third room.

"No, not very far but I am drenched and don't know the roads well, so am walking carefully," he said. I had to press the phone hard against my ear to make sense of what he was saying.

"Did you eat anything?" I asked Sid. Realising that Sameer was still standing, I simultaneously shook my head with a smile looking at him and pointed to the phone.

"Nothing. You keep the phone down. Let me figure out a way to reach home."

Ten minutes later, I called him again. He had reached home but he was waiting for the rain to stop so that he could go to Vivek's place to make the production preparation for the next day.

For the production to run smoothly, things were to be ordered from the city in advance. The things which were not available in the city were ordered from Delhi. But with his proactive planning, Sid was able to cope up.

Production was on track but it was not too long when Sid faced another issue. It was frequent power cuts, low voltage and fluctuations. Though the voltage improved at night, no labour was ready to work that shift. Vivek was able to persuade the labour to do night shifts but they turned it down every day. Work almost came to a halt.

"How was your day?" I asked during our daily chat. I was hopeful that he had sorted out the voltage problem.

"I am out. Will call you in thirty minutes," he said.

"Okay, but I hope all fine?" I asked him indirectly. I wanted to know why he was out so late. Eleven at night may not be late as far as cities are concerned, but for people in industrial areas, it is like midnight as people start the day early to work in shifts.

"Yes all fine, I am at a local roadside dhaba cum pub. These are locally called ahatas. I will tell you the story once I reach home."

"Dhaba cum pub?" I asked impatiently. He was in a hurry but I could not wait to know what could have taken him to a pub. Like me, he too felt giddy even with a few sips of tea or coffee.

"Will tell you. Wait for my call," he said and disconnected the call as sounds of people howling and singing could be heard in the background along with the blaring sounds of truck horns.

He called me an hour later. "I had thrown a party for the labourers. Vivek suggested that they will cooperate in night shift if I could arrange a small alcohol party. I asked Vivek to do it on my behalf and that I would sponsor it. But Vivek said it would be of no relevance if I didn't join them. So when you called, I was sitting there with a Coke. And the good news is that tomorrow onwards a team of six labourers is coming to work the night shift until I complete my work."

Braving the power cuts, whims and fancies of workers, location challenges and the terribly humid weather, Sid returned home after completing his work in a record three weeks' time. It was a dream come true for him.

"He must be sleeping?" I asked my mother. I had called home hoping to talk to Sid at length.

"Yes, he is sleeping," Mom responded, sounding sad.

"What happened?"

"Don't know, why all this happens to him."

"Please tell me mom, what happened?"

"I cannot say. Talk to your dad," she said on the verge of crying and handed over the phone to Dad.

Dad told me that Sid's left eye had become blood red. Explaining to me patiently, he said, "Need not worry. He will be fine soon. He is on medication and sleeping at the moment. I took him to the doctor and he said that exposure to colour and extreme heat has done this to his eyes."

After a week, Sid's infection got better, though the redness didn't go. But he could not stay back any longer. The next day afternoon, he had to meet the lawyer in Delhi and in the evening return to Bangalore. For the meeting in Delhi, Sid had to leave in the evening but on mom's insistence, Sid stayed back one more day.

Saharanpur's close proximity to the capital of the country is an added advantage. It is only a four-hour train journey to Delhi. The IIT Roorkee Saharanpur campus where we lived was earlier called IPT (Institute of Pulp and Paper Technology). It is strategically located between Duncan Goenka group's Star Paper Mill on one side and CPPRI (Central Pulp and Paper Research Institute). The campus is a complete world in itself with all the facilities and state of art Swedish designs of the buildings, houses, hostels, auditoriums and gardens. However, there is a disadvantage. It is located outside the city. But since the time we started travelling to Delhi, the disadvantage was transformed into an advantage as one of the city's railway stations was near to our campus.

Back to Bangalore – "I have a surprise for you..."

"How is your eye now?" I asked Sid peering into his left eye. It was still red but I wanted to know if it was painful.

"Better now," he said and made way into the house with one bag on his shoulder and a Skybag which he dragged.

"But it is still red," I said taking off his shoulder bag.

"It will go with time," he said as he set down his bags in our room.

As he freshened up, I started by asking the most important questions.

"How was your meeting with the lawyer? I hope you could make enough time for it?"

"The meeting was good. I met my lawyer for the first time in person but didn't feel it was our first meeting," he said wiping his face with a towel after the wash. "I had thought of him to be a very elderly and serious person, but he is very young. And the meeting went well. He was again appreciative of the recordings I have done."

I took pride in knowing that the lawyer appreciated Sid and jumped to my next question. "First step to your dream has been accomplished with the fabric in your hand. But tell me one thing... do you need to go to Panipat again or is it over?"

"Isn't over yet, but I need not go to Panipat, instead I will go home. The fabric needs to be stitched."

Thinking for a few minutes, he continued. "It is a hundred metres of fabric. I have brought it home and washed it. Mom helped me and we dyed it too. See my nails are still black," he showed me his blue-black nails.

"How did you wash so much fabric at home?" I asked amazed.

"Don't ask! It was so heavy after soaking it in water. We washed it in the bathtub. My body is paining even now," he said pressing his arms.

"But why dye?"

"Without the dye, the entire hundred metres DPOL fabric looked the same. Only after dying it you can see the different colours, texture and embedded design," he said.

"Hmm... okay, so when do we get it stitched?"

"When we go home for Diwali. For now it sits in the trunks and almirahs. Mom and Dad helped me wrap it in cotton voile with Odonil to keep it fresh," he smiled.

"Aah, royal treatment given to your creations already," I said. "But you did go through a lot of hardship," I added remembering the tough days he had spent at Panipat.

"Don't be sad for what happened. I am fine now. And guess what, I have a surprise for you!" Sid said.

"What is it?"

"I have applied for the fashion week."

"Fashion week?"

At the first, I could not understand what he was saying. Then I recalled that he had twice mentioned his desire to participate in a fashion show. He had said that he would attend a fashion show the day he walks the ramp.

"Yes, the Lavender Fashion Week?"

"Great, then why apply only for Lavender, apply for others too. By the way, what are the other fashion shows in our country?"

"Lavender and Willows are the two popular shows in the country. Lavender is conducted in Mumbai and Willows in Delhi. In both the shows, only established designers exhibit their designs. This leaves almost no scope for the fresh talent to enter the fraternity. But Lavender does offer a chance to young designers. It invites applications from young talent for their New Gen initiative. However, they select only six applications from across the country."

"Ok, so you have sent in your application for the New Gen show?

"Yes, for the August 2008 show. They not only seek applications, they ask for a garment too."

"Garment?" Could not think of any garment he had that he may have sent for a fashion show. "You mean you have sent a garment too?" I looked at him in surprise and excitement, waiting for him to divulge the details.

He smiled and said. "I have sent a coat made from the DPOL fabric along with a skirt. I have also provided a write-up on DPOL. Now hoping that the way DPOL has been appreciated internationally, it will be in India too."

I was happy. Sid had come a long way.

This is not how you meet a CEO of a company

"Stop over feeding them! Not illness, but they'll die of over feeding." I said to Sid as I entered our room to find him peeping inside his aquarium with fish food in his hand.

Everyone was asleep when I left for the walk, but on my return the house was bursting with the usual energy. Met Rajat in the porch. He was wiping the mirror of his bike. Impeccably dressed in jeans, a t-shirt, shoes and not to miss the goggles and hair set in spikes, he was ready to go out. He was always dressed to impress so it was difficult to say if he was going to college for breakfast or to date a girl.

Inside the house, Aditya was getting ready to go to his NGO. Anupam was in the living room reading Ayn Rand's *The Fountain Head*. Half door closed, Harsh was sleeping. And in our room, Sid was watching his aquarium. The fish had started to die, so the aquarium was under close observation over the past few days. Sid suspected the tiger fish which we added to the aquarium was carnivorous, but I was almost sure that over-feeding was killing them.

"I didn't feed them. Was just looking at the angel fish... she is slow today."

"She'll be fine. Come, let's have breakfast."

It was Sid's first Sunday morning after his return from home. To make him feel like home, on my way back from the morning walk, I had brought breakfast for him.

"Breakfast? You went to Food Days?" Sid asked in surprise with eyes wide open.

Walking uphill four hundred metres to Food Days was tough. But it was tougher for our housemates. Like others we didn't just walk uphill, we dragged ourselves in our food deprived state. The absence of a kitchen in our house was the reason.

And if ever, in an attempt to improve the karma, anyone ever volunteered to go to Food Days, the person was loaded with requests. And the requests were not limited to our home, they poured in from our neighbours too.

"Yes, have got idli sabmbhar and chow chow bhath," I said catching on my breath.

Sid served it feeling indebted.

"Breakfast is the most important meal, you should not skip it," I said to him as he poured the sambhar from the small polythene pouches into our bowls.

No college meant skipping meals for not only Sid but Rajat and Harsh as well. Earlier they had breakfast, lunch and dinner at the college cafeteria, but now after passing out of college they neither went to college nor did they go to Food Days.

"I think we should buy a microwave," I said after having my first spoon of sambhar. It was no longer hot and tasted bland. "We can at least re-heat our food and may be cook at times."

"Cook? For that matter, do we have a kitchen?"

He was right. Two years back when I tried to set up the kitchen, the condition wasn't this bad. But today, it was ten times more crowded. Our kitchen was so popular now that it was branded as a college project pool, where almost every day little groups of college students were found scouting for relevant project work, which they could reuse with some modifications.

The sink, slab and racks were overflowing with charts, socks, bulbs, tree branches, thermocol, glowsticks, paints, mugs and what not. And the portion of the slab that was visible was stamped with the muddy shoe marks.

"Someone at the door... you keep eating, I will be back," Sid said.

He returned with a courier parcel. He had not been selected in the Lavender Fashion Week. They had returned his dress. He also gave me a letter, which came with the courier.

"Hmm... does this make you sad?" I asked him after reading the letter. It was a silly question but Sid had to be questioned because he wouldn't express his feelings until asked specifically.

"Hmmm..." he smiled and rolled his eyes to look at the walls of the room – a standard way that many boys use to hide their emotions. "I was looking forward to getting selected but this is not the end of the world."

"Yes, of course," I said cheerfully to keep him encouraged.

"And anyway, it happens twice in a year. It has been returned for the fashion week to be held in August 2008 but I can apply again in December for the show to be held in February or March 2009."

"And December is just here," I said and counted August till December on my fingers in mute. "Hardly four months away."

"Yes, you are right. And this reminds me that the Foerbes group CEO wants to meet me to know more about DPOL."

"Okay...?" I said.

"I met him at the Textile conference. Since then we have exchanged emails but have never met," Sid said attacking my chow chow bhath with a spoon.

"Don't you dare..." I said pulling my plate away.

"Just for the change of taste... please," he pleaded.

"Hmm... okay just one spoon."

He jumped at the offer and dug his spoon in my chow chow bhath and said, "So he is visiting Bangalore with his team next weekend and wants to meet me."

"This is great. Finally there are people who understand your work."

As usual, a glimmer of hope was enough for me to ride on the waves of a dream. "By the way, what did you just say? Where did you meet him?"

"I told you about it. You forgot?" he said as he approached my plate with his spoon again.

"Stay away... talk from a distance," I said, holding the plate close to my mouth with the spoon in my other hand.

"You got me wrong. I was just keeping the spoon back," he smiled and said. "I met him in the Textile Conference – Bangalore Chapter. It was held just two months before you arrived."

"Yes, now I remember. It's the one you chaired too. 4000+ textile and fashion students attended it. And the conference was held at an engineering college, right?" I blabbered, non-stop in one breath.

"Yes!"

"See, I remember."

"I am responding to this email. Can we go on Sunday to meet him?" Sid asked as he sat with his laptop.

"We? What would I do there?"

"I have to meet him in a hotel near Bangalore Central. You be at Bangalore Central, I will quickly finish the meeting and join you. Then we will explore the food court there. Heard it is good. We can go shopping too. We might find a microwave of your choice there."

Agreed that we were food deprived all the time and he was excited about the food, but he was after all meeting the CEO of a company. But his plan did not have even a pinch of seriousness which a meeting with a CEO of a company deserved.

"Are you planning a meeting with a CEO of a company or planning a day out?" I asked him after listening to his elaborate plan.

"Don't give me that look," he said. "I know you are thinking I am being careless. But trust me, it is not going to be a life-changing event. I have attended many such meetings. There were times when I took these meetings very seriously and when things didn't work out, I was broken and took a long time to get back on track. But now I go relaxed. If it happens it is well and good. If it doesn't, something else will."

> **A rejection is nothing more than a necessary step in the pursuit of success.**
>
> **—Bo Bennett**

The next weekend we reached the mall early. As planned, we had our breakfast at the food court. After sometime, Sid left for the meeting.

"How was it?" I asked. It had taken him more than two hours to return.

"It was okay. Let's talk about it once we reach home. Did you like any microwave?"

"Not exactly," I replied disappointed.

Deciding to buy the one available at the electronics shop near our home, we headed to the food court again to have lunch and pack dinner.

"Before the meeting started, the CEO in a very disinterested tone said that he had just forty-five minutes to come to a conclusion," reaching home, Sid narrated the incident to me.

"He may have been preoccupied, but why disinterested? It was he who had called you."

"It was to build pressure. I know this from so many such meetings I have attended."

"Ok, go on."

> **Every failure has a lesson to teach. This is how we accumulate experience. And experience cannot be taught. It has to be lived.**

"We discussed the present garment construction and design scenarios. It was followed by my presentation on what DPOL could offer. He was quite impressed, though he pretended he wasn't."

"What makes you think he was impressed?" I asked.

"All through, he asked back to back questions and very relevant ones. And if not this, look at the most evident reason. He began with saying that he had only forty-five minutes for the meeting but he ended up speaking to me for more than two hours."

"Okay, but what was the agenda of the meeting?"

"It won't be any fun if I tell you the agenda right away."

I hated to wait but had no choice. Taking a long breath, I prepared myself to hear him out.

"It was a lot of information sharing but at the end of the two hours also, I sat unaware of the agenda. It was difficult to digest that a CEO, that too of Foerbes, who has travelled half the world was sitting on a Sunday afternoon with me only to share information. Finally, not seeing the meeting going anywhere, I thought, since he didn't seem to have any agenda, I should put forward my agenda. So I told him that I was looking for funding to produce and market my product."

"What did he say to it?"

"He did the most unexpected thing."

"And what's that?"

"Hold on, telling you... you mind passing the water bottle to me?" Sid said, deliberately testing my patience wearing a smirk on his face.

I was impatient and angry for the suspense he was building, but I contained my emotions and passed the bottle to him.

"He offered me ten lakhs for DPOL," Sid exclaimed.

"My goodness!" I knew DPOL was great and all but never in my wildest dream had I imagined it could be worth so much.

"What did you say then?" I sat upright to give apt attention to the climax, "I would have fainted hearing this."

"I wasn't prepared for this but I was able to contain my excitement because I never thought of DPOL as something which I would want to sell. It is my passion. So I thanked him for the consideration and said 'no' to the offer."

"Hmm... okay. But he may consider to fund as well. Did you not ask him again. I mean after saying 'no' to sell it?"

"I did but he declined to fund it. However, he has offered to meet again. Now he wants me to quote a price that I think is correct for my technology."

"Talk to Dad about it," I said. I have always wanted to be like my father so whenever there was a situation, I was keen to check my father's reaction.

Sid laughed. "That's the first thing I did when I stepped out of the meeting. He said not to even think about selling it."

Did I tell you about Armani?

I was excited about reading *Business Maharajas* by Geeta Piramal *again*! This was the third time I was going to read it after I finished reading *Losing my Virginity* by Richard Branson. I found all entrepreneurship books very inspiring. Now and then, I read out snippets from these books to Sid too. Not that he required any motivation but I did it for my happiness.

"I think it's time we buy new books. Shall we go get some?" Sid asked me.

"You want to go? Or you are asking me because I am reading the *Business Maharajas* again?"

"No, no... you know we have not bought any for a while." Every three months, Sid and I bought books. Dad had made this a ritual since we were kids.

"I know, but isn't it early? It is just five. We can go an hour later," I said.

"I don't think too many people will be here this evening."

The evening gatherings at our house had become weak. Sid's classmates started to leave to join work in different companies. His classmates with whom he had to go to Bangladesh had also left. However, things in our house didn't change much. Rajat and Harsh had joined Bangalore-based companies while Aditya and Anupam also continued to stay in the house. They were now in the fourth year of their college. I was going to my office while Sid continued his usual work.

For a change, I did not pick any biography or entrepreneurship book, rather I chose a book by Dr Brian Weiss, *Many Masters Many Lives.* Sid as usual picked up an encyclopaedia. He is fond of big books with big pictures.

Book shopping followed by dinner – it was an evening well spent. I went to sleep as soon as we got home. I had to wake up 5:30 am but forcing myself to sleep didn't help much. I got up at 1:30 am to find Sid awake. He maintained that he was most productive at night.

Seeing him engrossed, I wanted to know what he was doing but I did not ask. I didn't want him to think that I was checking on his sincerity.

"Awake?" Seeing me awake, he asked.

"Yes, trying to sleep though."

I resisted asking what he was doing, but he spoke up himself, "I was thinking about the progress we have made over the last one year."

He was in a reflective mood. We took stock of the events over the past year.

» *Court case – almost won*
» *NIFT innovation award – won*
» *Final Patent – submitted*
» *DPOL Collection – If not in Bangalore, we developed it in Panipat. Only stitching is pending.*
» *Publications – done and going on, our information website seems to be in good shape now.*

» *Lavender fashion week – rejection*
» *Foerbes CEO meeting – we don't want to go ahead .*
» *Funding – hasn't happened but we are still trying.*

"I think we have started it late. What do you think?" He asked his usual question again.

"Why do you keep forgetting Armani's story?"

Complement each other to keep going.

"You nailed my question. How apt! Did *I* tell you about Armani?"

"Yes, it was you who told me that Armani started his career as a designer at the age of forty-five. He was a window dresser before he founded the brand Armani. And I could fit this response to your question because it was just a week back that I was reading about Armani and his very close friend who had encouraged him to start the brand."

"We have inspiring stories around us but we forget to apply them to the situations we face in our life," he said.

"Don't worry, we have each other to remind us of these stories," I said. "And coming back to your question. It is never late to start, but then it is always good to start early. And you are an early starter. So relax!"

"Had it not been your support, I would have not achieved what I have today." At midnight, we were in a mutual admiration mode.

It is very important to feel good about oneself. Do it yourself and do it often.

"You see, I have a photographic memory. I remember things so well and that's how I can remind you correct examples all the time."

"Ok, enough! Where did your photographic memory go when you wrote your IIT entrance exams?" he jibed.

He was happy and it felt like the right time to talk to Sid about this one thing that was on my mind for the past few days.

"What do you think about moving to Delhi?" I asked him.

He was listening. After a pause, I continued, "There isn't any need for us to stay in Bangalore. You can do what you are doing from Delhi as well and we would be closer to our parents also."

To my surprise, he said. "Yes, you are right, but you have your work here."

"I can ask for an internal transfer to Delhi."

"Hmm... yes we can move but discuss this at office only once we are back from holidays," he said. We were going home for Diwali.

"It's late. Sleep now. Shall I put off the lights?" I made an attempt to force him to go to bed.

"Give me just two minutes," he said and turned towards his laptop. "And if you are awake, can you please come here for a minute."

"Hmm... tell me," I asked going to him. I looked at the screen of his laptop. "What is this?"

"It is the email from the Central Silk Bureau Director who wants to meet me regarding DPOL."

"So what are you thinking? Will you go?" I asked.

"There are some officials in the Silk Bureau who are notoriously known for poaching the work of others and publishing it under their name. A similar request came during our college days too and it is then that my professor, who encouraged DPOL had warned me about the Silk Bureau. I didn't go earlier but this time I will. I will be careful about divulging the details."

"When are you going?"

"At eleven tomorrow."

"What do you want from me?"

"Can you respond to this email?" he almost pleaded. He didn't like writing emails. "In the meantime, I will change the water of the aquarium. See the water looks dirty," he said.

No wonder, he was most productive at night. Who else could think of cleaning the aquarium at midnight?

"I will write your email but don't change water now. It is 2:30 am! The fish are sleeping."

"No, they are awake!"

The next day, when I returned from office, I asked Sid, "How was your meeting?"

"Rahul Patna had come along with me. It was the same old story. The director asked a lot of questions. I felt he doubted the potential of DPOL and had made a mistake. I got carried away and in an attempt to prove my points, divulged a few details. But when Rahul kicked me under the table, I checked myself."

"What happened then?"

"I requested for his approval to use the Silk Bureau technologies and equipment to develop DPOL."

"He agreed?"

"No, he declined, but cleverly continued the discussion. However, unable to get the complete answers he could not hide his desperation any longer. Gradually the discussion got heated and came to an end."

"So you have one more event to add to your experience," I said after listening to the narration of yet another pursuit.

He smiled and nodded.

Dad's friend's repentance on naming his son Sid

Sid always had one thing in the pipeline. Just few days before leaving for home for Diwali, he told me that he had come to know that FCDI was promoting ethical and green fashion. They were keen to work with upcoming designers.

Sid felt that this was the right opportunity and forum for him to present his work. He wrote an email to FCDI but there was no reply. Few more reminders followed but still there was no reply. He then came to know that a good reference could help him get a response.

Sid spoke with Dad. Dad knew the CEO of the company that sponsored the Willows Fashion Show that was organized by FCDI. But Dad didn't agree to talk to anyone. Sid convinced Dad that he just wanted a reply to his email and a true feedback. And finally with Dad's help, there was a response. They wanted to meet Sid.

A date was fixed after the Diwali week.

We are lucky to be born in an information age with information accessible anytime, anywhere. Just as we spend time on Facebook every day, if we spend even ten minutes to read about what's happening in our area of interest, it can keep us going. If we read about what we loved doing as a kid, we may discover our passion. This helps us to remain forever young and never retire in life.

It was nice to be home for Diwali. There were other reasons to celebrate as well. Not only had Sid finished his college, he had won the award as well. And it was almost obvious that he'd win the case too.

From early morning, friends and families had started coming over with sweets. In the evening, we also visited them with gifts.

"Why dinner, Mom?" Sid asked mom. After having visited a few places, mom disclosed to us that we were to join Kaushik uncle's family for dinner.

Sid and I never liked attending weddings or going to parties and dinners. That's why mom had been secretive about the plan.

"This was due for quite a while and they have been asking about you for so many days. Uncle and aunty are fond of you."

Already standing outside of their house, we had no choice.

We were also fond of Kaushik uncle and aunty so we didn't really mind. As kids we visited their home during summer vacations. They had two daughters and a son. The eldest daughter was Sid's age, the second daughter two years younger and the boy was the youngest. He was still in school.

The dinner was followed by a chatting session. Everyone seemed to be enjoying the evening. Sid was talking with uncle while his two daughters and Dad listened. Mom was also happy discussing dinner recipes with aunty. The young boy ran around the room playing with his remote control car.

I thought dinners were not that bad and we could attend our house parties at least. But just when I was beginning to believe this, things changed.

"Your college must have been over now," uncle asked Sid.

"Yes, uncle," Sid replied. He didn't know what was coming.

"Thank god you could finish college. I came to know of your high court case," he said laughing.

"So what's the status?" aunty asked. She dropped her discussion with mummy and turned towards us to be part of this discussion.

"I have almost won it," Sid replied.

"Good good... and where have you been placed?" uncle asked Sid. Then looking at Dad he said, "Must be in Bangalore with a nice package. After all, Bangalore is the place."

"Uncle, I didn't take up the job," Sid replied.

"So it didn't happen?" Uncle asked anxiously, "Or did you turn it down?"

"I turned it down."

"But why?" he asked in a rather loud voice. I feared to think what he would have done to his kids if they had done something like what Sid had.

Realising he was pretty loud, he toned down to ask further, "Why did you do this? Don't you realise that you are troubling your parents."

There was silence though Sid and Dad still smiled.

Uncle was still not done. He continued, "Parents want to see their kids settle down and get married so they can do away with the responsibility. Isn't it, sir?" he asked my dad who was still smiling.

"Sid has developed a technology. He wants to work on it and I am happy to see him do what he wants," Dad answered with contentment.

Seeing Dad speaking in support of Sid, uncle got confused. Until now he thought he was representing a parent in his conduct with Sid. But when it went kaput, he patted Sid's back laughingly and said, "Okay great hmm... scientist... nice."

Just then his son came and stood near him. "You know, Ashu's name is Sid too," he looked at his son and then looked at Sid to say. "I named him after you because I wanted him to be like you... but now I sincerely hope that he does not become like you," he laughed out loud.

"I mean... sir can manage this but I can't..." he said when he realised a moment later what he had said. But it was too late. The happy Sid had withdrawn from the discussion.

Dad read Sid's silence. He knew what could follow. He immediately steered the conversation in a different direction by enquiring the health of uncle's parents.

It worked. Sid calmed down after some time. However, there was a time when Sid would answer back aggressively but with more and more criticism coming his way, he had learned to take it in his stride.

The most recent humiliation was bestowed upon him when he was home after his Panipat trip. When he was spreading his fabric in the garden under the sun to dry it, dad's colleague took a dig at him. Uncle said, "Don't worry, kid, enjoy life, have good food, make good health, you will get a job."

Sid politely replied that he intended to set up his business. Paying no heed to it, uncle smiled sarcastically and walked away. He knew what Sid was doing. Dad had mentioned to him about Sid's plan but he never bothered to understand it and every time he saw Sid, he said the same things.

Inspiration from home

"Dad, where are you sending all this?" Sid asked dad pointing towards the chairs, tables and coolers, which were being loaded in a garden wagon by the household help.

Dad and I were watering the plants when Sid joined us.

"This is old furniture. Now you both don't stay here so I am moving it to the garage. Will get these polished to keep them termite free."

"Why do you need to do that? Just let it go, dump it."

"No, all this will be used very soon," Dad said.

"But where?" Sid asked.

"When you set up your business. they'd cost a lot if you were to go to buy them."

Yet again I was inspired by my dad's wisdom. It was just the previous night that the Kaushik uncle episode had taken place. I thought, if not at night, we'd discuss it in the morning. But instead, with no mention of it, Dad was making plans to contribute to Sid's dream. Dad always emerged unaffected.

Mom added, extending a cup of coffee to Dad. "Especially when you start up, unexpected expenditures are incurred and re-use of this furniture will give you respite at that time."

Defining a family dream makes the dream coming true so much easy.

It was a priceless moment and a glorious addition to innumerable such instances where Mom and Dad reflected the faith they had in Sid.

Our vacation was over. Dad joined us for the meeting in Delhi. Sid presented his work at FCDI. He also shared the testimonials he had received from all over the world. But FCDI displayed no interest in it. It was a brand new experience at a place where we were most hopeful. Until now, things hadn't worked out because people wanted to buy the technology or they wanted to get it in their name. However, they had all appreciated the technology.

"These experiences are part and parcel of life. Similar things happen in a job and here you are doing it for yourself. So just go on," Dad said.

"Hmm... yes. Another experience added to the portfolio," Sid said.

"We are planning to move our base to Delhi," I said to Dad. Sitting at the airport with heavy hearts, I felt the situation demanded we discuss something else.

"This is good, but don't do it for your mother and me. Focus on your career. We are fine. But if you really think it does not matter you be in Bangalore or Delhi, then come, we will be the happiest."

Sid was still gazing at his shoe laces.

Dad placed his hand on Sid's shoulder and said, "Anyway, Sid is coming in March to get his remaining collection stitched. And I think the final hearing of the case will take place around that time. We can discuss your move to Delhi at that time in your Mom's presence."

"Yes." Sid replied, "But I'll be coming alone as she has office."

"Doesn't matter, you can represent me in the discussion," I said.

Looking at me, Dad said smiling, "But remember one thing. Those who first decide on location and then on career, do not go far."

4

An Unexpected Set of Events

Satyamine fiasco

"I think, now you can discuss about the transfer in your office. In the meantime, let me also give one more try at raising funds," Sid said to me as the aircraft prepared to take off.

Sid met Abhay. Abhay ran a consulting firm that acted as a bridge between the VCs and the start-ups. Sid told him that he had already spoken to most of the VCs, angels and the Foerbes CEO, FCDI, Silk Bureau, etc. But Abhay said he had a new idea to approach them."

My manager also agreed to transfer me to Delhi but asked me to wait until the end of January. He reasoned that since Christmas was just a month away, so finding a suitable opportunity for me in Delhi wasn't a great idea as most of the people were away on their annual leaves.

Sid got busy with Abhay in revamping his presentations packs for the VCs. Simultaneously, he spent time interacting with students interested in green fashion. He also shared his research updates with the international journalists who had become good friends. With the close down of work in Christmas season, I also helped Sid.

After the Christmas and New Year break, charged up with dreams for the year 2009, I reminded my manager to initiate my transfer to Delhi. He reciprocated with the same urgency and right away spoke to the HR in Delhi to find work for me in the Delhi office on priority.

To my surprise, just two days later, HR came back to me with two suitable opportunities. They suggested I get further details on both the opportunities and identify which suited me more. A discussion was set with a Delhi manager the next day itself.

To prepare for the call I opened my Outlook email at 8:30 am. I saw the Delhi manager had cancelled our meeting without giving any reason.

I rushed to my manager's cabin to find out if he knew the reason. But the moment I stepped out of my bay, I saw hundreds of people standing in groups near the coffee area on our floor. I walked briskly to join my colleagues.

Satyamine had gone bankrupt. The phones rang non-stop. Families and friends had called after seeing the breaking news on the news channels. A group of MBA students who had joined recently were worried about their education loans. Another group discussed EMIs for homes and cars. Some girls and boys had even started crying. However, there emerged a group that appeared happy too. I wondered why. And then I heard their plan of becoming millionaires. They were buying the Satyamine shares that had touched rock bottom.

The chaos increased with time, but no one came to explain the situation. Managers had literally locked themselves in the meeting room. It was speculated they were not allowed to interact with the employees.

In the afternoon, word was sent out from the managers that the news was not a hundred percent correct and everything was going to be fine.

But it got worse. Things changed overnight. The credit card companies blocked the cards of Satyamine employees. The debit card limit was reduced. Telecom companies started pestering us to pay the bills right away. This was the immediate impact and the situation worsened over days.

Few days later, Satyamine started publishing the lists of people to be sent on forced sabbatical, which everyone knew would end in termination of their jobs. Employees openly started looking out for jobs. Their managers also helped them.

It was disheartening to see an institution crumble down but it was worse to see how the competitors exploited Satyamine employees. They offered salaries much lower than their current salaries. But Satyamine employees had no choice. It was better to earn less than not to earn at all.

I also had only one option. It was to look for a job outside Satyamine. I felt very bad because Satyamine was my first workplace. It gave me my first onsite and was the company I wanted to work for my entire career.

I was compelled to look for a new job when my manager was about to leave. I aggressively looked for jobs and attended telephonic interviews. But it got stuck on the issue of salary. I faced instances when HR laughed at me saying I had no right to state my salary expectations.

It was humiliating and disheartening but I went to office every day even if there were a handful of people around. Some had left and some preferred to stay at home to prepare for interviews. I kept myself busy by constantly looking for that one job where the HR would not laugh at me. The rest of the time I spent on reading about new business ideas and entrepreneurship on internet.

Reading keeps our mind stable and strengthens it to dream even in adverse conditions.

"I hope you are not disturbed with what is happening and what am I asking, that can't be you!" Sid said.

Lost in my thoughts, I was sitting alone in our room with a pen in my hand and a diary in front of me.

"No, no, not disturbed. I was thinking that as nothing much is happening in office, I can start exploring the handicraft business," I had read on internet about jute.

"Jute is still common, why don't you focus on banana fibre? It is a soft fibre and can be twisted for its flexibility. You can make many things out of it."

"Banana fibre? I have never heard about it... Who told you about it? Dad?"

"Dad would definitely know about it but I know of it from college. Learnt about it in Hampi."

"Hampi?"

"Don't tell me you've never heard of Hampi?" he laughed at me. "How dumb!"

It was an attempt to coax me to fight with him and get out of my gloomy state.

"Whatever! Tell me about it now."

"Hampi is a UNESCO world heritage site about five hundred kilometres from Bangalore. The place has both religious and historic significance. I have been there as it is compulsory for all the students from our college to go there and do cluster development projects."

"What is the religious and historic significance of the place?" I interrupted.

"I knew you will ask this." He teased me. "Will tell you about it when we go there. But for now I want to tell you that if you decide to work on banana fibre, Amit AD can help you. He stayed in Hampi for the longest period of time and developed many products. You know, he even created chappals (bathroom slippers) with the fibre?"

Sid called Amit AD and asked him to get a few sample products. Amit was the accessory design (AD) student so he was known as Amit AD. He was one of Sid'd best buddies and was also his first roommate when he joined college. I had also known Amit AD for over four years.

Sid woke me up. It was 12:30 pm. Amit AD was standing tall with a shoulder bag and back brushed long hair. It took me a minute to recognize him as I was meeting him after two years.

"Nice t-shirt, Amit" I said. On top of a pair of rugged jeans he wore an orange tee that had horizontally torn rows on the front to reveal a Radha Krishna image in the background.

"Thanks... and sorry to keep you waiting," he said and extended a pack of Cadbury chocolate to me. "This is for you."

"I should have got one for you. Why did you get it?" I said as I accepted the chocolate.

"No, no... I had to get it for you. I am sorry for not coming to meet you for so many months. And today also I have come so late. I expected you would be mad at me."

"It's okay... I know you were busy."

Amit was working on a design project with an MNC and his office was sixty kilometres away from HSR.

"And what's with the long hair, Amit?" Sid said pulling his leg. "Heard you have scaled the girls' charts with this Arjun Rampal look."

Amit blushed and hurriedly pulled out the products from his bag.

"For now let's focus on banana fibre."

I had a wide spread of products in front me. There were pen holders, hair clips, bangles, slippers, hand fans, bags and what not.

Amit was happy to help. He quickly gave an overview of the demand of banana fibre products, from where to source the products and how to engage in the business.

"But it is not going to be easy," I said as we started talking about the risks and challenges.

Sid interrupted, "At least start it. You will contribute to the employment of so many people by promoting their products. Who knows later we merge it in our business. It can be the CSR (corporate social responsibility) of our business."

As he spoke, Sid proved yet again that he was a visionary. Things were not looking bright on the funding front but he had no doubts on his dreams.

Never let go of your dreams. Never stop dreaming more because dreams are what keep us alive and give a meaning to our life.

"Hmm... Sid is right. We must make a start at least, and if required, we can visit Hampi too," Amit suggested.

"Yes, Heera would be glad to meet you," Sid teased Amit.

"Oh, yes! It's been a long time since I met Heera," Amit laughed.

"Who is Heera? She lives in Hampi?" I asked anxiously.

"Suspense..." they both said in unison.

If not the VCs, Bali ka Khazana will fund us

We decided to buy products from the NGOs and sell them. We also decided to connect the NGOs with the companies that required customised gifts for Diwali, New Year and corporate events.

"Apart from Hampi, we can source banana fibre products from Chennai too," Amit handed me a fluorescent green paper on which he had scribbled the names of various NGOs using a magenta sketch pen. Designers are colourful in whatever they do.

"You took so long... we have almost finished the discussion," I said to Sid.

He had stepped out to take a phone call.

"The call was over long back. I was with Sunil feeding the horse," Sunil was Sid's classmate and he had recently shifted with us on a temporary basis.

"A horse?" Amit asked in a state of shock. "You mean a real horse?" He looked back and forth at me and Sid seeking an answer. "Don't tell me that you guys have a pet horse now. This house is crazy, specially you two when it comes to animals."

"Yes, a real horse?" Sid said.

"But I didn't see it when I came. Where is it?"

"Come I will show you." Sid said.

"Okay..."Amit got up in excitement.

"So here it is. His name is Chetak," Sid introduced Chetak to Amit. "And Chetak this is Amit," he said rubbing Chetak's forehead.

Amit's happiness had no bounds. He smiled ear to ear on seeing Chetak standing bold and strong in our porch. Chetak looked beautiful. His brown coat was shining under the sun.

Carefully watching his steps, not to stamp Chetak's droppings, Amit went close Chetak to touch him. Happy and excited, he opened a flurry of questions. "Where did you get him from? And will you be able to keep him... I mean how can you clean so much shit every day? At night, will he come inside your house?"

"We found him," Sunil who was feeding the horse with gram and pulses answered Amit.

"What do you mean by we've found him? It's not a dog or cat. It is a large and beautiful animal. You don't spot them on roads roaming just like that."

"Okay, relax." Sid intervened. "Chetak is not ours. He just comes to us in the evening to have some gram. He belongs to an old person who lives in a village behind HSR."

"Animals also know which house to come to. But man! This is a lot of shit to clean," Amit said as Sunil poured a bucket full of water to clean the porch and ramp.

It sure was lot of shit to clean everyday but it was immense happiness to meet Chetak every evening. He came every evening to display his gratitude for what we had done for him two weeks back.

A month back, I had spotted Chetak outside our house near the park area. Grazing, it limped as he moved forward. Its hind legs were tied with a rope to restrain him to small steps but the limp was because of an invisible injury on his left hind toe. I looked for his owner but could not find anyone. I felt bad for it but I could not wait longer. I was getting late for office. To my delight, I met Chetak at the same place the next day also. Again I could not find its owner. This happened for a week every day outside our house. Finally, I decided to wake up early on the weekend and look for the owner.

I stood outside my house. An hour later, a lean man went near Chetak and signalled him to follow him as he jumped to sit on his bicycle. He told me that he had got the horse from the army cantonment. They had let him go because of his injury. Now he used Chetak to carry clothes around. He was a washerman.

I asked him to free his hind legs as he already had trouble walking. From next day, I saw Chetak at the same place but he had no ropes on his legs. But the surprise happened two days later when Sunil called me to show Chetak standing right outside our house. Not sure if he understood what I had done for him, but that day onwards, he started coming to our house in the evening. He would come and touch the gate of our house with his nose. Sunil fed him gram. Chetak would stay for an hour and leave after gifting us with two kilograms of his droppings.

Animals never forget any act of kindness done to them. Be kind to them. Your small act can mean a lot to them. So step ahead and help.

"Did you find anything yet?" Sid enquired if I had found a suitable job in Delhi. After introducing Amit to Chetak, we returned to our room.

"No, nothing. I am so sorry. You are also stuck in Bangalore because of me."

It was February now but I had not been able to find any job and the chances of losing mine at Satyamine increased with every passing day. Many employees had already been sent on forced sabbatical. Many had left to join other places.

"No problem. Don't worry and take your time. I asked you

only because I was thinking that since we may be leaving Bangalore soon, why not visit Hampi," Sid said.

"And what about your work?" I asked Sid. He was busy with Abhay.

"Nothing positive on the funding part. Abhay has asked me to pitch the designers now. And I can do that only when my collection is ready. So I will pursue the designers after I return from home."

"When are you going home, Sid?" Amit asked.

"Next month." Sid replied.

"Okay, we can go to Hampi," I said. "Monday is a holiday. On Friday I will take a day off," I decided instantly.

Immersed in work, I had forgotten to live. I had studied in Bangalore for two years and had been working there for the past one year but I had never stepped out of Bangalore. Work can wait, life can't.

"That was quick," Amit said.

"She is a Cancerian. Very moody. You never know what's coming from them," Sid explained.

"But why just Hampi? Why not some other place?" I said. I suddenly felt free and had many ideas jumping in my mind.

"I am not able to find any funding and Hampi is my last resort. I am hopeful I can unearth some fortune there," Sid said.

I laughed, "Come on you guys... give me another place."

"Sid is right. We must go to Hampi and don't laugh. It is true that we may unearth some fortune there and fund Sid's business."

"Stop kidding, you two. And tell me... from where did the fortune come in Hampi?"

"Believe us," Amit spoke to me with modulation in his voice to match the narration of *Vikram Betal* and *Panchtantra* series on Doordarshan in the 90s.

"King Bali's (reference from *Ramayan) khazana* (fortune) is buried in Hampi and when it rains, the rivers wash away the mountains and bring along the rarest of rare jewels for the people of Hampi."

"What are you saying? Crap! In that case the people of Hampi must be the richest. Let us also go and live in Hampi."

Amit said, "Trust me, and in addition to Bali ka khazana, it is also believed that in earlier days traders used to come to Hampi for trade. While returning, the fear of getting robbed made them hide their jewels in the mountains and the bridges. So now when it rains people stand under old bridges or near mountains. Some turn out to be lucky too!"

"If it does not rain when we go.... then?" I asked pulling their leg.

"Don't take us lightly. We know places where we can dig and unearth the fortune," Sid said.

"Huh... if you unearth fortunes this way, it is the government's property."

"Correct. We will also give it to the government, but in turn we will ask the government to fund our business. I am sure for a fortune, the government can happily fund us," Amit supported Sid.

"Okay, enough! Now stop fooling around with me. And if all this was to convince me to agree on Hampi, then you have been successful. Let's go to Hampi."

Looking at each other, both of them flashed big smiles on their faces, "Okay then we will leave for Hampi this weekend." Sid confirmed the plan.

"Amit, come let's go and book three train tickets to Hospet?"

"But Hospet? You said we are going to Hampi," I asked stopping Sid.

"Hospet town is the nearest bus and railway station to Hampi. From Hospet, the Hampi ruins are fourteen kilometres away. After reaching Hospet we will take the local bus or auto-rickshaw to Hampi."

Hardly ten minutes and they were back with the tickets. "Tadaaaaa...

tickets. We are off to Hampi!" Amit waved the tickets at me.

"That was quick!" I said and returned to reading the book in my hand.

"Hey come on! Hampi deserves excitement. And look at you, no sign of excitement at all! Probably I need to tell you a few more stories about Hampi," Amit said.

Sid also added, "Trust me, you will love Hampi and you'll repent why you had not visited the place earlier. Do you know Hampi is also believed to be the birth place of Lord Hanuman? We can visit the exact place where Lord Hanuman was born. It is a temple now."

"Yes, Sid is right," Amit said placing two pillows under his arm. He was in story telling mode. "And Hampi does not only have historic and religious significance, it is mysterious too. The local fables talk of the fairies visiting the Tungabhadra river on a full moon night. And the recent mystery is that there are unseen forces which do not let Hampi to stay connected to the world. It is the third time that the bridge built to connect Hampi to the city has collapsed."

"How did I not know of this place until now?" I said. "And who are the locals there?"

"It is a mixed group but the famous locals are the Lambanis. Years ago they came in a group from Rajasthan and settled in Hampi. Today, their colourful outfits, jewellery, intricate hairdos and dance forms define the culture of Hampi. Apart from the locals, you would hardly find any Indians there. The place has tourists from all over the world. In fact, the restaurants are also Italian and French and they serve the most authentic tastes that you cannot find in Bangalore also," Amit replied.

"Can't wait to visit Hampi now." I smiled.

"We will meet my friend Heera too."

"Ahaan Heera! Okay, tell me honestly, isn't Heera one reason why you are so fond of Hampi?" I asked him.

"Yes, of all the reasons, it has to be Heera," he said and laughed. "Heera is my mother's age but it is true that I go there for her. She works with a local trust to promote banana fibre products."

"What! But when Sid teased you about Heera you didn't say anything."

Both laughed aloud, "We were just making you curious about Hampi," Amit said.

"Not good! Hope all that you have told me today about fairies visiting the Tungabhadra river and the broken bridge is not false."

Seeing my scepticism, Sid took over, "No, no, not at all. For that matter we didn't lie to you about Heera also. She exists and we will go to her cave. And the cave reminds me about the famous cave of Hampi where King Bali fought the demon. We will visit it too. And you know when Bali returned to reclaim his kingdom, he also fought with Sugreev as he had become the king assuming Bali was dead. So Hampi has sculptures of Bali and Sugreev fighting in different poses all over."

"Wow!" I said.

"See I told you, Hampi deserves excitement. Now you are set to visit Hampi!" Amit said.

Mysterious Hampi

We arrived at Hampi at six in the morning. The sun had not assumed all its power. The auto ride from the station to Hampi on this slight winter morning was heavenly. Hampi welcomed us throughout our auto ride with never-ending green paddy fields. Its scenic settings were peaceful and divine. The air was light, fresh and fragrant. Hampi was absolutely untouched.

Standing at the entrance gate of Hampi town, and looking at the people around, it didn't seem like a place in India. It was after entering the main gate that I could see Lambani people. They were selling things like coloured cotton lamps, mirror studded belts, embroidered skrits and tops. Some sat on the ground and some had set up shops on a platform with wheels underneath it. Behind their setups, on both sides of the road, there were restaurants, juice shops, internet cafés, travel agents and basic utility shops. It was the Hampi bazaar.

"Not a step more. Tell me where should we stay?" Tired of walking with a bag on my shoulder and another in hand, I asked. The road was muddy, so could not even drag my bag on wheels.

"Want to live this side or across the Tungabhadra river?" Amit asked. We were standing at a place where people were boarding ferries to cross the Tungabhadra river.

"Near the temples," I said.

"Temples are all over. So don't worry about that. If we live this side, we'll see the night life and get good restaurants. If we cross the river then that side is more untouched and we get big villas to live in. Heera too lives on that side."

We didn't cross the river and decided to start seeing the places as soon as we freshened up. We had just three days in hand.

The concept of accommodation for tourists is pretty interesting in Hampi. The locals convert one or two rooms of their houses to guest houses. Some houses also convert the top floor to roof top restaurants.

We found a room for the three of us. It was a bright and airy ground floor room overlooking the waters of the Tungabhadra river. The coconut trees on the sides of the river were just a few metres away from our window.

After taking bath, we grabbed a map of Hampi and made our way to the most famous restaurant of Hampi – Mango Tree. We sat on the steps facing the Tungabhadra river. People were dispersed on far off terraces of this vast mountain restaurant. After a sumptuous lunch, we saw the famous swing at the Mango Tree. Fixed on a tree in the centre of the restaurant, it went straight up in the air towards the Tungabhadra river.

"We can either take bikes or we can walk around," Amit said.

"But bikes won't go everywhere and when we go to the other side of the river, we cannot take bikes so I think we should walk around," Sid suggested.

"What are they wearing?" I asked as I noticed people from different nationalities dressed in a similar manner.

"This is Hampi's local dress," Sid said. "We can get it for you. There is a small home shop. Girls from our college bought some good stuff from there last time."

Men, women, kids, all wore colourful loose cotton t-shirts with Hare Rama and Aum printed on them and the bottoms were loose too. They wore the mirrored belts of Lambanis, silver bangles and anklets as accessories.

Tired from the journey, we could not cover much on the first day apart from roaming around in Hampi bazaar. But we made it up in the next two days.

The second day, we woke up at four and covered the temples on our side of the river. The temples ruins had battles between Sugreev and Bali in the form of beautiful engravings. We also visited ancient ruins, mountains, rivers and met local people and tourists. We spent the evening in Hampi bazaar, had dinner at an Italian restaurant and walked by the river to look for the fairies.

The third day was the longest day. We had to return to Bangalore the same night. After our morning temple visit, we had guntu pongal in a home which was serving breakfast to earn some money. Then we went to see Virupaksha temple and the stone chariot.

"When are we meeting Heera?" I asked Amit.

Heera had come to our side of the river to assign the handicraft work to the locals. We were to meet her and go along with her to the other side of Tungabhadra river to see her cave.

"She will meet us at Hampi Bazar in thirty minutes. Let us also go there," Amit said reading a message on his phone.

Dressed from neck till toe in a jet black robe, Heera looked mysterious. Followed by a quick exchange of greetings, Amit walked ahead with her, while Sid and I followed behind.

I could not take my eyes off her. She must have been in her fifties and definitely had the grace of age but some things were strange about her. Her head was covered in very fine, tightly knotted plaits. She had smeared her eyes with a thick black eye liner. Her wrinkled face was shining as if she had washed her face with oil. She also had a strange fragrance coming from her.

"Had she not been Amit's friend, I would have feared her," I said to Sid.

"Shhhh..." Showing me finger on his lips, Sid smiled. "Don't worry. He has known her for many years."

"She doesn't look like an Indian."

"She is from Belgium. She came to Hampi as a tourist when she was in her twenties. Since then she has been living in a sadhu's cave. The sadhu passed away a few years back, so now she lives there alone. She earns her livelihood from the trust Amit told you about."

Reaching the bank of river Tungabhadra, we stood in a queue to board the ferry. The queue mostly had tourists but there were locals also who carried with them cycles, fodder for cattle, etc.

Heera was famous. After we boarded the ferry, the locals took turns to greet her and she too returned their greetings with the same enthusiasm. This made me a little comfortable in her company but it didn't last long.

"That mountain top you see?" Heera said pointing to a far away mountain. "My cave is there."

"Have you changed your cave? It doesn't look like the one I visited," Amit said very confidently.

Listening to their conversation, I stepped aside to check the route leading to the mountain she had pointed at. I could clearly see that to go to her place we would have to get off the main route and then cross the rocky terrain formed by a river gone dry. After that it was a steep climb to her cave.

I murmured to Sid, "Where is she taking us? What will she do to us? Let's cancel the plan."

"It won't look nice if we change the plan now."

"What do you mean by *won't look nice*? She may cook and eat us up. Don't you see her nails?" I said pointing to her sharp nails, painted black.

"We are three, don't worry," Sid said.

"We've come to see history and I suspect we will become history in some time," I murmured.

A rigorous physical drill landed us at Heera's cave. It was an isolated cave. Outside the cave, there was a small hut. It was absolutely quiet until two dogs started barking. Heera ran towards them. We followed her. There were two ferocious dogs chained at the entrance of the cave.

Heera hugged them to silence them but at the sight of us they were on a barking spree again. We immediately got back to the hut and waited for Heera to join us.

"I think we should leave. I am hungry," I said to Amit and Sid. I feared the place.

"Hmm...okay," Sid said staring at a cat that was sitting inside Heera's hut on a rod that supported the thatched roof. Amit too appeared lost. He too looked around in suspicion.

Heera joined us in some time and as planned, after spending five minutes with her, the three of us got up to leave immediately.

As we descended Heera's mountain, I was glad to have come out of the place safely. We went to the trust office where we enquired about the banana fibre products and had lunch at their Hoova café. After this we walked to see the mysterious broken bridge. On our way Amit also took us to a restaurant that he had designed.

"I think we have covered all the places on our list," I said eating a bread roll. The owner of the restaurant that Amit had designed insisted we at least have some snacks.

"Yes, from our list, the only thing left is the Hanuman temple," Amit said

"Great...but tell me, what about the fortune you guys were to unearth?" I asked.

Amit grinned looking at Sid.

"Fortune? Yes, we will unearth it. It is only 4:00 pm. We have a lot of time. The bus for the station is at 9:00 pm," Sid replied and laughed.

It was a steep climb to Hanuman temple. Amit stayed back. We took the stairs. Soon we were joined by a group of people who had come from Madhya Pradesh. They sang holy hymns all the way. It made our experience much more beautiful.

When we reached the top, it was absolutely quiet. The white Hanuman temple was shining under the bright sun and the only sound was the sound of the cool breeze. It felt as though the earth had been born just a few minutes back. We offered prayers in the temple and also saw Anjani mata (Lord Hanuman's mother) cave.

Amit was waiting, so we were in a hurry to leave but before descending, we sat for few minutes on a mountain top next to the temple. It is said one should always sit in the temple after offering prayers.

"Hello guys," an elderly tourist greeted us with a smile. Wiping her face with a hand towel and taking a sip from her water bottle, she sat beside us.

When we had reached the mountain, she was standing there with her arms wide open in the air. Eyes closed and holding her feet tight on the mountain, she was breathing in and out.

Lucie had come from Canada and she visited India every two years since she was twenty.

"Meet my daughter," she said as her daughter came towards us. She had gone to check on their shoes.

"Her first time in India," she smiled. "India is one place where I wanted to visit with her before she turned eighteen. And here we are!"

"What do you do in Canada?" the usual curious me asked. Sid looked around with no interest in the conversation beyond the initial smiles he exchanged with them.

"I am a fashion design teacher in Canada," she said.

Instantly, Sid turned to look at me and told her. "What a coincidence! I am a design student."

For the next twenty minutes, Sid and Lucie spoke non-stop to each other about the differences and similarities in the subjects between Canada and India.

"We got to leave. Amit is waiting," I interrupted hesitantly.

"Oh ok... sorry to keep you guys," Lucie said.

"No problem... It's just that a friend is waiting for us. But it was a pleasure to meet you," I said.

"Same here, I wish we had more time at hand," Lucie said.

"We live in Bangalore. Let us know when you are in Bangalore. We can meet," Sid said.

We exchanged our contact details and bid adieu to Lucie and Zoe. They were coming to Bangalore the next day. They stayed back to watch the sunset from Matunga hill.

"It was a sign!" I said to Sid as we collected our shoes.

"Yes an absolute sign and it is this fortune we had come to unearth in Hampi," Sid said smiling.

"It means that we are on the right track!" I said. We both were talking about the coincidence of meeting a design teacher near the temple.

"Yes, that's God's way of telling us to keep going," Sid said.

We didn't discover any jewels but the fortune we had discovered was a sign straight from God.

Entrepreneurs are also big dreamers. To remain motivated, they observe and absorb signs literally anywhere, at any time and in anything.

Junior Johnny Lever

"Sirrr.... Sir... Sid Sir..."

As Sid, Amit and I took turns to freshen up, a voice approached us from the always open doors of our home.

"That has to be Pawas," Sid said.

"How dare you go to Hampi without me, Sirrr...."

Sid was right. Clad in a light brown kurta over dark brown trousers and rubber slippers, Pawas was standing at our room's door.

Like many students who frequented our house, Pawas also came over often. His visits became more frequent after my return from Sydney. I was also fond of him.

Unloading the colourful and over-stuffed bag from his shoulder, he settled on the floor. Pawas was Kritika's junior. Just like her and other design students, Pawas always came loaded with patterns, colours and fabrics.

But there was a special thing which Pawas carried along as well. It was his infectious smile and the trick to make you laugh. His name was Pawas but by his looks and the talent to spread smiles around, anyone would confuse him with a young Johnny Lever.

"Sir, please do something," Pawas said. "Sir, we all have so many hopes from you. But you took the award and sat quietly," Pawas said to Sid in Johnny Lever's signature Bollywood style by rolling his eyes and modulating his voice.

We smiled at his performance. Amit, who was washing his face in the washroom said, "We knew that with all your drama, you would have not let us cover Hampi in three days, that is why we didn't take you."

"Oh... Amit sir, you are also here," Pawas said peeping inside the washroom and resumed his drama. "Sid sir, you just can't sit tight, please do something. Sir, are you listening?"

Pawas went on and I rolled with laughter and Sid tried to control his in vain. Pawas was a walking and talking entertainment channel; not only us, but everyone in college loved him for this.

"You should be in Bollywood," I said to him as always. As Johnny Lever's look-alike, I sincerely believed that his place was in Bollywood.

He also, like always, assumed a pose and delivered his standard dialogue in Johnny Lever style. "Why you want to send me away? I am providing exclusive entertainment. You not happy?"

We could have not laughed more. But he didn't stop. "Now let me please please plaeaseeeee... talk to Sid sir."

"Sir are you listening...?" he began pestering Sid.

"Okay, enough, my stomach and mouth are aching... can't laugh any more," I said pressing my face between my palms.

At last Sid replied, "I am on it, Pawas. It will happen soon."

"I don't believe you are doing it enough else why is it taking so long. Okay, tell me what are you doing?"

Pawas looked up to Sid and wanted him to start his brand of clothes after which Pawas wanted to expand the brand.

Sid laughed, "I am going home after two weeks. I will talk to you after coming back. But in the meantime, I have an idea and I need your help."

"What is it, sir? These days you don't tell me anything. See I didn't know you were going home. Why are you going, sir?"

"I have the final hearing of the court case and I have to get the DPOL stitched, so I will be away for a month at least."

"Sir, but everyone in college says you have already won the case."

"Not yet, Pawas. The final hearing is left."

"Okay okay... and sir, you were saying something about the idea you have," Pawas reminded Sid.

"Oh yes... I want to make a movie on you. Would you act in it?" Sid said recollecting his thoughts. He had forgotten about it. With his non-stop questions, Pawas could do this to anyone.

Sid spoke with Pawas about the movie. No, it was not a comedy. It was a movie on OCD (obsessive compulsive disorder). When Pawas was spreading happiness around, his life wasn't a happy one. He was suffering from severe OCD.

It is a disorder where a person follows strict rituals which are self created like washing hands over and over again, remembering horrid pictures from newspaper the whole day, imagining blood all around while taking a bath, and so on.

Likewise, Pawas also followed a set of rituals. This was the reason he always wore a kurta over his trousers. Wore only rubber slippers and used no leather products. He also displayed the most common OCD symptom of washing hands over and over again.

It started for him as a fear of contamination when he was in class 9. When he returned from outside, he didn't enter house without taking a bath. He took bath in the garden with a pipe and so that no one saw him taking a bath, he would return in the night. The rituals increased with time and consumed all his energy. He had no energy left to spend on studies. As a result, being an extremely creative boy, he could not do well in his studies.

"Annnythingg for you sir..." Pawas said with tears rolling down his eyes. "And thank you so much sir for finding time for it. The movie will be of great help for many like me."

In the past, we had often discussed about making a movie on OCD but had not been able to get down to it.

"You just give me the script sir and I will handle it..." said an enthusiastic Pawas after wiping his tears with a tissue he always carried. It was a sign of OCD to fight the fear of contamination.

Sid wanted to send the movie to a documentary film competition and festival called Kiran. He could be busy later, so he planned to shoot it soon.

OCD did not fall under the subjects showcased in Kiran. But with a pressure to send the movie to them, Sid wanted to complete the pending task. He was doing this for a social cause.

A high level script was ready in two days. It was quick because we knew the subject well enough. And in the following week, Sid and Pawas completed the shooting. They shot the movie in the college campus, near the HSR layout lake, and in our house. They had roped in Amit AD also for some shots.

"Sir, when will I get to see the movie?" Pawas asked Sid one day when he saw Sid browsing through the movie clips.

"Don't worry, you will be a hero soon, Pawas," Amit said. He had appeared from nowhere and was again in hurry to leave.

He had come to confirm our next day's plan to go to the handicraft exhibition.

The exhibition had artisans and handicraft business from all over the country. We directly went to the banana fibre products stall.

Pointing towards a lamp which was size of a globe we used in geography classes, I asked, "Is this also made of banana fibre?"

"It is a parrot lamp. And yes it is made of banana fibre," the man at the stall answered and placed the lamp in my hand. It was very light.

"So you liked anything?" Amit asked.

"Not only like, I am buying a few."

We became the buyers. It was our first step to execute our business plan.

"Where is Sid? I have an update for you both," Amit said. He had come to meet me a week after the exhibition.

"Sid has left for home today morning."

"Oh okay.... It is about Pihu. It is a Chennai based NGO. I spoke to its promoters. They can provide us banana fibre products so can we go to Chennai to meet them over this weekend?"

"Going to Chennai? Not possible. Can't take leaves in this critical time. If I ask for three days off, they will send me off permanently."

Coincidentally, Pihu's coordinator was to visit Bangalore. Amit scheduled our meeting on a Sunday afternoon in CCD on M.G. Road.

We sat in the garden area. The man asked us to help Pihu sell the banana fibre laptop bags to the corporates. The bags were beautiful but they were fragile. I doubted if people would buy them. I asked him to give us some other products as well to market. But he insisted that we work only on laptop bags.

In the following days, we contacted offices to sell the laptop bags. We also looked for places where we could retail the handicrafts we had bought from the exhibition.

The shop owners demanded unreasonable rent for even a small corner of their shop. It was a lesson for me. I learnt the importance of owning a retail space. I promised myself that someday if I owned a retail space, I would be generous. It was sad to see that on one side in Hampi the people were making all possible efforts to earn a livelihood and on the other side, being in a position to promote the handicrafts of artisans, the retailers didn't cooperate.

The retail plan foiled. Pursuing the companies for laptop bags also didn't work out. As expected, people thought the bags were not robust enough to protect laptops.

Seeing these failures, we gave a new face to our business. We did freelance consultancy to offer end to end design services for our clients. And it worked well. With not much running around, we churned a good number of proposals. Amit was happy designing while I wrote proposals and found a creative vent, instead of crying over what was happening in office.

I am Fearless now

"You went with one bag but what is this extra bag you've brought back?" I asked Sid as he walked inside the house dragging two bags behind him, "Did mummy pack this big a bag of chocolates for me this time?"

"It is more than chocolates, Sid replied. He was beaming with happiness.

"Okay. But first tell me, how was your final hearing? Who had come? Does the courtroom look like the ones we see in movies?"

"Yes, it does," he said laughing. His cheeks bounced up and down as he laughed. Even a few days' stay with parents does this to children.

"I will tell you everything, but before that take this," he handed me two *Business Standard* magazines.

Whenever we went home, the first thing our father did was to show us our study table. Underneath the glass of the table he would have laid down beautiful pictures with quotations. Above the glass, he displayed the magazines and articles that he wanted us to read. The other monthly subscribed magazines like *Business Today, Business World, India Today* and others were stacked in the cupboard. In our absence our parents spent endless hours in our room to prepare it for us.

Dad reached out to us in a different way. He used limited words and the power of his actions. Under the glass of the table there was also one or the other message for Sid and myself.

I once found a picture where a father was holding his daughter on his shoulder and above it was written, 'Each day I see my pride growing. My daughter. My Hero. ' My father had placed it for me. For Sid, there was a picture, where a small boy was standing in a green meadow and looking at the aeroplane in the vast blue sky. The caption read, 'Little boys never stop dreaming of flight.'

Tirelessly, dad prepared us to follow our dreams and achieve something in which we could help others too.

This time, I could not go home so he had sent the marked up magazine and articles for me.

"Thanks and tell me now, how was your hearing at the court?" I said after carefully placing the magazines by my bedside. I always keep the magazines and articles from my father near my bed or pillow and read them religiously before going to bed.

"The setting was similar to Bollywood movies. The judge sat on a raised platform. In front of him, on one side I sat with my lawyer and on the other side there were three people from my college. I didn't recognize them. But after sometime I noticed, the man sitting on the right most corner was staring hard at me through his glasses. I finally recognized him. He was the governor of the Bangalore branch."

"Did you also stand in the enclosure to give your version of truth?"

"The case had been running for two years so no discussion happened. The lawyers spoke with each other. After sometime the judge gave the judgement. The college has been asked to make changes in their strictures so that no other student faced what I had."

"Just that? What about the revision of your marks?"

"As a corrective measure, college had already included my revised marks in the final marksheet and they had also suspended Mugdha Singh. In addition to this, the court has asked the college to demote Mugdha Singh. She was to become head of the department in a few days. Now she will lose out on the position. The court has also passed orders for the transfer of my director."

"Wow! That sounds like a good judgement. You must be happy."

"Yes, I am very happy. Definitely for the victory, but I am also happy that Mugdha Singh did this to me."

"What? You are happy that she gave you less marks and you had to go through this trauma? It is only because of her that others kept you average and you missed being the topper."

"Yes, because this whole incident has made me fearless. I have already seen the worst."

He was right. Had Mugdha Singh and the other teachers who supported her given Sid the marks he deserved, he would have just topped his college. What's great in that? Year after year the college produces toppers. But the experience and wisdom he attained out of this case was going to make him a winner in life.

"Okay, now it is time to find out what's in your bag," I said as I rolled his bag to bring it into our room.

"Take a guess," he said.

"Hmm... I can't," I said impatiently.

"Ok then... watch out!" he said and opened the bag. "This ennnn... tire bag contains DPOL garments."

"Wow! So many colours!" The bag was bursting with shades of green, yellow, red and aqua blue.

"Yes, just have a look," he said and started placing the garments around him.

The DPOL collection had seemed like a distant dream but today it was in front of us. I gave a soulful look to all the garments that were spread in our room.

"All these created from just threads but with so many benefits!" I said.

Sid's DPOL technology weaves threads directly into the fabrics of desired shapes. It thus reduces the use of cloth and water too. In turn, production time and labour is also reduced and that is how DPOL produces eco-friendly garments.

Amazement lit up my face and emotions flooded my heart each time he displayed his creations, picking them one by one with tender care and pride.

"Where are the stitches?" I ran my hand across a pink coloured top and asked.

"Minimal stitching is one of the features of DPOL. You can produce the garments with limited stitches and that's why you can't find them."

"Amazing!"

"Apart from this, the other features of DPOL are continuity of designs, proportionate designs, non- repeatable designs and seamlessness. You will see all of these features in the other garments," Sid said.

"I got it. Your dragon jacket had continuity of design, right?" I said. The jacket had a dragon that covered its back and from above, the shoulders the dragon came to the front.

"Yes, you got it right," he said. "Okay, see this waist coat now. Can you tell me, how is it different?"

"Dart (vertical plate) at the front but design still continuous," I said and took it in my hands.

I was surprised to see that despite of the shape of the waist coat, the design of the bamboo was continuous.

"How is it possible? The design gets cut when we make anything from a printed fabric."

"This is DPOL!" he smiled.

He went on quizzing me on the features of DPOL as he showed me a complete women's collection of shirts, skirts, trousers, dresses, etc. Sometimes it looked khadi and at times it felt like silk. Together the collection was a state of art with motifs of Radha Krishna and elements of nature.

"And do you know that with DPOL we can assure our customers for a one of its kind garment. It means, no copy of a dress would exist if we want!"

"This is brilliant! And now that we have the collection, we can do so many things," I said as we both folded the clothes.

"Yes, so now our next step is to do a photo shoot of this collection and for that I have to look for a model," he said.

"You should have no dearth of models in your college," I said.

"It seems like that but it is a challenge to find one. But not to worry, I have a junior. His name is Karan. He does photo shoots. Will ask him if he can arrange for the model and also do the photo shoot."

Sid spoke to Karan and all the arrangements were done. Our model was Diya, a VJ on MTV. Diya was Karan's childhood friend.

The day before the shoot, Sid selected the dresses for the first shoot, ironed and hangered them.

Dogs of HSR

"How was the shoot?" I asked Sid after I got home from office. I was expecting that he would have definitely started the shoot.

"Not as easy as I thought. The location turned out to be a big issue. We finally started the shoot on the college terrace but it wasn't a good day for shoot, the sun was playing hide and seek. You know the Bangalore weather. Hoping tomorrow will be better but yeah, one good thing is that the model is very cooperative."

"The weather may delay the shoot but it will happen. The best part is, you have a good model," I said.

"Yeah..." he said and suddenly we heard raindrops pattering on our window panes. "Shhh.... can you hear that? It's raining again." It was a sudden downpour. We went to the porch.

Harsh, Rajat, Aditya and Anupam were already in the porch waiting for the rain to slow down. All of us, again in our food deprived state were hungry and couldn't wait to get dinner.

"Your turn, sir..." Aditya said to Harsh. Aditya was circulating a tiny packet of Haldiram aloo bhujia. It was a heavenly respite.

"Wait...can you hear someone crying?" Rajat silenced us all.

"Can't be inside the house," Aditya said and we all ran outside.

"Sounds like a dog howling in pain," Harsh said sitting on the ramp in front of our house.

He peeped on both sides of the ramp. There was a drain under the ramp. The same drain ran in front of all the six houses in our row.

"Can anyone show me some light? Mobile or match stick?" he asked.

"Are you crazy? It's raining, how can we light a matchstick or use the mobile phone light?" Junior or senior, no one spared any chance to pull Harsh's leg.

The howling increased but we were still running around in frenzy to find a way to light up the drain. Someone turned on the bulb in the porch. There was some light now but the drain was still dark.

Finally we decided to wrap a newspaper in polythene, place it inside the drain and light it with the match stick inside the drain. Harsh lay down flat on the ramp. Two of us took a firm grip of his ankles. Inside the drain, Harsh removed the polythene to light the newspaper. But it was a flop show. The bright splash of light fizzled out within seconds.

"Can we wait for the rain to stop to bring them out?" someone asked demanding further action.

The rain was pouring hard. With the cold breeze around us, some had started shivering and sneezing.

"Here is a torch," Sid gave me a torch wrapped in a polythene.

At a distance of two metres, there were four puppies. They were taking turns to balance on a slippery surface, which was almost immersed in water.

"We need to save them right now else they will drown."

"But how? Do we break the drain from that side?" Someone suggested.

"It is made up of concrete. You think it's child's play to break it open?" Rajat, our Tom Cruise said setting his wet hair in the rain too.

Suggestions poured in but we could not think of any feasible plan. Suddenly the howling of the puppies started fading.

I immediately got down on my knees to peep inside the drain again. The puppies were now neck deep in water. I lay down on the ramp and slipped inside the drain.

The drain had water only till my ankles but it was dark and the puppies were far away.

"Give me that torch," I said.

"But how will you hold it and slide inside?" Sid asked.

"In my mouth," I said.

I reached the puppies just in time. Water was about to touch their noses. Two in each hand, I moved backwards slowly.

The puppies were placed near the fire that was already lit using the old pizza boxes and chart paper. Within an hour of rubbing, warmth and pampering, they seemed fine.

It continued to rain that night. We brought them inside our house.

'To start' is most important

"You know what! Last night, I shared a picture from my shoot with my journalist friend in the US and see he has already published it," Sid said to me and scrolled down a webpage to show me the picture.

"Wow! This looks amazing!" I said looking at the knee length green coloured DPOL dress in the web article. "So have you completed the photo shoot?"

"Yes! We concluded it yesterday."

"That was quick!" I said. It was only a week since he had started the shoot. "Did you shoot all the dresses? I saw you iron only a few of them."

"Few dresses are still left. We will do it later."

"You can shoot them yourself and Kritika can be the model."

"Let's see. I will talk to Kritika. The biggest step was to begin the shoot. The remaining can be done at ease."

Fear of the unknown is bigger than reality. Just take a leap and start. The rest all follows.

Sid showed me the other pictures from the shoot. He placed the laptop on my pillow.

"What? You didn't like them?" Seeing no reaction from me, he asked.

"May be I don't know... but I think the shoot could have been better," I said reluctantly. I actually meant that I didn't like the pictures at all.

"I know what you mean. You can say you didn't like the pictures. I won't mind," he said smilingly.

"The background is so dirty. The pictures aren't very bright too..." I blurted it all out. "I mean after all this hard work why such a mediocre photo shoot?"

With a hearty laugh he said, "You don't worry. These are raw images. I actually shouldn't have shown you these."

He closed the laptop. "We will revisit the pictures after two days."

We took a break and decided to go out for a walk.

"It is cold today. You go. I will join you in a minute," I said searching for my jacket in the cupboard.

"What is this?" I heard Sid's voice outside. He sounded amused and in a moment he was laughing.

Wearing just one sleeve and with the rest of the jacket in my hand, I ran outside. The porch and staircase was filled with almost a dozen of puppies and their two mummies.

It was drizzling outside so they had come in. Sid went to bring his camera.

"Hey, do you see those four puppies we saved? It seems they have brought the whole family today," Sid said as he zoomed his camera on the four.

The four were the only ones who huddled together while the others crawled about on the stairs and porch. It's true; you make best friends in tough times.

"Our house is always packed and it seems we will have no room outside as well," I said.

"Tell me how is your handicraft business coming along?" Sid asked, stepping out.

"We have stopped looking for retail space. However, we are still trying to find clients for Pihu. And as usual, the design consultancy work is going well."

"Good... and don't worry about the products we have bought. We have a long way to go and we will definitely use them. At least you helped the artisans in your small way by buying their products."

"What's up with you? Your product is ready. The photo shoot's done. When will you talk to the designers?" I asked.

"Very soon," he said and after a pause said, "Actually, in total, I have three things on my list. Will talk to the designers, will send the movie to the film festival and the third thing I will tell you later."

"You can't do this. Tell me, what is the last thing?"

"Not the last thing. Say the next thing. I may add more. But this next thing has been decided. It is in my mind. I am not telling you right now. But you are free to take a guess."

He gave that cruel smile of his.

"Fair enough... I will also not tell you whom I met in the morning while going to office," I said.

My trick didn't work. He laughed and quickly started scribbling the points he had mentioned on the Post It. I anxiously looked for point number three, but he had scribbled a funny face with tongue instead.

Manavraj – Country's liquor baron designer friend

"Please tell Manavraj that Sid is here to meet him," Sid asked the only man at the ground floor of the building where Manavraj had called us to meet him. It was seven in the evening.

Manavraj was a famous designer from Bangalore. He showcased his work at the Willows Fashion Week. A regular on page 3 of the *Bangalore Times*, he was also seen watching Formula 1 races, sitting along his friend, the liquor baron of the country. We were meeting him under the scheme of 'meeting the designers' for DPOL.

"Do you have an appointment?" asked the man.

"Yes, I have an appointment and he knows me well."

Sid had met Manavraj when he was in college. He had shown Manavraj his 'the only' DPOL sample, the black and white dress, he had at that time. Fascinated by the continuity of the design on the dress, he had asked Sid to create a collection for him. But due to the challenges of producing DPOL in Bangalore, Sid could not develop the collection for Manavraj.

Now more than a year later, Sid had called up Manavraj. He remembered Sid instantly and was keen to meet him when Sid informed him that he had developed a DPOL collection.

We stood in his dimly lit studio. It had clothes scattered all over. A big pile of clothes sat on a table. More clothes were hanging over the handle of a chair that was like a throne from a palace. On two sides of a wall sized mirror there were two small bulbs. They reflected in the mirror. This was the only light in the room.

"Who would wear this?" I asked Sid pointing to a coat.

It was a large dark brown coat and was covered with tiny crocodiles, marigolds, balls, sun, pens, trees, boots, apples, aeroplane and a hundred other things. The size of computer icons, they were embroidered in all possible colours. It must have been difficult to make it but from a distance it looked like a kid had pasted stickers on the coat.

"You can come with me," the man returned to take us with him.

We climbed a tight staircase along the side wall of the studio. On the first level, a door opened to a room that had mountains of fabrics, sacks of laces, buttons and threads. The walls were used to hang dresses on the hangers and nails were used to hang scissors and other design equipment.

The second floor had tailors working on the machines and a man dressed in a green blazer, mustard coloured pants, red shoes and super white curled hair was giving them instructions.

The man who was leading us stopped at this floor and went inside the room. After a minute he came back and took us to the third floor.

"That mustard pants... was he Manavraj?" I asked Sid.

"Yes," Sid said.

"How are you? We are meeting after a long time," Manavraj said and shook hands with us. We were sitting in a tiny room on the third floor, which he had converted into his office.

"Yes, it's been more than a year," Sid said.

"Yes...so can we have a look at the much awaited collection that you have finally developed?" he said and ran his hands on the white long table in front of us to push aside the papers, scissors and threads to make room for us to show him the collection.

"Wow, this is gorgeous... look at this," he exclaimed in happiness seeing the twelve panel knee-length white and bottle green skirt that Sid displayed on the table. "All the Radha Krishna motifs are different, right?" he stood up to have a better look.

"Yes," Sid said.

"And no printing, no embroidery. This is unbelievable!" He was turning the fabric inside out to see how it was done.

"This is one of the features of DPOL. Look at this dragon jacket. It has no stitches on the shoulder. The dragon starts from front and ends at the back. No cuts, no stitches."

"Amazing amazing...purrrfect... Have not seen anything like this ever... I love it. DPOL is so cool," he gushed like a schoolgirl.

"Thanks..." Sid said.

"I have told you time and again and I say it again, I love your collection and I will be very happy to work with you. Tell me how you guys want to go about it," he said and pulled his chair to sit down.

Sid looked at me. It was my turn to speak.

"We are looking for co-branding. When you sell our garments it should have our brand label too along with yours."

"No, no, I think there is some misunderstanding," he said flabbergasted. "It will be like this... I will give you my design. All you have to do is to develop it in DPOL style and give it to me. And I will pay you for this. Simple! Isn't it?"

He wanted us to work for him like any other vendor. Like any person who does embroidery or printing for him.

"Mr Manavraj, we wish to be a brand one day. We have no intention to do outsourced work," Sid said.

"There is no chance of co-branding. What are you talking? Who are you? No one knows you. I am a brand. How can I put your name next to mine? No, no, no... this can't happen," he was in a state of disbelief on our proposal.

Sid and I sat silent. He realised what he had said. He toned down and made another attempt, "Okay... see, your goal to establish your brand name is to finally earn good money for you. Right? But I am already giving you good money. And you are also getting a privilege to work with me, a national level designer. And if you think you are going to earn a name like me.... forget about it. It will take ages. So think about it and work for me."

I smiled, got up and started folding the dresses. Seeing me fold the dresses, Sid took them from my hand and stared putting them into the bag.

"Okay, tell me the price of this skirt," Manavraj picked up a skirt from the table and asked us. We didn't respond and continued packing our samples.

We were clear, it was not going to happen. Establishing our brand was the first priority for us. We were never after money. This man's fundamentals didn't sync with us so there was no point talking.

When we didn't answer, he asked again, "Tell me the price."

"We don't want to sell," Sid said. Our bag was packed and we were ready to leave.

"Thank you very much for your time," Sid said to Manavraj.

He was perplexed. He wasn't able to understand what had happened a few minutes back. It all showed on his face.

"You can leave your products as samples... I mean... if you wish," he fumbled.

"One more down!" I laughed and said to Sid on our way to home in the auto.

"I sort of knew that he would not agree to our proposal. Not everyone demands what we demand. So what we want and desire won't come easy. After all, it isn't a small thing," Sid said.

"True. Not every seed turns into a tree. But the seed which we have will grow into a huge tree. Let me tell you this story about the seed and the rock?"

I narrated the story to Sid as we sat curled up in the centre of the auto to protect us from the cold wind and rain.

Many seeds, too small and insignificant lie under a rock. The rock does not let them grow, but the seed that dares – sprouts. With time it also twists and turns to overcome the pressure of the rock and finally manages to become a giant tree. The mighty rock that was not letting the tree grow now rests on its foot whole life long. The same rock that was not letting it grow gets the shade from the tree in summers and warmth in the cold chilly winters.

"So by the rule of nature also, we have to grow. We have to just keep trying. These people we meet are like big rocks. Don't get disappointed by these events. We are the daring seeds," I said.

Revealed: The third point on Sid's Post It

"Paawass.... how are you Paawas...." I sang and jigged as I entered the room on seeing Pawas.

He was sitting next to Sid. They both were looking into Sid's laptop. With the strange sounds coming from the laptop, I could make out they were editing their movie.

"Gud guud gooood..." he replied increasing his pitch and the size of his smile. Suddenly he turned sad. "I want your help. And you better consider it to be very, very important. It must be like top priority."

"Okay, I will. Now tell me what is it?" I asked.

With a very serious face, he said. "See, I have given such good shots but Sid sir is editing out all of them. Pleaaaseeee stop him."

I felt bad for Pawas and turned to Sid to talk to him. But Pawas started laughing.

I realised I had made a fool of myself. He was just acting. I tried to hide the transformation of my expressions from sad to wonder to anger to back to normal but Pawas caught me. "Don't tell me you got serious," Pawas said.

"Can't believe you are such a big drama queen, Pawas. Look at you, so much over acting."

Sid interrupted us. "And don't disturb me. Be quiet."

"Let him do his work. You come here and tell me how are your studies going?" I called Pawas and patted the mattress on my side.

"I have already failed two times and if I fail this time, the college will throw me out." My question made him sad.

"This time you won't fail. Write and learn it. You will be able to recall everything in the exam," I said but cautiously watched him in case he was making fun of me again. This time he wasn't.

So I continued, "If you never fail you will not learn anything, Pawas. What matters is that you be sincere with what you do. And that you have been. You have immense talent too. So stop worrying. You will make a very good living and make your family proud too. And if you listen to me, I insist that you go to Mumbai at least once. You belong there."

Pepped up with the talk, Pawas instantly jumped and stood up. Rolling his eyes, this time he enacted a drunken policeman.

I rolled in laughter when Aditya called out from another room. "Pawas, shall we leave?"

It appeared Pawas had been waiting for Aditya and they were going somewhere.

"Ok, bye. I will come to...mmo..rrow," Pawas said. Still acting, he slowly stepped back to leave and bumped into Aditya.

"Nautanki," Aditya laughed holding Pawas at a distance to avoid their heads banging. "Come let's go."

"But where are you guys going?"

Pawas popped out from the side of the door. "We are going to an NGO to teach kids."

I should have guessed. Aditya was associated with many NGOs and Pawas had a golden heart. They both coming together had to be for a good cause.

Sid finalised the movie. The next day he was sending it to the film festival, Kiran.

"You wanted to know the third point from the Post It, right?" he said looking at the Post It in front of his nose on the wall as he stretched his back.

Seeing him stretch his back, frustration and anger overpowered me. "You must not sit continuously in front of your laptop," I said. Working in IT, I suffered from terrible back pain and didn't want to see him repeat my mistakes.

When frustration and anger subsided. I realised that he had offered to tell me about point 3.

"Ok... yes, tell me what is point 3? You were saying something," I was very curious but I feigned disinterest.

I asked keeping my eyes on my laptop. This was my display of disinterest. He could any moment decline to tell me if I displayed my interest. It was one of his traits, which I knew!

"Point 3 is.. I will apply again to the Lavender Fashion Week."

"What!"

"Yes! So the coming week I will complete the photo shoot of the remaining collection. Will do it on the terrace. Have spoken to Kritika too. She will be the model."

"Oh nice... Sounds like a plan."

"Once the photo shoot is done, you can tell me which dress to be sent, and alongside I will send the picture from the shoot too."

"Picture from this shoot?" I asked.

Worry was written on my face. I hadn't like the pictures. I had told him earlier too but I wondered if he had considered my opinion.

"Yes... oh are you still scared of the pictures from the last photo shoot?"

Sid called me to look into his laptop.

"Is this the same photo shoot?" I could not believe my eyes. The pictures he now showed me could be printed in a fashion magazine right away.

"Yes, the same photo shoot and a similar photo shoot can be done on our terrace too, though there is a problem."

"What's the problem? With no rain, it's been a clear sky the past few days. And unlike college, you don't require any permission too. It is our terrace," I said.

"I know but the problem is these dogs. I will have to lock them down somewhere. They were barking when we were making the movie. I want the terrace without them. I can't spend time erasing them from the background."

"Lure them for some fresh bread outside the main gate and lock them out."

"Yes, will have to do something to keep them out for a few hours."

Greenmodelz Magazine, Eco Fashion Edition, Jun-July-Aug'09

Seeing the pictures of the DPOL photo shoot that Sid had published on the internet, an Indian green fashion magazine offered to cover DPOL in their magazine.

"Why are you laughing?" he asked.

"It is their standard presentation to sell the ad space in their magazine. They want us to buy an ad space," I said. "We do not have enough clothes to sell, then why will we give an ad."

"I know," Sid too laughed. "I thought they wanted to write about the green fashion initiative and the DPOL work. But Ad?"

We turned down the offer.

"Can we decide which dresses are to be sent to the Lavender Fashion Week this time?" Sid said.

We decided to send a crimson red and black dress.

"We need some embellishments. Some satin rosettes maybe," I suggested.

Sid instantly placed a few white satin rosettes on the dress. It looked perfect.

"Do you think it will be selected this time?" he asked me and waited with conviction to hear from me as if my saying yes meant that it would be selected.

"Yes, it should get selected and if they have read about DPOL, it should be the first dress they would select this season."

"Let us see. And hey, we also need to name our collection. DPOL is the technology but what will be the brand name?" Sid said.

We had demanded Manavraj to place our label next to his label but we till date didn't have a name for our brand. I sat with my laptop to think of a suitable name while Sid scribbled the qualities of DPOL garments and called them out aloud to me. The qualities were – rich fabric, design elegance, graceful, one of its kind, state of art. We named our brand 'August'.

He closed his eyes, smiled and opened his eyes to say, "August it is!" He was very happy.

Sid prepared a story that explained why August was the best name for his brand and shared it with his journalist friends.

"Hey, the fashion magazine coordinator has replied to the email. She wants to talk and I am sharing your mobile number," Sid said as soon as he finished updating his group about August.

She called up immediately. I told her that giving an ad wasn't our requirement at the moment.

She ignored my requirement and said, "The price is negotiable. Let me talk to my management and we can give you a good quote."

"It is very kind of you. But we are not interested at the moment."

"But why? Our magazine is published once in three months. So your ad will remain for three months in the June-July-August 2009 edition. We will give you a good price."

"But..." I tried to explain but she didn't let me speak.

"Ma'am, please first check the price in the email I will be sending you and then you decide," she said in hurry and disconnected the call.

She called back three days later to offer ad space at a discount of ninety percent.

I was shocked to hear this.

"But still there is no point for us to give the ad, right?" Sid repeated to check if the price slash had changed my mind.

"Yes. No point for giving the ad," I said. We did not have enough clothes to sell.

Sid said no to the offer.

A 'what if' Situation

"We will soon have to start selling and making money," I said to Sid. Sometimes it was frightening to think about where we were headed.

"I don't see us getting funded but I have hopes from fashion shows."

He explained the business behind the fashion shows. He told me fashion shows were visited by buyers from all over the world. They attend fashion shows and give business to the designers. Big business takes place during fashion shows. Buyer-seller meets are also organized to facilitate this.

He continued, "The buyers either take up orders or consignments with the designers. In the case of orders, they buy outright. But in the case of consignments, buyers keep a stock of designer's garments in their stores. On the sale of garments, they share a percentage of the amount. And the dresses which are not sold are returned to the designer."

"Just assume, don't take me wrong, in case our dress does not get selected at Lavender this time also... then?" I said.

"Fashion shows are not the only resort. Even if we don't have buyers, we will invest to make DPOL collection and take this forward. And anyway, fashion shows help designers make a label. But my journey begins after making a label. I want to make a brand."

He was overwhelmed. It was clear from his emotional answer. He didn't tell me the plan. He shared his desire. I didn't disrupt him and instead, continued to understand the model of business we were about to enter.

"What is the difference between a label and a brand?"

"A label is for designer clothing. Designers give a name to their work for retail. Labels are stocked in designer stores where only a specific section of society goes. The clothes are expensive too. But brands are like UCB, Levi's, Lee and so on, everyone buys them."

Listening to him, I had a plan in my mind. There were many designer stores in Bangalore. I suggested we could approach them directly and explore the retail opportunity.

"Yes, you are right. People from outside India want to buy DPOL clothes and why go far, Manavraj so very much wanted these so I'm sure there will be a demand. We sure can try this."

We had a good sales pitch too. DPOL had many unique design features. The stories of DPOL were also included in the Discovery website, 'Tree Hugger'.

"We are looking at June. We will soon move to Delhi. I just hope I find a job in Delhi before my name is featured in the sabbatical list," I said with a heavy heart but controlled my emotions. I didn't want Sid to fear that our pact was in danger. "So, let's utilize this time and visit the Bangalore stores."

Sid wrote to the designer stores and also shared our catalogue. But out of the twenty stores, we heard back from only three. And when it came to fixing a meeting, two got cancelled in the process. One store owner was on a vacation in Malaysia, the other store owner declined to meet us saying she stocked only Lavender and Willows designers. Only one store owner accepted to meet us.

"Is this the state of things? You work so hard to meet people who are not even serious about what they are doing? We will have to think of something else," I was angry

"I understand what you are saying, but who said we are dependent on them. But since we are here in Bangalore, let's go meet this lady. You suggested this option, so now when we have started this, let's give it our best shot," Sid said. "And by the way, I have some good news for you."

"What is it?" I asked with no interest thinking he would be making up some good news to cheer me up.

"The ethical fashion magazine lady called up."

"Again?"

"Yes and guess what... they want to print the August ad in their magazine for FREE!"

"What!" I was surprised but I was happy too despite knowing that the situation was still the same. We had no clothes to sell. "But what do we wish to achieve by the ad?"

"It will be more of an information ad and not a sales ad."

"And has she agreed to it?"

"Yes, she left it on me to design the ad for August. Though she wants the same picture on the ad, the one from which she had picked up our details," Sid said.

"Unbelievable! And now we can talk about this ad when we go to the designer stores as well. Finally, we have someone who wants to write about us in India too," I gushed with happiness.

"We have an appointment with Ms Shelly," I said to a lady in the designer store.

"I am not aware of any appointment that ma'am has today," she said and looked at us blankly. "Anyway, let me call and find out."

We looked around. The store was beautifully done with soft lights. Beautiful sarees and other Indian ethnic wear for women added to the beauty of the store.

"Apologies but ma'am had forgotten about the appointment. Do you guys mind going to her residence for this meeting?"

Unlike the designer store, the house wasn't a designer home. The first floor was a property dealer office cum residence. A white board with red paint said so. The second floor had chartered accountants. The name plate had metallic characters. The third floor belonged to the lawyers. It had no name plate but it was busiest with people in black coats making their ways in and out. It felt the whole country was being run from the three floors of this house.

After reaching the top floor, an old lady who was sitting with piles of files on both sides of her table showed us to a room, "Give me a moment. I will send Shelly."

"I am Shelly," said a large woman with short hair. Dressed in a white kurta and jeans, she came towards us.

Just like everyone, she was impressed with the collection. But she also expressed her inability to keep our collection.

"My clientele is women who are above the age of thirty-five. You know women with rich husbands or the women who earn themselves and are in big positions – they are the ones who have money," she said.

And, continued, "If they come to my store, I would want them to buy an expensive designer label rather than a western wear which would not earn me much. You see, people are still reluctant to spend a big amount on western wear."

She explained further, "I mean why waste space in my store

when I can earn more by selling heavy ethnic wear. When you produce ethnic wear with DPOL, I can definitely work with you. Your designs and fabrics are gorgeous."

The month of June took us to the different designer stores in Bangalore. Our collection packed in a bag, we went everywhere we could think of. But the response was the same: either they stocked only Lavender and Willows qualified designers, or they sold only ethnic wear to earn more money.

"There is a designer store in this mall on the second floor at the corner. Have you noticed it?" I asked Sid while having lunch in Transit at the Forum Mall in Koramangla.

It was our favourite mall since my college days. When Sid visited me from the HSR layout, we always had our lunch and dinner followed by movies here.

"Yes, there is one. But what about it?"

"We can try it too. I am hopeful here because it is between a designer and branded store. It offers a lot of western designer clothes. They stock multiple labels."

It was again a well done up store with good interiors and good lights. Sid had a look at the various labels and the quality of clothes. We decided to talk to the owner.

"Can we get the contact details of the owner of the store?" I asked the sales lady in the store.

"We can't share the details," she replied carelessly and walked away.

The store supervisor was no better than the sales girl. She noted our details on the last page of a register and said she would share the details with her madam and if she would be interested, she would contact us.

"It is so strange that people are not ready to work in a professional way. Everyone is so unapproachable," I grumbled.

"All this is leading us to do something big. Think about history.

Maximum rejections have been faced by the most successful people so just enjoy the journey," Sid said. "And see the strength of your thought process – when girls of your age approach a store to buy things, you think of buying the store itself so that you can start a chain of stores for your brand.

Plate full

"Cotton Design International (CDI) is conducting a t-shirt designing competition. The top three national winners will be awarded cash prizes worth rupees one lakh, seventy-five thousand and fifty thousand. And these designs will be adopted and retailed by an international clothing chain," Sid said to me.

A non-profit organization, CDI was devoted to the promotion of cotton. To celebrate the international year of natural fibres, CDI was conducting similar competitions in ten countries.

"Only three designs out of the whole country? Would it not be a waste of time to participate in it?"

"I am sending my entry. And you are also sending one," Sid said.

"I am definitely not going to make a fool of myself. I am telling you, you don't participate either."

"It is some brain exercise. Let's do it for fun," he said.

I wasn't convinced but since Sid was participating, I could not stop thinking. Sitting in the office bus, browsing for jobs and while having lunch – finding a winner design was the only thing on my mind. In the evenings Sid and I discussed the designs.

"How do you like these? We need to finalise one," Sid asked me a week later. He showed me his top three designs on his laptop. He had created them using Photoshop.

After a long discussion, during which we were on verge of fighting many a time, we selected a design.

"This is a winning design," I said.

The design we finalised was a vocabulary crossword where the properties of cotton were highlighted. This crossword was to sit on the front panel of the t-shirt.

"Yes, looks like it. If it gets selected, it will be easy for them to print as well. And I wanted to show you one more thing," he said and picked up his notebook and frantically searched for something by turning the pages.

"Here it is," he said and placed the notebook in front of me.

"Look at this dress and this one too and tell me which one you like more," he showed me two dresses one by one turning the pages of his notebook.

I turned the pages a few times to decide, "This one," I pointed to the first dress.

"Okay and now let me show you something," he smiled and said.

He half folded the second page to show the two dresses side by side and said, "Ok now tell me, which one you like more."

"Now I like the second one," I said pointing to the picture on the folded page.

"But..." Confused, I took few seconds and said, "No...the first one I like more... Aahh... actually both are good."

"You know what?" he said. I looked at him to know why he was laughing.

"You can actually like both because both the dresses are same!" he said pointing to the two dresses.

"Can't be!" I was sure and I insisted.

"It is! Take a look again," he said and watched me carefully as I looked at both the dresses.

"I can't find any similarity," I said feeling frustrated.

"Both are exactly the same. The only difference is that in first picture it is the usual style and in the second picture it is top down."

"Top down?"

"Yes!"

I compared the two pictures again and this time the second picture appeared to be the top down version of the first dress.

"It is unbelievable. Fantastic!"

"You liked it?" He asked.

"Yes, yes, very much," I nodded my head. My eyes were still fixed on both the designs.

"Great, so I will design a few more of these and get a sample created of this very soon."

"Yes, you must. You never know when you have to use it," I said to Sid. I actually wanted to say that if he didn't get selected to Lavender this time also, maybe next time he could send this design. But I quickly cleared my mind of this thought because I desperately wanted Sid to be selected this time.

"I know," Sid said and got into thinking mode.

I feared, he too might think of what I had thought a minute back so I quickly changed the topic. "Are we visiting any more stores, meeting any designers or is there any ongoing discussion with VCs?"

"Nothing now. I am just looking forward to moving to Delhi and funding our business ourselves."

"In a week or two, Lavender will give us the results," Sid mentioned on our walk back home after breakfast at Food Days on a Sunday.

Apart from the love that blossomed in every corner of HSR – all credit to the college – it was also a place to find peace and smell flowers.

"And when is the final patent coming? Isn't it almost a year since you filed it?" I asked.

"Yes, about to complete a year so it may come anytime now."

"Time flies. A year ago you had completed college," I said as we walked at a snail's pace. "Hey, is that Pawas?" I asked Sid suddenly seeing Pawas take a turn into a lane.

"Pawas!" Sid shouted.

Pawas stopped and smiled. We walked quickly to get to him.

"Where are you going so early in the morning?" I asked. He was standing under a Gulmohar tree which was ablaze with orange flowers.

He laughed, "Where can I go? No one wakes up this early. But I knew you both would be awake so had gone to your house."

"Okay. You look happy. What happened? Finally you've found the love of your life or are you going to join Bollywood?" I smiled and again pulled his leg.

He blushed and said rolling his eyes, "No, no, nothing like that yet. But nothing less," he said.

"What is it Pawas?" I asked.

"The exam that I was fearing to fail... I passed it. Now there is just one practical left which everyone can pass. It's just grades."

"This is great news. Come let's go home and celebrate," I said happily. I had bought Coke, chips and some cake just the previous night. It was my idea of a perfect celebration.

"They have grown so big. Don't you feel afraid when they jump on you?" Pawas asked nervously when our gang of dogs came running towards us as soon as we entered the lane of our home.

"They won't come to you. Don't worry. They are waiting for their food and it is in my bag," I told Pawas.

"Sid sir told me you both will move to Delhi very soon. Is it true?" Pawas asked me.

Sid was feeding bread to the dogs. Twelve of them had stopped Sid outside.

"Yes, it is true. We will be closer to home if we move to Delhi. And eventually everyone in this home also will be leaving Bangalore. Harsh wants to go to Dubai and Rajat to Delhi. Aditya and Anupam also have passed out of college."

"Time flies. It feels just like yesterday that you returned from Sydney," Pawas said taking a deep breath. A very rare moment when he spoke with seriousness and aplomb.

But it didn't last long, and Johnny Lever again possessed him when Sid entered the room.

"I will be bored here. Pleaaasseee don't go. You guys can't just leave me like this and go."

"I am going to establish our brand. You come and join us once you finish college," Sid answered Pawas as he washed his hands after feeding the dogs.

"Yes sir, please do. I will come and work on the ethnic wear. Will design totally dangerous dresses."

"Dangerous?" I asked in surprise.

"Aah... you don't understand dangerous? It means, full on heavy, beautiful, princess style, out of the world dresses in baby pink, peacock blue and carrot red colours," Pawas explained every detail and fabric with actions. "The dresses will have full ornamentation done with zardozi and net on the neck and sleeves. Will get the borders of the dresses studded with small mirrors. Cut work on the torso..."

And such were the expressions of Pawas that I actually drifted into a dream world akin to the tales in the Russian story books I had read as a child.

As he went on, Sid and I enjoyed watching him speak and express himself.

"Okay tell me what gift do you want from me?" Pawas asked me coming out of his dream world.

"I want to see you wearing normal clothes – a shirt, jeans and shoes. Not kurta pajamas and slippers." I didn't take time to say this.

I wanted to see Pawas break his OCD ritual.

"Okay, tell me, when are you going? I mean leaving Bangalore?" Pawas asked instantly.

"We will leave as soon as I find a job in Delhi."

"It will happen very soon."

"What will happen soon? You will dress up like I want or we leave for Delhi?" I asked.

"Everything. I'll dress up as you want. Your job in Delhi. Your shifting to Delhi. And Sid sir's brand," Pawas said.

The interview in the movie hall

"Guess what! I got a call for a role in IBMS." Freaking out with happiness, I told Sid.

"Great news! For Delhi?" Sid said equally excited.

"No, Gurgaon."

"Doesn't matter. It is equally good," he said.

Our excitement was equally proportional to the time we had waited for this day. It was a year's wait. August 2009 is when I received this call and it was exactly one year after Sid passed out of college in August 2008.

"Do you see how wonderful life is? Things happen just at the right time. We were actually done with Bangalore. And it happened, "I said.

To have passion is undoubtedly THE most important characteristic of an entrepreneur. The second and equally important is unending positivity, which entrepreneurs derive themselves. They join the dots of the past and present events in a way that makes them believe that everything happened at the best time and in the best manner.

"Yes, you are right. It is time to move on. But Bangalore will always be remembered. It is here I became a graduate and you a post graduate, DPOL was born here and the patent was also filed here," Sid said.

"True, Bangalore will be special," I said. "We visited Hampi and found the dogs here as well."

"Yes, what an experience!" Sid said, "And it is for this experience that everything seems so clear and approachable today."

"Let this happen first." I stopped Sid who was more overwhelmed than me by this one call from a placement consultant, who must have been sitting somewhere oblivious of the amount of happiness he had given us.

As asked for, I shared my resume with the consultant. After two days he called me to tell that based on my resume, I was selected for the interview and in next four working days I would receive a call from Lata, a manager in IBMS.

"You know this landline number from Bangalore?" I asked Sid showing my phone to him. We were watching the movie *Love Aaj Kal* in PVR cinemas at Forum Mall on a Friday afternoon.

"Don't know. Take the call," he looked at the flashing screen of my mobile and quickly turned to watch the movie. "There's a song going on right now so you can run out and take the call."

Until a year ago he didn't watch Bollywood movies, but he could not take his eyes off even a song these days. I was right about him imitating me since childhood. My favourite food became his favourite food. My favourite colour became his favourite colour. These random thoughts flooded my mind.

"These people call me to enquire about DPOL since you have given all of them my number. How unfair is that? You sit and watch the movie and I have to run outside to take your DPOL call," I grumbled.

I didn't want to take the call. No different from Sid, my eyes were fixed on Deepika Padukone and Saif Ali Khan dancing away on the streets of Delhi.

"Pick it up and say 'hello' at least, else it will be disconnected," he hurried me.

It was my interview call from IBMS. Lata had called up. I ran down the stairs of the movie hall and asked her to wait for a few moments, until I reached a quiet place.

A quiet place in a movie theatre! Wasn't it an oxymoron? I sulked and ran around frantically until I finally parked myself outside a toilet that had a yellow board outside it saying 'Caution. Cleaning in Progress'.

"I am so sorry to keep you waiting," I said catching my breath.

"You are watching a movie on a Friday afternoon. Isn't it a working day for you?" This was the first thing Lata said to me. It is usually seen that the moment the interviewers start taking the interview they start acting like a boss. Lata was no different.

"I am on leave today," I conveyed it sharp enough to display my dislike for her question.

I must have been out of my mind to do this at a time when I desperately needed a job. But I realised it only after the damage was done and just wished that she did not take revenge during the interview.

She explained the role to me and asked a series of questions. At the end it felt she was carelessly reading the standard pre-listed questions because she asked me what she didn't think I was entitled to answer.

She asked, "Why do you want to join IBMS?" Then without giving me a chance to answer she said, "Aahh... this question isn't applicable for you. I mean Satyamine is doomed. So you will take anything that comes your way."

It was still less for a revenge I had expected. I was tempted to answer back again, but I controlled myself and let her take her assumption as the answer to her question. My concern was to move to Delhi and not explain to her that there were enough good roles in Bangalore too which I had not taken up.

"Anyway, thank you for your time. I will share my feedback with our recruitment team. If you are selected you will hear from us in two or three days' time."

It wasn't a pleasant discussion so I kind of knew that she was not going to write a good feedback. The next morning, the placement consultant called. I feared but instead he told me that I had been selected for the second round of interviews and that I would receive a call from the practice head soon. It was a new presales practice which IBMS was starting.

"Did you receive any call from IBMS?" The consultant called me a week later to know the status.

"No. No one called me yet," I told him.

He said he would find out the status and let me know on Monday as it was already Friday evening.

"I have an intuition that very soon we will go to Delhi," I said to Sid. Friday was the night of long conversations.

"Any update from IBMS?" Sid asked.

"No, still waiting for the next round of interviews but I have a feeling that we are going to Delhi soon," I said. "I was thinking, is there anything we need to do before we leave Bangalore?"

"Nothing I can think of," he replied. After a pause, he added. "Mintraz is doing good. There is news that Mintraz has been able to raise good amount of funding from the angel investors."

For the past few days, Sid and I were talking about Mintraz. It had suddenly emerged in HSR layout. Started by a group of IT professionals who had returned to India from Silicon Valley, this company was printing customised t-shirts and coffee mugs. And since their two-storey building was near our home, Sid and I often discussed them whenever we walked past the building.

We also heard stories of it growing fast from Kritika's seniors who had taken up jobs in Mintraz in large numbers.

"Yes, I read about it in the *Economic Times*," I said. I religiously read the Emerging Business section in *Economic Times*. It was my source of self motivation.

Sid suggested, "How about going and speaking to one of the founders."

"But what do you want to talk to them about?"

At two in the morning, Sid literally sprung up from his bed. He turned on the lights and answered me as he searched the internet to find out about the founders of Mintraz.

He said, "We know what we have learnt from our experience of getting funding from venture capitalists and angels. But why not we go listen to someone who has received funding?"

Sid slept only after writing to the email IDs he could find over the internet.

The wait was over

"What is it?" I whispered softly to Sid. Head tilted to balance the phone between his ear and shoulder, Sid entered the room with a big parcel. He placed it on the table, showed me a thumbs down and walked out.

He was talking to the panelists of a design scholarship that was sponsored by Mercedes Benz so I did not ask aloud.

Sid had qualified for the final round to receive this design scholarship to study in Kingston University. Every year the institute selected one idea to fund. For years, China qualified for the finals but Sid was the first Indian to make it to the finals.

I reached out to the courier on the table to find it was from Lavender. Sid's dress was not selected this time as well. Tears flooded my eyes. I could not imagine what Sid must have been feeling. I knew he would not express his disappointment so I had to make him talk about it.

I immediately washed my face and prepared myself to give him a pep talk. Multiple stories flooded my mind but to my surprise, Sid came laughing after the call. Without saying a word to each other, we both laughed together for the next few minutes.

It is true that it stops hurting after a certain point of time. We had also almost reached the stage. And that's how we could manage to laugh after seeing back to back rejections and criticism over the past one year.

Sid opened up the dress, straightened it to remove the folds and gently placed it in his DPOL bag.

The day you start laughing at yourself is proof that you have reached a stage where failures don't deter you.

"I will not send any more DPOL to Lavender. They can never understand it," he said.

We didn't discuss about it further and went out. We bought new fishes for our aquarium, had juice and sandwiches at the new juice corner and returned with bread for our dogs.

In moments of failure, 'eat loads' and 'be with animals'. It is therapeutic. You don't need to smoke and drink.

Sunday flies for everyone. I prepared for office the next day while Sid browsed through the internet.

"Yes, yes, yes..." he jumped in euphoria.

"Calm down. What happened?" I said switching off the iron. I was ironing my shirt.

"I have won the second prize in the t-shirt design competition. Come here. Read this for yourself."

"This is unbelievable! Does this means your design is among the three best of all the entries received from all over India?" I asked after reading the email.

Adding to the feel good factor, Sid said, "I read this somewhere that they had received around six thousand entries."

"This is amazing and well deserved! Your design was indeed

brilliant and I am glad the judges could also pick it amidst the vast pool of entries they received," I said and patted his back. "Good, good!"

"Have to tell you one more thing."

"What is it?" I asked. Sid never stopped surprising me.

"One of the founders of Mintraz has replied. His name is Ravikant. He has agreed to meet us tomorrow at five in the evening."

The next evening, we stood outside the Mintraz office. It was the same two storey building which we had been crossing for so many months.

"Where does Mr Ravikant sit?" Sid asked the boys who were on a smoking break outside the building.

The boys showed us a door. The ground floor was cluttered with cartons that had t-shirts and coffee mugs overflowing from them. Wary of not stepping on them, we made our way carefully to reach the staircase.

The right side had loud music and people walking around. In front of us there was a covered cabin where a meeting was going on. Ravikant appeared from the boardroom to our left.

He told us how Mintraz was founded and what they had done differently to receive the funding. He also shared the three basic qualifications to receive the funds. There should be a strong board of directors. Business should already be running when you start to look out for funding. You should be working on your venture full time (can't be an employee in any other organization).

"The meeting that is going on in this closed cabin is with the investors. And these happen very often now," Ravikant mentioned as he stepped out to see us off. "So there are the not-so-good things too that accompany funding."

He indicated that with funding the owner's idea and business may be hijacked. They may lose the freedom of doing what they wish. The initial team which finds the business also disperses over a period of time. Owners can be fired from their own business.

But that's all what is bad. Good things are truckloads. Along with many known benefits, funding also makes you part of a network. This network includes the other businesses funded by the same investors, which can become clients to each other's businesses.

After meeting Ravikant, our journey to look for an investor came to an end. The evening turned out to be very important for us to wrap up from Bangalore on a happy note without any regrets, ready to begin a new journey in Delhi.

"Thanks. It was pleasant talking to you," I said ending my interview call with Taresh who was going to head the new presales practice in IBMS.

After an hour of the interview, he said that soon I would be contacted by the HR for further formalities.

"It seems I have been selected in IBMS. We can start packing now," I said to Sid, balancing myself as I was still in momentum. I had come running and sliding to reach him in a hurry.

"Wow! Is it?" With happiness he jumped off his chair.

"Yes finally, we are going," I said and absorbed the fact by taking a look at the things around me. Suddenly everything appeared to be very temporary and I felt detached.

"Fishes we will return to the aquarium shop. Mattress, table, chairs and bathroom stuff we will leave here. We will carry only books, clothes, microwave, computer and laptops," Sid summarised our plan for the move. "I will take quotes from the courier companies so that there is no last minute rush."

"Now I hope the offer letter comes soon," I said. I was worried because a friend told me that IBMS took the longest time to roll the offer letters, sometimes taking even six months.

"It will come soon and anyway, your last discussion with the HR is still pending. You can then tell him that you will need time to plan your move from Bangalore to Delhi. He may then tell you, when they will give you the offer letter," Sid suggested.

"Hmm...yes, you are right," I said. "By the way, have not met Pawas for many days... you have any news of him?" I asked.

The IBMS call came after Pawas said that 'it will happen soon'. I anxiously wanted to give him the news.

"Think of the devil and the devil is here," Sid said

"What a transformation! Life is changing... look at you, boy!" I exclaimed looking at Pawas.

"All this is for you," he blushed and said.

He was formally dressed from head to toe. He looked dapper in a blue shirt, black trousers, a black belt, and black leather shoes. Within a minute Pawas was surrounded by everyone present in our house.

"Is that you Pawas?" "Going for a date hmm... ?" "You look handsome man." "Dude you never dress up like this then why today..."

These were the only questions which could be heard in the house for the next ten minutes.

They surrounded Pawas and took him to the living room.

"No, no, don't sit down, sit on the chair. Your trousers' crease will be spoiled," I said to Pawas after he returned in the room and tried sitting next to me on the mattress.

He blushed and sat beside me.

"Pawas, finally we are moving to Delhi. I may get an offer from IBMS. And this all happened after you told me that *it will happen soon*."

"I knew it would happen. I had an intuition so I dressed up for you and was confident to hear this news from you today," Pawas said and then paused. "The '*It*' had three things – my gift to you, your job and moving to Delhi – these two, done but the third is pending," he said and turned to look at Sid.

"I know what you are saying. The third 'it' is that we make a brand," Sid replied smiling.

"See, he pretends he is not listening. But he listens and remembers too," Pawas said.

"Pawas, I wanted to talk to you about something that is troubling me since the day it was decided that we are leaving," I said.

"Is there really something with which I can help you?" he said. "I am so helpless myself, I wonder if I can be of any help to anyone."

"Only you can help. I am worried about the dogs. Can you feed them after we are gone? Only for a few days, until they are bigger and able to fend for themselves."

"Don't worry, I will feed them," Pawas assured me. "But where will I find them once you are gone? I don't think they will be here in this house."

I took a breath of respite, "Most likely they will be here. I will talk to the landlord to let them stay here until they grow up a little and I am sure he will agree. He is a kind man. The rent he collects from us, he donates that for the cause of girl child education."

"Good man he is. I will also meet him if I happen to catch him around. Anyway, why are we talking like you are going tomorrow," saying this he remembered something, stood up and left. The OCD always kept him engrossed in back to back thoughts.

Pawas was a lucky mascot for us. Each time he came, good news followed.

The next day I received the call from the HR. He asked me to confirm an earliest possible joining date so that I could be given the offer letter.

Satyamine wanted people to leave as soon as possible. My manager gave me an early release. I conveyed my joining date to IBMS. My offer letter arrived exactly after two days.

Goodbye Bangalore

The last night at the most happening house of HSR layout was very dull. We were the last ones to leave the house. Harsh and Rajat had left for Delhi. Anupam and Aditya had moved to a new house nearby. Eventually, the house which once was bursting with life stood barren with empty rooms, missing curtains on windows, old mattresses lying toppled up in corners, old plastic buckets with soap dishes and empty shampoo bottles in the bathroom.

We had also sent all our things with the movers and packers a day before. Now left with just two cabin bags and two check-in bags, which we were to carry with us in the flight next morning, we spent the day like a traveller in our own house using the things from our packed bags and putting them back again.

When we had nothing to do sitting inside the house at around 11 pm, we decided to take one last walk outside our house.

Our gang of dogs was happy to see us out at this hour and joined us. They walked by our side as we took repeated nostalgic rounds of the dimly-lit street. Half of the sodium bulbs were conked out but no one bothered about the maintenance.

"What do you think about our stay at Bangalore?" Sid asked me.

"It has been an incredible experience," I said. "As we discussed the other day, it's been a tremendous learning experience at both personal and professional fronts, which includes education, inception of ideas, direction for entrepreneurship, friends for lifetime, courage to dare – the list is endless."

"True, but what do you have to say about the things which didn't happen? I mean, I agree we are happy with what all happened. It's been an experience. But wasn't life a little harsh to throw innumerable rejections at us?" Sid said.

"This reminds me of one of the interviews of Mr Amitabh Bachchan where a journalist asked him – So, what's the most terrible truth in Bachchan's life and how has he dealt with it? Without dwelling on specifics, he quoted a line from his father's work: 'Mann ka ho toh achcha, na ho toh zyada achcha'. It's good if some things happen according to your wish. But if they don't happen, then it's all the more better because then what happens is according to the wish of God. And God always wishes the best for you. We just need to do our duty and leave it at that."

Sid smiled after I finished answering his question. I hoped I had answered his question.

> ***Mann ka ho toh achcha, na ho toh zyada achcha.***
>
> **– Dr Harivansh Rai Bachchan**

5

Delhi it is! Windfall of good surprises

Cheap living gets you far

Anyone coming from a long term onsite booked houses and bought cars but I did neither after my return from Sydney. It was for the investment pact between Sid and myself. My only investment had to be Sid's dream. And today it was a respite to realise that we entered the pact at the right time because after two years, having made all the attempts for funding and partnering support, it was clear that it was us who were going to fund our business.

We were fortunate that our parents were also ready to support us. However, we reserved the option to seek their help only if things went out of our hands.

Continuing the trend to save, we rented a small apartment in Vasundhra Enclave, Delhi. We got ourselves a low maintenance Maruti Esteem. With these two basic things, we were ready to kick start our journey in Delhi.

Cheap living gets you far!

In the first week of October, I joined IBMS. Sid too worked on DPOL documentation, answered DPOL research queries and conceptualised new designs. In addition, he also supervised the renovation of our house in Greater Noida where we had to move as soon as it was done.

Life in Delhi turned out to be very hectic. We found ourselves, most of the time in the car driving to Greater Noida, IBMS office and during the weekends, we were on the road exploring Delhi for our business.

We drove more than a hundred kilometres every day on an average. Thus, very soon the situation demanded our next step to conserve for the future. We converted the car to CNG and we were set to run around in the most economic model.

Living simply is half the battle won – we were really good at living simply and frugally. Half of our worries were taken care of by our selection of an economic car and a modest-sized house with a very reasonable monthly rent.

"You think we should try Hauz Khas village once again?" I asked Sid one morning when he was going to drop me to my office in Sector 62, Noida.

To retail our clothes, just like we explored Bangalore, we wanted to explore Delhi too. But I was wary of asking because our past experience visiting the place had not been very fruitful.

Sid agreed. We both were mostly on the same page when it came to our pact and dreams.

In our past experience, we had been to a store selling western wear. We had a word with the salesgirl and expressed our desire to meet the store owner. There was another lady who was listening to us. As soon as we finished speaking to the salesgirl, this lady quickly made her way into a room and banged the door. She was the store owner. The salesgirl told us. She yelled and called the salesgirl. Few minutes later the salesgirl returned to tell us that her madam doesn't meet people who just walk into her store.

We were just making an enquiry. It could have been communicated in a proper way. There was no need to make a hue and cry out of it.

Another instance had taken place. A lady had opened a fashion retail store. She did everything right – the marketing, the sales events, etc. But the store failed miserably. What went wrong? The reason was that more than doing business, the lady was interested in the extravaganza around it. She didn't meet any customer. She maintained that one needs to be pricey in his/her availability. When customers arrived even after taking appointment, she made them wait. It was her idea to show how busy and important a person she was. The store was obviously bound to fail!

It is important to understand that no one has time to cater to our fancies. Everyone is important. If we act pricey, we will surely lose not only customers in business, but friends in life too.

When we think we are superior to others and make ourselves unapproachable, that is when we cease to grow.

I joined IBMS but as destiny had it, I was again identified to work with ANZ region. The ANZ bids demanded me to start at 7 am. Some days I started work at 4:30 am too. But the benefit was that I was done by 3:00 pm. This early start and early end of the day worked as a blessing for me.

"I know it is late but we need milk," I reminded Sid as he parked the car.

There was dense fog on the Noida-Greater Noida Expressway and we also made payments to the labour, made arrangements for sand, bricks and cement.

"No milk at all?" he asked. Milk was very important as a glass of Bournvita was our breakfast on most days.

The market was just a ten minute walk from our home.

"You remember the t-style competition?" Sid asked me when we slowed down on seeing that the lights of the Mother Dairy kiosk were still on.

"Yes, I remember."

"They have sent an email confirming the date for felicitation. I have forwarded you the email."

Coming back, I read the email and congratulated Sid. He congratulated me back.

We congratulate each other for our achievements. We do this not only for the pact, but because we feel we co-exist.

Few days later, we were again discussing Cotton Design International for a fashion design competition called Design Celebration they were organizing. Sid wanted to participate in it.

"It is a fashion competition conducted as a reality television series on TV," he said. "The designers compete with each other to create clothes within a time limit using given materials. Just like the weekly eliminations in Big Boss, the contestants are eliminated here as well," he said.

Sid decided to send his Upside Down dress concept for the competition. I wanted him to send this concept to Lavender and not Design Celebration, but I didn't stop him.

"Your Upside Down is a terrific idea. Take it from me. You are in the competition," I said.

The Upside Down dress could raise curiosity in anyone. The dress could be worn in a regular way for office and in the evening, it could be turned upside down to make it perfect for a party.

Sid sent his entry for Design Celebration and immediately got onto converting the sketches into sample dresses. Irrespective of getting selected or not, he wanted to develop the upside down collection.

He was busy supervising work at Greater Noida, yet he took out time to develop his sample collection. He started by making brown paper patterns followed by muslin cloth. It was the most difficult part of the process and he did it himself.

"In my career of thirty-five years, I have not seen these kind of patterns," a seasoned craftsman at the export house said. Sid had achieved the extraordinary.

Sid was selected for the Design Celebration north zone regional auditions.

It was finally happening for Sid. And the best part was that he didn't have to rush to create a garment. It was already ready.

Cotton Design was organizing the Design Celebration competition in the morning and the felicitation ceremony for Tee-Style was in the evening at the same venue.

Who was she?

"Let me know when you need me," I told Sid settling on a sofa in the hotel lobby.

The place was nearest to the plug point I required to charge my laptop. Despite knowing well in advance that I would be busy this day, I could not take leave due to an important bid.

Sid was in the hallway attending to the competition requirements. I was required at the time of presentation. I had to wear his dress. He required two girls to wear his dresses in front of the jury to showcase the two looks side by side.

We had requested a girl in our neighbourhood to be our model but unable to find another girl, I was going to be the second model for Sid.

"Are you done?" Sid came to ask me after an hour.

"Yes, I am almost done. Just five more minutes."

He sat on the floor impatiently waiting for me to finish sending my email.

"It is time for the presentation, let's go," he quickly wrapped up my laptop power cord on his hand, closed the laptop lid, grabbed it and ran towards the hallway. I too rushed behind him with the half-opened laptop bag in my hand.

As we waited in the queue for me to dress up in his garment, I saw Sid looking at a girl at some distance.

"Who is she? Do you know her?" I asked him as I closed the chain of my laptop bag.

"Looks like Kritika," he said still looking in her direction.

"No... she isn't Kritika," I said stepping out of the queue to take a look at the girl, "And what would she be doing here?"

"In fact, she can ask me what I am doing here because I am not a fashion design student but she is. I am a fashion technologist, you're forgetting that..." he said.

"She may be participating in the contest. You wait here. I will go and see."

Sid walked up to the girl and started talking to her. It had to be Kritika. Sid and Kritika were meeting after more than a year.

For some reason, the best of friends had stopped talking to each other before leaving Bangalore. I didn't know the reason but I faintly remember that the last time I had seen them together was when they were fighting. Sid had called up Kritika's parents to tell them she was severely ill which she didn't like. She didn't want to bother her parents. Though at last doctors in Delhi said that it was good that her parents brought her to him for she had a stomach infection which had to be treated immediately.

I feared they would burst into a fight again. But I was surprised to see that they seemed happy all through the ten minutes of their conversation.

"It is Kritika. She has also been selected for the competition," Sid said to me flashing a broad smile.

"Had she been your friend still, she could have worn the dress for the presentation. She knows the catwalk too. I am not comfortable doing this but there's no option," I said.

"She can wear my dress! Yes!" Sid turned to run towards her.

"But do you think she will agree?" I asked. A few heads in the queue turned to look at me. I had been loud because Sid was already a distance away from me.

"Yes, she will," he was confident but I knew it would be a 'no' from her.

"What happened?" I asked him. He was back within two minutes.

"Good news for you. She said yes."

Sid was very happy. He pulled out the dress from my bag and walked up to her again in a hurry.

It was a respite to know Kritika had agreed to wear Sid's dress. Considering they had not been talking for the past one year and today they were also competing with each other, it would have been a tough call for her, if it was not for the wonderful friendship they had shared for four years.

The presentation started. Designers took turns to present their dresses. Kritika too presented her dress which she wore herself.

After her turn, she changed into Sid's dress and turned into a model. Until now, designers had only one model to showcase their designs, but when two models walked in side by side during Sid's turn, the audience went quiet.

The two judges also could not hold their excitement and welcomed the idea. But things changed when the third judge, who was also the senior of the other two, did not appreciate the concept.

"You could have made a reversible garment," he advised Sid.

"Reversible is common, I wanted to do something new," Sid answered.

Sid's reply didn't really go down well with him. It clearly showed on his face.

The results followed. Kritika won the competition and as expected, Sid did not qualify for the second round. However, the day was still special. Sid had connected with Kritika after one long year and also received the award for t-shirt design in the presence of mom and dad.

Lavender and London

It was again the time of the year when applications were invited for the

Lavender Fashion Week 2010. The show was to be held in the month of March. And as I had wished, Sid sent his Upside Down dress to Lavender.

It was the same dress that was rejected by Cotton Design International. He wanted to add some embellishments to it before sending it. However, busy with the renovation work, he could not find time and the last date of submission approached. He sent the dress as it was.

But perhaps Delhi proved lucky for him. Sid was finally selected for the Lavender show.

Sometimes things happen when we stop chasing them – the same happened with Sid. Having sent the dress without embellishments, Sid didn't hope to qualify this time. He did not even track the result dates as he used to earlier and came to know of his selection only when the Lavender coordinator called him.

What doesn't work at one place can be a hit at another place.

For the Lavender show Sid had to make double the number of dresses because each of his dresses had two looks. So in all he was making twenty dresses, out of which six pairs had to be selected for the ramp walk. Conceptualising this big collection had to start immediately. Sid worked day and night to accommodate this new activity with his daily work.

"What do you have to say about getting selected to Lavender this time?" I asked Sid on seeing a catalogue that had a colourful set of stamp size fabrics pinned up side by side on its pages.

I had seen a similar thing in the kitchen of our Bangalore house too. So I instantly knew that Sid had started the preparation and was in the process to decide the colour palette.

"They only have four or six positions across India and you know just two or three selected every year and these usually have a direct or indirect connection to Bollywood. This leaves just three or four seats.

For these limited seats, there's a lot of talent around but all I can say is that this time my timing was right."

"By the way, what do you call this? I am forgetting the name..." I asked him showing the catalogue.

"It is a swatch book."

"Okay," I said and kept it aside to pick my laptop bag. "Are you ready?" Sid was coming to drop me to office.

"Yes," he said.

"Car keys?" I reminded him.

"Got them," he said as we ran down the stairs, "Have sent you an email. Check it once you reach office and then we will discuss it."

"Okay, but what it is about?"

"If you believe it and if it is not a spam, it is an email from the London Museum of Art. It is most likely to be a spam because it sounds too good to be true," he said.

"What?"

"Yeah, read it. It will be fun. So many spam emails these days can confuse anyone."

Reaching office the first thing I did was read the email.

Dear Sid,

We are currently developing a new temporary (6 month) exhibition at the Science Museum, London, due to open in June 2010. In the exhibition we aim to explore how innovations in design, science and technology can improve sustainability and reduce waste in the fashion industry. We aim to cover a number of stories ranging from natural/sustainable fibres to new colouring and finishing processes to designing for durability and recyclability.

I was very interested to learn of your Direct Panel On Loom technology. Might it be possible to display a garment manufactured using this technology at the Science Museum for a period of approx 6 months (Jun-Dec this year)? Do you have anything else that might be suitable for display at the museum, e.g. video or photo footage of garment construction?

I'd be grateful if you could get back to me as soon as possible.

Best wishes,

XXX YYY

The Science Museum, London (UK)

Wellcome Wolfson Building, 165 Queen's Gate

"I have read the email. Want to talk to you about it," I called Sid after half an hour. I had waited for him to reach home.

"You think it is real?" he asked laughing.

"Of course... did you not reply to it yet?"

"Don't be annoyed, if I say that I didn't even read it completely... forget about replying to it."

"What! It's been a week that you are sitting on this email. You should have at least passed it on to me."

He laughed louder, "Okay, will discuss this in the evening."

In the evening, Sid replied to the email and the next morning itself he received the response. I knew it wasn't spam but Sid believed it only when he received the reply.

"The London Museum has invited you to showcase your DPOL patented garment at the London Museum of Art. This is wow!" I said to extract some reaction out of Sid.

He smiled.

"Just a smile? Come on, tell me more about it. Did you register yourself at the London Museum?"

"No, I didn't and I am equally surprised. I really want to know how this has come about!" he pressed a tiny bit of his tongue between his front teeth. "I think either a journalist or a professor must have referred me there."

In days to come, many emails were exchanged with the London Museum. We also came to know that only nine garments were included in the top green innovations in the field of fashion. DPOL was one of them.

But this invitation to London Museum came with a lot of hard work. There was a detailed process which we had to abide. They asked for multiple forms to be filled and presentations to be prepared. It required the content to be created for the first time. It was challenging but we soon realised how important the process was. We ourselves were surprised by the new discoveries about DPOL.

London Museum valued DPOL and it felt like an honour. They looked at it from different perspectives. The perspectives, which we had taken for granted and never thought of stating explicitly.

Presenting DPOL in this new light saw Sid attending late night phone calls, spending prolonged time on his laptop for Skype calls.

Things happened at lightning speed. In the meantime, the Lavender Fashion Week also assigned Sid to a mentor. Here on, the progress of the work was to be reported to the mentor.

Hi guys,

Congrats on being selected to the New Gen show to be held in March '10. You are among the elite few chosen from a very large number of entries. It is also your first step in the real world of fashion. First impressions last a lifetime , so make the most of this wonderful chance.

You have been selected on the basis of the work submitted by you to the jury and I do expect that the clothes for the show will be in line with those that you had submitted.

I would request each of you to mail me the following:

1. The theme of your collection, 2. The colour story for your collection, 3. Sketches of the clothes for the collection, 4. A list of accessories for the same.

Once again let's work together, kick some butt and make the New Gen show the best at the fashion week.

Warm regards,

LK

It was time to ship the DPOL garment for the exhibition to London. An insurance cover was arranged. They made arrangements for the pickup and delivery. A FedEx man came home with a big box to pack the garment.

It was overwhelming to witness so much honour being bestowed upon the DPOL coat which we had decided to send for the exhibition. It was the same coat which was rejected from Lavender Fashion Week, the first time Sid had applied. It took time but fate changed for this recycled cotton yarn coat. And the wait was worth it. Because it had suddenly turned into a super garment and was soon going to become the talk of the world.

The invitation from the London Museum of Art finds its meaning in one of the sayings of Paulo Coelho.

Ever since the goal found out that you were travelling towards it, it has been running towards you.

—Paulo Coelho, *Manuscript found in Accra*

It is what happened with Sid. He was so carried away after getting selected to the Lavender Fashion Week that for the moment everything took a back seat. He even ignored the email from London Museum. However, he always held high dreams for DPOL and worked diligently towards them, so this time the goal found him. He didn't apply for London. They found him. The goal had found him.

What was rejected by Cotton Design was selected in the Lavender

Fashion Week. What was rejected by Lavender was invited by London Museum of Art. And it remained there for two years. The six months exhibition was extended to two years.

When you are rejected, take heart and believe that better things are in store for you.

6

Lavender Fashion Week 2010

Before the show

"Did you check whether you have your passport?" I asked as we saw Sid off at the airport. Mom and dad also looked anxiously waiting for him to answer.

"I know you have kept it in my bag. Old prank of yours. Won't work on me this time."

"No, I didn't!" I said making myself loud and clear. It was eleven in the morning and the airport was crowded and noisy.

"Come on, don't joke! I am going," he said pulling his bag on wheels to make a move.

"Hey, listen," I said laughing at his over confidence on me. "There was so much to do that I forgot to check. But I had told you last night to put it in," I completed my explanation fuming with anger, frustration and helplessness.

He was still walking away with confidence. Seeing his casual behaviour, I hoped that he was just trying to irritate me.

But it didn't take even seconds for my hope to shatter. He had not brought his passport.

"I have my driving licence, I think it can work," he said.

"You thinnn...kkk... it will work! It has a very old picture of you and they may turn it down like last time. It will be your day if you can get an entry with it!"

I was surprised as Sid stayed calm.

Like father, like son? I thought for a moment on seeing him manage the crisis but this thought soon gave way to the thought about his carelessness.

I bent my head to see the security personnel at the gate. Out of the four guys, only one guy appeared to be clearing the line fast. He was a happy face too, "Go to gate no. 3. In the meantime we are going home to get your passport..."

We started for home and he ran towards the airport gate. It was a long queue so we could not wait to see if his licence would work.

"I am in," he called up to inform. He was laughing.

"Your show will go well. The chaos that always accompanies all your endeavours is over," I said.

If anything goes wrong in life. Take note. Good things will happen soon. Every event has a chaos attached to it. The sooner it gets over, the better it is to smile through it.

Sid left for Mumbai one week ahead of the fashion week. He had to attend to the dresses and stage rehearsals. Mom, dad and I were to join him after three days.

He was going to live in the pilot hostel with his best friend Abhinav, who was a pilot. The pilot hostel was Hotel Hyatt, the venue of the show.

"What is a slip?" It was the first thing Sid asked me when he met me.

After checking into a hotel, we had come to meet Sid. We had to wait for him. Sid and Abhinav had gone for the dress rehearsals.

"Slip is what girls wear under a dress if the dress is flimsy or transparent."

"Right. See I told you it is required only when the dress is transparent," Sid said to Abhinav feeling helpless.

"Don't worry. There are few tailors around. Let's get one stitched now," Abhinav suggested calming Sid by patting him on his shoulder.

Something was wrong and I wanted to know what but Abhinav changed the topic and greeted us.

"Did anyone offer you water, tea or juice?" Abhinav said as he touched the feet of my parents and looked at a group of pilots who were standing behind him.

It was quite a sight, seeing all the pilots in shorts and t-shirts.

"We were comfortable. There was a small boy who did not leave us alone and we had a good time with your Jazz Billu too," Dad said.

"Okay Kariappa you are talking about. Uncle, he is not a small boy. He is a pilot," Abhinav said.

"He seemed like a school boy!" I said.

"I am sure that he was Kariappa. Where did he go?" Abhinav said.

"He will be back in ten minutes," I said. Kariappa had told me that he was going to collect some stuff from a friend who lived in the same hostel.

As we waited for Kariappa to return, Abhinav said, "Let me tell you an interesting incident which happened with Kariappa at the Dubai airport. After reaching the Dubai airport, he reported the arrival of flight in the office. Seeing him, the lady on duty ran away shouting some words in her language. Kariappa and his crew were amazed. Few minutes later the lady came with her team. She wanted her team to see the smallest pilot she had ever seen in her career of fifteen years."

"What stories are you telling about me?" Kariappa walked in and placed a cat food packet on the table.

"Thank you, Kariappa. I completely forgot about it," Abhinav said.

"Thakur was leaving for his flight so he called me to collect it. And anything for Jazz!" he winked.

Jazz Billu was a stray cat the pilots had found. He had been badly injured in a dog-cat fight near the pilot's hostel. The pilots took him to a vet and he had to amputate one of his hind legs to save his life. That day, he was jointly adopted by the entire pilot hostel and he was named Jazz Billu. But he was weak, so he was on a special diet. Pilots started getting food for him from the US. And now after two years, Jazz Billu was so used to the tuna and cat food from the US that he did not eat any other food. So any pilot who went to the US bought food for Jazz.

Sid was still looking worried. "What are you thinking now? We'll get the slip in some time," I said.

"You should have come with me for the rehearsals," he appeared miffed and I could guess there was more to it than just the slip.

"We had discussed that I wasn't required. And then I did not have any leaves also."

"You were required. I realised this the first day itself. They asked me to bring my assistant."

"Ahh... then what did you do?"

"Abhinav came along as my assistant. Luckily he wasn't flying. He is on training for a new aircraft."

"Good it is. Then, what is the problem?"

"It felt like a dream come true when we collected our badges and walked into the hotel lobby with our bags filled with dresses and accessories to dress up the country's top models."

"Sounds like a fairytale?" I said listening with rapt attention, without batting an eye.

"You thinking that you missed the feeling?" he asked.

"Yes!"

"Well, then hold on. Reality strikes," Sid said. Abhinav gave a mysterious smile. "We opened the door to get into the dress rehearsal room. Trust me, it felt like unveiling a beautiful future."

"Oh, yeah, I can understand," I said.

"The room was flooded with models and designers," Sid said.

"But it was a beautiful flood of beauties, colours and perfume," Abhinav said with a broad smile.

"Making our way, we went and parked ourselves in a corner to see what was happening. The room had designers dressing their models. Initially it seemed chaotic and an uncontrolled crowd but soon we noticed a strong built fair man controlling the proceedings of the room. He spoke like a woman but he had arrogance and authority. He called the designers turn by turn for the dress rehearsals. We spoke to a few designers who had completed their rehearsals. I felt it was going to be easy."

Sid hadn't mentioned any problem till then. Impatient, I could not hold myself. "What could have gone wrong? You had all your dresses stitched as per the size chart they shared. You had an adequate number of dresses. You had matching shoes and headgear too."

In the background I assumed there could have been an issue with the number of models required to walk the ramp. The upside down concept required double the number of models. Two models walking the ramp side by side.

"This reviewer's name is Harit. When my turn came, I went up to him with my models. As expected, the rehearsal went fine. There were just a few general comments. And there was one model who wanted a slip."

"Big deal! We will get the slip now," I retorted.

"It wasn't a big deal earlier but it is a big deal now," Abhinav said and looked at Sid.

Sid explained. "Today when we went to the rehearsals, Harit reviewed the changes he had suggested. But just when he was going to give the final approval, this model who had asked for a slip came and tapped him on his shoulder. Both of them stepped aside to talk. And out of nowhere, Harit asked me, 'What are the points I told you yesterday?' I told him the four points. I had memorised them and had corrected them too. But he flared up and said that you cannot be so casual. Take your collection and go. Come back with a slip and the points noted down on a paper."

"It seems the model said something about you to Harit that angered him," I said.

Abhinav added, "Yes, you are right. In fact, Harit and this model shared a hearty laugh after Harit snubbed Sid."

"It is definitely not the right behaviour. But tell me, did he not ask you to take the notes the previous day when he was speaking to you?"

"No," Sid said.

"Did you see other designers do it?"

"I didn't notice anyone holding any notepad. You come yourself tomorrow. It is chaos inside."

"And why didn't you take the slip along with you the next day?" I said.

"How could I arrange it overnight? Yesterday I returned late and today morning, I told the model that I would give her the slip in a while. But she didn't wait and complained to Harit."

"So what now?" I said.

"We are coming back from there. We have to go back at six in the evening for the final dress rehearsals."

"Okay, don't worry we will get a slip now," I said to Sid and to make the conversation lighter I turned to Abhinav. "So Abhinav, what do you have to say about what all happened?"

"That model created a fuss out of nothing. I saw other models using their own slips."

After a thought he added, "And I think the issue was not the slip. I suspect, the problem started because Sid didn't give any special attention to her. So she created a scene. And of course Harit would listen to her."

"What special attention?" I asked.

"Shazia is a senior model. She is famous in Dubai and India and has been in the industry for many years," Abhinav said.

I smiled. "I am impressed to see that you know the people you are working with so well. But I am wondering, even after knowing so much how couldn't you guys not manage the situation?"

"No... I mean yes... but we know just this," Abhinav said and stopped abruptly.

Sid picked up from there, "Don't ask him, he has been sitting there on the couch flirting with all the models. He has their phone numbers on his fingertips. They went crazy when they got to know he is a pilot."

Abhinav snapped back laughing, "Because of this, the others were good to you too. But Shazia is a different case. She had her airs so I didn't talk to her beyond the initial introduction."

Abhinav was embarrassed. I asked Sid, "But why is Harit reviewing? I thought Lokendra Chatwal was your mentor."

"Yes, he is still my mentor. But before we see him, the rehearsals have to be done with Harit. Lokendra is busy with his own show too. He will come for the final review."

"So who is Harit? A designer or someone from the panel who selected you guys?"

Sid fumed and answered, "I should not say this, but he is nothing. You look at the way he speaks. Belittles you in every statement he makes. Holds not even an iota of respect for you. But he has all the respect – I mean *love* – in the world for the models. You will be embarrassed to see what all they do in front of you while talking to you."

Not able to contain his frustration, he went on. "You see for yourself what happens there. I worked hard to find my worth after years of hard work. I didn't work to stand in between two people pampering and spoiling each other right in my face and not even looking at what I have created."

Focus on the bigger picture

"Darling, can you come here for a sec?" Raising her eyebrows with a sign of losing patience, Shazia called Harit while I was trying to attach a safety pin on the neckline of Sid's dress which she was wearing.

"What's the matter, my butter ball?" Harit asked walking up to us.

On seeing Harit, Shazia threw my hand aside saying that this wasn't working. I felt humiliated but I didn't react and stepped aside handing over the safety pin to Harit.

This one model was onto something. I thought she was done troubling us when she herself suggested that she would wear her own slip but I was wrong. Now she had another issue. She complained to Harit that it was a deep neckline.

"Let me try that on you, honey," Harit said and I witnessed the embarrassing moment.

A simple task of putting a safety pin had turned into giggles and whispers. I definitely did not belong there and wanted to leave immediately, but I had to be there for Sid.

"So finally this one done," I said managing a smile and giving the dress to Sid.

"How dare she snub you!" Sid said.

"It's okay, focus on the bigger picture!" I said.

"And yes, we are not done yet," Sid said. He was holding a wine coloured dress.

"What's wrong with this now?"

"Nothing wrong, but Shazia has made it a scene. Seeing her, Rhea also has an unnecessary demand."

"And what's that?" I asked.

"She tried to pull the dress on top of a sweater and complained that the dress was tight under the arm. I mean will she wear the dress on top of a sweater and go on the ramp? Finally I made her take off the sweater and the dress was perfectly fine."

"So it's sorted now, right?"

"No, it isn't. She still wants it loose under the arm."

"Not a problem. We will take care of it. But the good thing is that Shazia'a issue is sorted," I said.

It was 11:30 pm by the time we were done but the hotel lobby and the dress rehearsal room were still buzzing with action. Designers were running around while models changed into different outfits.

"So what's next?" I wanted to know if we were good to leave for the day.

"I am looking for Sanket. Tomorrow we have to set up our stall. Sanket, who is the coordinator for the stalls is going to give us the details. I have to also collect the schedule for my show on the ramp. He asked the designers to see him before leaving for the day."

"Is that Sanket?" I asked Sid pointing to a guy who was talking to a model.

It didn't take me long to recognize him. The back pocket of his jeans was filled with entry passes.

"Yes, he is Sanket. Let's wait, he'll come here."

Sanket handed over a few papers to Sid and informed us about the next day's schedule. The next day was the inauguration of the fashion week and the New Gen show was scheduled for the third day of the fashion week.

"Why the third day?" I interrupted to ask.

Sanket replied, "It is the senior designers of the country who do their shows at the onset of the fashion week. The night and weekend slots are also for them."

"Why so?" I asked.

"Because they have a celebrity guest list who can come only at night or over weekends. But that's just with the shows. All the designers will have their stalls opened on all days starting tomorrow."

Sanket asked us to return the next day no later than seven in the morning to set up our stall. He explained the location on a map and handed over a copy of it to us.

The stalls were set up by eleven the next morning, and at twelve an established designer was to inaugurate the fashion show with Bollywood celebrities walking the ramp for him.

I asked Sid, "Do New Gen designers not get to attend the fashion shows of the senior designers?"

"No, they have a long celebrity guest list so there are no seats available."

"Not even the inaugural show?" I asked.

"No, not even that. And anyway, leave that. I have to attend the buyer-seller kick off meeting at twelve. You stay at the stall and I will be back in an hour," he said and left in a hurry.

A few seconds later he returned, grabbed a notepad and pen from his bag and said, "This is where a notepad is required. I don't want to miss even one piece of information about the buyers."

I could understand his curiosity. I recalled the time when we were so desperate to find a buyer that we also discussed how a buyer looked like. Our main motive at the fashion show was also to get buyers. And finally, we were officially going to meet them.

"How is it going?" Sid asked me as soon as the other New Gen designers who had come with him to visit our stall left.

"Only the six New Gen designers have set up the stalls. The coordinators told me that established designers come only for the show. The stalls will be managed by their team," I showed him the stalls of established designers that were lying vacant.

"How was your buyer-seller meeting?" I asked with excitement.

"It was well-organized with a good attendance. This is the list of the buyers who work with Lavender," Sid said giving me a three-page list of buyers. It had the buyer/store name, store location, email address and contact numbers.

It was the happiest moment for me. I could already dream a whole world of opportunities it would open for us.

"You mean to say that all of these are expected to be here?"

"Yes and those who register ad hoc as well. Apart from these, there would be many visitors too. They also bring business."

For the coming two days, the stalls were visited by a number buyers. Page 3 and television celebrities were also seen. Bollywood celebrities also visited the show after they walked the ramp for their designer friends.

Newspapers, web media, radio and television did extensive stories on the New Gen designers. Sid's upside down concept was much talked about. It was all great and overwhelming but I didn't find any genuine buyers. The same was the story of other designers.

The buyers said great things about the collections but didn't place any orders.

The show

"Can you come here? Right now!" Sid called me on my phone. He was talking in a low voice though in the background there was loud music and people talking.

He had called me from the show area, where the New Gen designers were asked to report at 6:30 am. It was the third day and show day for the New Gen designers.

I came with him as I had to keep a few hangers at the stall. I had not gone to the show area as it was only the designers who were required backstage.

"Ok coming... but will I be allowed there?"

I was surprised. It was just thirty minutes that he had gone there. And it was lucky that I had not left. We had decided that I would leave after keeping the hangers and come back for the show at nine.

"I am sending a coordinator. Come with him," saying this he disconnected the call.

Sid looked worried. The backstage was full of buzz but he sat alone in a quieter corner. Near him there were hangers of the collection belonging to the New Gen designers.

"What happened? And where is your collection?" I asked.

"Rhea, who has to wear the wine coloured dress has denied to wear it. She says she hasn't tried the dress after the alteration in the armhole. And unless she tries the dress, my collection cannot be steam ironed. That's how you see everyone's collection on the hangers except mine," Sid explained.

"Where is Rhea? We can ask her to try our dress."

"She is inside the makeup room," Sid pointed me to a make shift square room behind him. "I have checked with her thrice in the past hour, but each time she says she is busy and will take ten more minutes."

"Can we talk to this man to start ironing our dresses? While he does so, I will also try talking to Rhea."

"You see that girl there?" Sid showed me a girl standing at a distance. Surrounded by the coordinators of the fashion week, she was shouting at everyone.

"Yes," I said.

"She is the head of this year's fashion week management team. Her name is Zara. She has said she would not let my collection be ironed until all my dresses are ready. Even if it means that my collection does not go on ramp today. So you see, it is complicated!" Sid said.

"Rhea will try the dress," I said feeling determined.

"We don't have time. The man who has to iron the clothes has to leave in some time."

"Does Zara know this?"

"Yes, she knows and says she does not care."

"How dare she say that?" I fumed with anger. "And why would she do this to you?"

Zara could have allowed the dresses to be ironed. She could have also asked Rhea to try the dress. Rhea would have not turned her down.

"Don't know exactly but what I know is that Zara is friends with Harit. And Harit does not like me because I discussed my experience of the dress rehearsals with Lokendra. And today morning, I also came to know that wisdom prevailed on Shazia and she wore her own slip under my dress. Lokendra had asked Harit to sort the slip issue with Shazia."

"So did you not talk about the present situation with Lokendra? He is your mentor. He is the best person to help you out of this."

"Yes, I called him. He said he has come to the hotel and will be coming this side in some time. But I just hope he arrives before this ironing man leaves."

"You should have explained it to him over phone itself," I said. I was impatient and had fixed my eyes on the two entry points to the backstage.

"I wanted to but he was in a hurry and asked me to wait for him."

With no sight of Lokendra, I could not wait any longer. I picked up the dresses and went to the ironing section. I explained the situation to the staff and requested them to start ironing. They were kind enough to understand me. They decided to iron the clothes and keep them in their work area. Keeping them on hangers in the lobby could draw Zara's attention.

Next, I asked Zara if I could go inside the makeup room to talk to Rhea. She may have wanted to say no but by then Lokendra had arrived and Sid was speaking to him.

"Can you please try the dress Rhea?" I requested her looking into the mirror.

Sitting on a raised chair in front of a mirror, she was flipping through the glossy pages of a fashion magazine.

"You will have to wait. The hair dresser will start her work soon and after that I have to get my nails done. After all this, I will see if I can accommodate time to try your dress," she said not looking at me.

"I will take ten more minutes to finish this one. You can try the dress," the hairdresser, who looked prettier than many of the models around, said to the Rhea. She was doing the curls of the model who was sitting next to Rhea.

"Whatever… I need time. I am tired of doing the rehearsals with high heels," Rhea said. "And why am I even answering you guys," she snapped at the hairdresser.

I decided to stand behind her and wait till she was done. I looked around the room. The models were being attended by a troop of beauty experts. The room wasn't big so there was not much space left in between. Whatever space there was, models were trying different styles of sandals and shoes. The coordinators made their way in and out.

Having absorbed all the activities around me I realised I had been standing for half an hour. I stared hard at Rhea. Her hair styling had been postponed and her nails were done. She was free and noticed my stares but ignored me.

In the meantime, Sid came to me. He said that it was sorted. Before I could ask what happened, I saw Lokendra's assistant walk into the room with authority. He whispered something into Rhea's ear. She immediately got up and tried on the dress.

Grabbing the dress, I hurriedly made my way out of the room. Walking ahead of me, Sid stepped out of the room but I bumped into Harit. Blocking the doorway, he was posing with the models. People on both sides of the door waited for him to finish the head to head and cheek to cheek poses.

"I am sorry for this last minute rush. For once you had decided that you will dress up for the show and I foiled it," Sid said to me shaking his head.

"Don't worry. What is more important is that your collection is all set for the ramp," I said looking with pride at Sid's collection on the hangers.

Forty-five minutes were left for the show to start. Sid went to attend the designer briefing session and I went to receive our guests at the reception. Apart from the pilot gang and local guests from Mumbai, we had guests coming from Delhi and Pune too.

Fashion weeks are open only to invitees. It makes them a rare occasion to attend. It was evident from the fact that half of the seats were already occupied when the doors to the show area opened. Thankfully the seats were numbered.

I felt blinded when I entered. When my eyes adjusted, I could see a brightly illuminated ramp in the middle. It was covered with a silver sheet. I immediately drew a parallel from the NAFT fashion show where Kritika had presented her work.

There were hundreds of lights hanging from the ceiling and the bigger ones were placed on the sides of the ramp. The front of the ramp had the camera troupe of various television channels and magazines.

Soon the silver sheet was pulled off the ramp. An unseen man from behind the stage welcomed the audience and congratulated the New Gen designers who had made it to this platform after facing a rigorous national level competition.

The show started. The name of the first designer flashed on the stage. The music was played. Four models, in sets of twos walked in from the two sides of the stage and took positions on the stage under the four spotlights. The unseen man narrated the theme of the designer. After the narration, the music turned louder and the models took turns to walk the ramp and assumed their original positions. Two more models joined in and at last the designer walked the ramp with all the models to take a bow.

Finally it was the most awaited moment. Sid appeared from the back stage. It was overwhelming to see him walk the ramp with his show stopper. I almost choked with emotions and tears rolled down my cheeks. I remembered the day when Sid said that he would attend a fashion show the day he would walk the ramp. And it was not long back. It was just fifteen months ago. The music turned louder. Coming midway, Sid slowed down. He waved to mom and dad, smiled at me and went ahead to take a bow as his models clapped for him.

It was an absolute larger than life experience. I was awestruck but experienced enough to take the best shots.

An Interview and the Mexican order

"Can you send me few high configuration pictures of your DPOL collection? This is my email address," Vikrant Das said sliding his visiting card on the table towards Sid.

Vikrant was a journalist with a popular news and entertainment portal. He was covering the New Gen designers for his portal. When he came to know that Sid's DPOL work had been invited by the London Museum of Art, he wanted to do an exclusive story on DPOL.

"Can I send these pictures after a week when I reach Delhi? I don't have them on this laptop," Sid said pointing to his laptop.

"No problem. And yes, please share your picture too," Vikrant said and left.

Within a few minutes, a middle-aged woman came asking for Sid. Smartly dressed in a khadi kurta with one hand in the pocket of her kurta and a pair of spectacles hanging around her neck, she looked like a journalist.

"Sid will be here in sometime. Please take a seat," I said rolling a chair towards her.

"It's okay, I will see the collection here," she stepped in. She carefully examined the DPOL collection. Along with the ramp collection, we had also exhibited the DPOL collection in the stall.

I wanted to ask if she was a journalist. Prima facie she looked like one. But before I could ask, Sid came in.

She was Shraddha. A buyer from Mexico.

She liked the DPOL collection. Hesitantly she requested Sid to do a DPOL collection for her in white. She wanted almost everything – coats, panel skirts, stoles, long skirts, mini skirts, halters, tops, waist coats and long kurtas.

"It can be done, but it will take at least two months," Sid said.

"No problem. I will wait. But I have one more request," she said.

"And what's that?" Sid asked.

"Tonight I am leaving for Mexico. So this needs to be sent to Mexico. I am so sorry about this extra trouble."

Sid agreed to her request. A discussion on the terms and conditions of the deal followed.

"The day you got selected for Lavender, I thought my dream to find buyers will come true. But the past whole week I saw my hopes being dashed. Trust me, it is a miracle that you got this order," I said to Sid.

I don't lose hope easily, but after four days of the fashion week when there were no genuine buyers, I gave up. The buyer-seller meet, which was inaugurated with all the fanfare didn't head anywhere. Its meeting room turned into a college cafeteria. The event coordinators were seen having good time with free coffee and biscuits.

"Congratulations, Sid. It's a big order," a New Gen designer named Priyank whose stall was next to us, wished Sid.

"Thanks, how is it going for you?" Sid replied.

"Not great. Retailed only two dresses and no order so far."

Sid and Priyank were soon joined by the other New Gen designers. Each of them had a tale of sorrow to share. If one of them had sold two dresses, another had done a little better by selling five. One of them could not sell any but he was approached by a store in Mumbai for consignments.

"I wonder when there are so many buyers roaming around, why are there not enough orders?" someone raised a question in the discussion.

Another replied, "The buyers roaming around are the ones who have registered ad hoc saying that they will start a business soon. With this they get an entry to the stalls area. They enjoy all the benefits given to a buyer. Seeing them wear a buyer badge, we also give all our attention and some of us end up giving the passes for the show when they ask for it."

So that is what was happening all these days. Buyers walked in, I welcomed them. With full conviction I answered all their questions too. But despite my sincere efforts, some fled away without saying anything and some went with a promise to come back. They left me wondering if there was anything wrong with our collection. But today I realised that they were looking only for passes to which I had not paid heed.

"Please re-open the stalls. Two of our special guests are coming," a coordinator came running and requested all the designers.

It was nine. We had already closed our stall. Others were preparing to close theirs as well. Charged with today's evening discussion, designers continued to shut their stalls. Seeing this, the coordinator secretly divulged the names of the two celebrity guests.

The names acted as magic words. It infused superhuman powers in all the designers. They immediately started doing the reverse. They re-opened their stalls. We were startled with the sudden buzz. We didn't re-open ours and wishing luck to the fellow designers we left for the day.

The next day was a relaxed one. The designers had started packing by the afternoon. It being the last day of the show, Sid was busy meeting fellow designers. Apart from the New Gen designers, there were close to forty designers who were exhibiting at the fashion week.

The Mexican order Sid had received was the biggest order any New Gen designer had received and there was no regret for not reopening the stall last night. Only one out of the two celebrities had picked two dresses from a designer but had not paid a penny. She haggled for the price and at last went away with the dresses saying her secretary would negotiate and take care of the payments.

7

After the Show

First order, first consignment and AIGHT was born

"I am Radha. I am calling from Hyderabad."

It was a bright sunny hot afternoon of April when I received this call from Hyderabad. Sid and I were in a market in Noida, buying things for the Mexican order.

"Yes... Radha," I said recalling if I knew anyone named Radha who I met in Hyderabad.

I had joined Satyamine in 2006 in Hyderabad. I hoped not to embarrass myself by not recognizing any Radha I knew from those days.

"I got your reference from the designer list we received from Lavender. Is it a good time to talk?" she asked.

It didn't take long for my mind to process that Sid must have given my name and number as his contact manager. "Yes, sure we can talk."

I walked towards a less noisy lane of the busy market. And it was absolutely not a good time to talk. But only I knew what this call meant to me. It was the first call for me where I had a buyer on the other side! How could I say 'no'?

I pressed the phone closer to my ear. I could hear only a part of what Radha said. I never expected my first call with a buyer to go this way. I felt bad. However, at the end of the conversation when Radha expressed her desire in keeping our t-shirts in her store, I was happy.

"How is the color? And where did you go?" Sid asked me holding a fabric in his hand.

"A buyer called from Hyderabad."

"Oh is it? It means people were right about Hyderabad being the place which gives highest sales for the designers."

"Looks like, but she is interested only in the t-shirts. She will call tomorrow to discuss the details."

"No problem. But did you tell her that for t-shirts we will do only orders?" Sid said.

"No, I didn't. But I think that's obvious. Isn't it? I mean who would take t-shirts as a consignment? Anyway, I will mention this to her when she calls tomorrow."

The next morning, Radha called again to discuss size and quantity of t-shirts. I was very happy but my happiness didn't last long.

She wanted to do a consignment. This meant unsold t-shirts would be returned to us. How could she expect this as the t-shirts were already priced low? I wanted to ask her but controlled myself.

I excused myself saying I required the designer's approval for doing the consignment for t-shirts.

"Would you want to do the consignment with Panaroma?" I asked Sid as I prepared to leave for office.

"Let's discuss this in the evening," Sid said as he collected the car keys, goggles and wallet from the study table.

In the evening, we discussed Radha's call. We were pretty sure of not doing the t-shirt consignment. But before saying no, we evaluated the pros and cons of the offer. We had not heard from any other buyer. So it wasn't a good idea to turn down the offer at hand. We thought if we started retailing the t-shirts now, later we could get an opportunity to retail our other products too from there. Also, we had the t-shirts with us already. There were only pros. We could not think of any cons.

"Ok then. Say yes to Radha," Sid said to me, busy changing the settings of his camera.

"What are you trying to do with it?" I asked pointing towards the camera he was fiddling with.

"Can you take a picture of me? Need to send it to Vikrant Das."

"Will take one in the daylight tomorrow," I dismissed his proposal out of sheer laziness, but my excuse was logical.

"He has been asking for one for many days. Don't want to delay anymore. I will forget about it tomorrow so click a few with different settings now. I will select the best one and send it right away."

The Mexican collection was dispatched ahead of schedule. Shraddha was happy. Her customers liked the products. She said she would soon place more orders with us.

"So! We have one international customer err... 'buyer'." I said as I threw my laptop on the back seat of the car and sat in the front seat. Sid had come to pick me up from the IBMS office.

"Don't be happy. She wasn't a regular buyer. She was the wife of an Indian businessman settled outside. They come as buyers, buy dresses and sell them to family and friends. Chances are very bleak that we will hear from her again."

"Then who do you think is a regular buyer?"

"Buyers who give recurring business. They have a store of their own where they retail your collection or they may have a brand which they sell in multi branded fashion stores."

"And what makes you think she wasn't a regular buyer?"

"Had it been the case she would have shared her store details. When I asked her the business details, she said she would tell me later."

"Okay, but she still remains special to me. She gave us our first order and a big one," I said.

"Yes, her order was one of the best things that happened to us at the fashion week. And the lady herself was nice too. But she wasn't a buyer," Sid said, pulling my leg.

He then smiled and asked me. "By the way, the order for Panaroma is ready too. Tell me what do you want as the name of our label for this order?"

"What ready? We already had t-shirts from the Lavender fashion week."

"I know, I am just saying. Come on, suggest a name for it. We can't name it August. It is a different product altogether."

"Hmm... I agree. Let me think of it," I said as I waited for him to unlock the massive iron safety door of our house.

"Think of a name that will connect with youngsters because t-shirts are mostly used by teenagers," he said and after few minutes suggested, "AIGHT, how does this sound?"

"What is that?" I asked.

"AIGHT means – I am alright".

"Hmm... I didn't know that. Sounds cool and young."

"And what do you think of my hairstyle? Isn't it cool too?" he offloaded my laptop bag from his shoulder and straight away walked towards the bathroom mirror."

I never saw him even brush his hair after his bath. He didn't really care about his looks and today he was looking at himself in the mirror. I was surprised.

"What happened to you? Is everything fine?" I smiled standing behind him as he admired his hair in the mirror.

He quickly came towards his laptop. "You remember the interview? The one for which we sent my picture last week?"

"Yes, I remember. Vikrant Das, right?"

"Yes. He has published the article. And he has written about my hair. Come here, read this."

The article published on the news portal was titled "*This designer is saving the world, one garment at a time*" and it read:

> *Fashion technologist and designer Sid is twenty-five years old. His unkempt hair and aloofness set him apart from the rest of the fashion fraternity famous for air kissing and schmoozing at the first given opportunity...*

Richard Branson crossed the ocean in the hot air balloon for us

"How was your day? Any response?" I asked Sid after reaching home.

We had shared the catalogue of our collection with the fashion week buyers.

"No response."

I got a little worried but I didn't show it. I was thinking if a list of hundreds of buyers also did not yield any response, then what will.

"Why not we start working on ethnic wear?" I proposed.

"I don't know the 'e' of ethnic. I can only do western wear," he said.

"I understand, but we can try it. I saw you have made many ethnic wear designs in your design book."

"True but converting them to real clothes, literally gives me a fever," he said.

There was silence in the room. He got back to playing his guitar and I started thinking of ways to get the buyers.

After sometime, Sid kept his guitar aside and came and sat next to me and said, "You are also a business partner. You start it, I will follow you."

I really wanted to do many things but my schedule didn't allow me to. It was difficult to manage a job and business together. So far

I was able to manage both because of my ANZ work timings but I was drained out of energy. On my return from office, I slept in the car while Sid drove around to go to the places we visited for our business. He woke me after parking the car.

For the next half hour, I proposed my plan to Sid. He listened patiently and finally said, "All this sounds easy but doing it is very difficult."

"Good it is not easy, that's why it is exciting," I said. "How can you forget Richard Branson?" I pointed to the book on my bedside. "Did he not start in garage by selling his *The Student* magazine? He had no money to pay rent for a space too."

Sid was listening. He was a Richard Branson fan too. I recalled a few more instances from the book and shared them with him.

"You remember the incident when Richard Branson ventured on a hot balloon to cross the ocean? He didn't know he was going to return alive. Still he did it for his dreams. He also once dived into water when he didn't know how to swim. He jumped into the water for the sake of his dreams. When he jumped, he knew just one thing that if he jumped into water, his aunt would give him a prize in terms on money. He wanted to use it for his business. He risked his life for the dreams. Do you still think that starting an ethnic wear line is difficult? Come on, you can't. Isn't doing ethnic a step towards our bigger dream?" Saying this, I concluded my speech.

"Yes, you are right," he smiled.

I asked him. "Are we not in a much better position than all those who we consider our mentors?"

"Yes, agree," he said. "Okay, so let's keep it this way. You tell me what needs to be done and I will do everything you say, without raising any doubts."

"The most important thing is design. And you already have the designs. The novelty and freshness of your designs have been appreciated everywhere we've gone, so I do not see any challenge in starting an ethnic wear line. But since you get fever at the mention of ethnic, so you tell me, what are the challenges you foresee if we were to start working on ethnic wear?"

"We don't have a factory," he said and looked at me with expressions that meant he had thrown the most difficult challenge on me that he could think of. He waited for me to give a solution.

But I didn't give it any importance he expected and instead said, "Go on, I am listening. Tell me all the challenges," I picked up my notebook to make a note of the issues he was going to mention.

"Ok, well... if not a factory, we need a place. We can take it on rent to install the machines."

Unknowingly he had proposed a way around a factory himself.

"But we will have to buy the machines."

"Okay, next?"

"We need a team of people like masters, tailors, etc. And not ordinary tailors, only export house trained tailors. Starting from day one, we need to pay them salaries. Are we ready for it? We would also need to source fabrics."

"These are the generic challenges. You do ethnic or western, you will require these. We were going to set this up for your western collection anyway. So while doing the western wear, why not do some ethnic wear alongside and slowly make a foray towards it?"

He was convinced. I suggested we take help from one of our aunts. In her late 60s, she used to run an export house in the 1980s. Her eldest son Rajeev bhaiya helped her in those days. They sold their factory long ago and Rajeev bhaiya who was around ten years elder to us managed someone else's export house in Noida. Very resourceful in this field, he had also helped Sid with resources when he was doing the Lavender show.

Rajeev bhaiya was happy to help. He immediately proposed that we buy an export house that he knew was on sale. He assured he would get us a good deal too. But we explained to him we did not want to set up our facility but wanted to outsource our work instead.

He was disappointed. His interest in helping us took a steep dip. He believed the first step to do what we wanted to achieve was buying an export house. But seeing that we were firm, he connected us with his team that could help us. He also told us the places in Delhi to source our fabric. He arranged a visit to a few export houses where we could see the kind of work being done.

It is not wise to invest all the money in buying big assets and block the money. Outsourcing is the new mantra for success.

"I have asked dada to keep his first floor open. He has no problem doing this because he has his last order being prepared here," Rajeev bhaiya said as we walked out of the factory.

He had made a temporary arrangement for our collection to be produced at the same factory, which he wanted us to buy. Dada was the owner of the factory.

"Master ji and Alam are the two people who would be here. They will help you in your work."

Alam stitched and Master ji endorsed the patterns done by Sid. It felt we were set for some time now.

"How is your work going?" Rajeev bhaiya called a week later.

I thought it was a general call but it had more to it. He had called to let us know that the export house had found a buyer and we would have to find a new place.

"After so much difficulty the work had come on track, and now this," I said. I was already tired after a long day at office. Sid had brought me directly from the office to the factory.

"Don't worry. I have a clear idea of what we want. We just need to make the arrangement for the setup," Sid said.

"What about Alam and Master ji?"

"I suspected this to happen so I had already spoken with Alam. He is happy to stay with us because he has faced problems due to irregular payments in export houses. But we cannot afford to pay Master ji."

"What is his salary?"

"It comes to sixty thousand rupees per month. Not a good idea to incur this expense when we are only beginning. But he is ready to help whenever we need and we can pay him accordingly."

"Okay, but we need a place where Alam can sit and work. What about that?"

"Same plan that you proposed. We need an export house where we can make an arrangement for our stitching. Let's go and meet Rajeev bhaiya. His factory is nearby."

We were in the SEZ zone on the Noida-Greater Noida expressway.

"Apart from this area, where else do we have export houses?" Sid asked Rajeev bhaiya.

"Sector 6, Noida. Many designers have their setups there. That's where we are going now," Rajeev bhaiya said in a hurry. "Give me ten minutes. Let me give some instructions to the supervisor and we can leave right away."

We visited two places in Sector 6. The owners of both the places were Rajeev bhaiya's friends and they readily agreed to help. Their first priority was to complete their export orders. However, they were ready to let Alam use the machines when the machines were free.

The arrangement wasn't feasible for us. We had our deadlines and we were paying Alam to work full day. The issue was still unresolved.

"Any other place where export orders are done?" Sid asked as we settled into the car.

Suddenly an idea struck Rajeev bhaiya, "Did you see the shutter in our lane that is always closed?

We instantly remembered it. We had parked our car in front of it to go to Rajeev bhaiya's house.

He said, "Sometime back, export house orders were done there but it was an unapproved setup so few months back the setup was closed. However, since the past one week, I am seeing some action there in the night."

We parked the car in front of the closed shutter. The ventilator was covered with brown paper. A peep through the slit of the main gate revealed tube lights that were shining on the pale whitewashed walls.

"Can you hear that sound?" Sid had heard sounds as he pressed his ears close to the shutter.

"I am telling you. This is clearly the sound of machines," Rajeev bhaiya said.

In the meantime, a boy peeped from the corner of the ventilator and then pulled up the shutter to step out, "What happened?"

He immediately closed the shutter behind him.

"What is going on inside?" I asked

"Nothing. Who are you?" he said looking at us suspiciously.

"Don't worry. We are not investigating anything. We need your help for our work."

"What work?" he asked.

"Export order," I said.

"I don't know anything. The owner comes in the morning. Come tomorrow."

"Can you give us his phone number, please?" Sid asked the boy.

He bent to get inside the shutter. Coming out, he handed us a tiny piece of paper with a number scribbled on it.

"Call before coming tomorrow."

The next morning we came to know that the two owners of the factory were Sanchit and Pranav. They turned out to be Sid's juniors from his college's Calcutta branch.

But our problem was still not resolved. They did not have the machines we required. Also, they were operating from this location on a temporary basis. They were on lookout for a place in Sector 6.

Reasons said it was daunting but passion said it was possible. We set out on our journey because we chose to dream.

We could not afford to delay the work. We took help from bhaiya's factory supervisor and bought three machines. They were the best brands but we bought them second hand. For the time being, we kept the machines at home. Sid started making patterns. He took two weeks to make the patters of four western and two ethnic dresses.

"I want to show the patterns to Master ji before we ask Alam to convert them into garments. But not sure how and where can I show these patterns to him."

"Don't worry, let me organize this for you."

I called up Master ji to check if we could meet him at his place. He agreed but he was hesitant with the idea of the meeting us at his home. He lived in a shared accommodation and it was an area where he did not want us to come. And he could not come out with us because he had to leave for Nepal to attend to a family situation in two hours' time.

This left us with only one choice. We wrapped the patterns and drove down to his place. We pulled the car to one side of the road in a vegetable market outside his house.

"How is this, Master ji? I want you to please endorse it," Sid said to Master ji.

It was extremely hot as I stood outside the car with black glasses and a scarf wrapped around my face. They were sitting in the back seat of the car. We folded the front seats to make place for spreading the big patterns that were cut out of the brown sheets.

"Sir, you do better than me," Master ji said after reviewing the patterns and then picked up the one he liked most.

"I am surprised by the simple approach you have taken to conceptualise this design. It is absolutely beautiful and I want to have a look when Alam converts it into a garment."

Alam's work started. He worked at our home to convert the patterns into samples of muslin cloth. Simultaneously Sid finalised the colour palette, embellishments and fabrics. Some work was outsourced to the women who had worked for us during the Lavender Fashion Week.

Circumstances were not conducive but we continued to work. Over time, it had become difficult to manage everything in our one bedroom. The patterns had to be kept straight. Alam also worked at home. One room was occupied with machines. This had left just the drawing room for us to live in.

If you walk only on sunny days you will never reach your destination.

—Paulo Coelho, *Aleph*

After a month, Sanchit and Pranav found a factory. Finally, the production of our clothes started. But the factory was located in the dirtiest lane of this industrial area. The building was old and dilapidated with crumbling plaster on the walls, and with giant-sized webs hanging from the roof. From the outside, it was difficult to make out that there could be a fully functional export factory inside.

The hot summers of Delhi are difficult to battle. The conditions were even worse inside the factory where there was the nonstop sound of machines, no fans and boiling water dripped from the only tap. The labour had their food at the tea stall under the tree outside the factory.

Spending long hours in the factory started taking a toll on Sid's health. He packed the food and water from home but the heat wave inside the factory was intolerable. The only respite was that he met Pranav and Sanchit at the workplace where they discussed their favourite topic – entrepreneurship.

The clothes got dirty during the stitching process as the floor was dirty. The workers touched the fabrics with grease and oil on their hands. A lot of time and money was spent on finishing the products.

As a corrective action, Sid identified two best labourers who worked on his garments and rest all were barred to enter the area. The problem was addressed to some extent. Sid did a detailed quality check on the dirtied garments every evening at home.

In three weeks, a set of fifteen garments were hanging on the wooden hangers in our wardrobe. The designs which were on paper once had become a reality.

The next thing was to organise a photo shoot for the collection, and then make the catalogues and share with the buyers. It involved substantial cost, effort and time. But we obviously didn't want to make any expenditure at this stage. Sid completed the shoot with me as his model. The shoot was done in our balcony early in the morning before I left for office or on weekends when there was sufficient sunlight. He used the sunlight for photography and to add a flash he used the white thermocol sheets. This is how our economical yet magnificent photo shoot was completed.

Make use of the resources you have at hand. But start. Don't look for excuses. Just start. Because only if you start, you will go places.

The UCB story – a brand, not a label

"We got to price these now," Sid said smiling as he walked inside the room to find me ogling at the collection in the wardrobe.

After pricing the garments, I felt we had been very conservative with the prices, "Aren't the prices low? We should include at least some part of the costing incurred in your efforts."

I meant the costing Sid saved by doing thing by himself like making the patterns, finishing the products, doing the photo shoot on his own, the price to hire a model, making the catalogue, etc.

"I understand what you are saying but we want to do business in volumes. Our aim is not to become a designer label but a brand like UCB," Sid said.

He wanted to sell more number of garments by keeping the price low rather than making same money by selling a few. With low prices he could reach more people. He saw it as his first step to becoming a brand.

"And do you know, why I said I want us to be like UCB and didn't say any other brand name?"

"No," I thought he said UCB just because we wore UCB a lot.

"Because we already are like them in a way. Do you know the UCB story?" he asked me.

"No."

"It is a brand started by brothers and sisters. The UCB siblings now have a UCB town in Italy but there was a time when the elder brother had sold the favourite bicycle of his younger brother to make the first collection of garments. See the similarity?"

"How?"

"Whatever you earn we put in the business without knowing what is going to happen in future," he laughed. "The only difference is that you give all what you have happily."

"There will be light at the end of the tunnel. Amen," I said and we both laughed at ourselves until our stomachs ached and tears rolled down our faces.

The day you start laughing at yourself, you prove that you are a true warrior in your journey.

"You know why we are able to take the risk with money and our careers and think BIG?" I asked Sid.

"Yes, because the parents we are born to are visionaries," he gave the exact answer I was looking for.

Dad always said, 'no pain no gain'. He insisted that everyone should take some degree of risk at least once in a lifetime to chase their dreams, because only those who take risks have the chance to taste success.

Whenever we spoke to him about rejections and disappointments, he said success will come, to have patience and hang on. If success doesn't happen when you expect it, take the failures as a journey to accumulate experience and prepare yourself for success.

It wasn't just us who suffered criticism. Our father too faced the same when his colleagues enquired what Sid was doing. But he remained unfazed and continued to tell us to define ourselves with what we had. 'Think BIG and make it BIG' – time and again he repeated this.

"Defining oneself with the help of what we have," I have come to appreciate it more as I have grown in age. There is a recent instance too when I heard Lizzie Velásquez speak about 'defining oneself' on a TED talk. She is a beautiful evolved soul but some call her the ugliest woman on earth. An excerpt from her talk is this.

Is it the people who wonder what I am doing going to define me? I decided, let the goals, achievement and success define me. Work your ass out. Use the negativity around to light the fire inside you and keep going.

I could be grateful and open my eyes and realise the things I do have and make them those things that define me.

—Lizzie Velásquez

We e-mailed the catalogues to the buyers. And in two weeks we were talking with eight of them. All of them were interested in ethnic wear and in combination asked for western wear too. It proved that ethnic wear was selling in India. It was also confirmed that people bought exorbitantly overpriced designer ethnic wear but did not buy a correctly priced western wear.

The coming months saw us doing business with designer stores across the country. We retailed ethnic wear under the brand name August and western wear under the name of AIGHT.

We were happy to earn less profit, but we wanted more customers to know our brand. However, we faced our share of challenges when we tried to set our rules in a business which already had its rules.

"Where do you retail in Hyderabad?" Saurabh Shukla, Sid's senior from college asked. He was in Hyderabad for a business tour and wanted to buy a gift for his sister.

Sid gave him the names of the stores in Hyderabad where Sid retailed August and AIGHT.

"Don't have much time, have a flight in the evening. I will go to the Banjara Hills store, I am close to it."

"That store has invited me many a time but haven't been there yet. So when you go, tell them that I am your friend."

Saurabh called up. We were waiting to hear good things about his visit to the store. But we were in for a shock.

Saurabh knew our price range and he was startled to see that the store had inflated the prices of our garments. They removed our price tags and had put their price stickers. As per the agreement, our garments were to be sold at the price we mentioned on the price tag. But with the inflated price, without our knowledge, the store was earning more than twice of what was agreed upon. Our sales suffered due to the high prices and neither did we get our share from the inflated prices.

Sid confronted the store owner but he refused to accept it. We continued to work with him in a hope that after the confrontation, he would not repeat what he was doing. We felt cheated and feared that this could be happening in other stores too. To deal with it, whoever we worked with, we kept them informed that we travelled often and may visit the store any day. Many wondered why we repeated this and never visited.

The supply chain played a strategic role in consignments. We tied up with a courier agency to deliver our consignments but it was a difficult process to manage. Sometimes when the stores returned the unsold garments, the courier boxes were damaged and the garments were missing. They saved money by using a local courier service. The condition of the garments received back was horrible.

If the courier boxes reached us intact, the store forgot to send a few garments. They didn't provide the sales report even after multiple reminders. When it was provided, it wasn't correct. There were instances when they didn't return a garment and it also didn't appear in the sales report. This meant that they had either lost it or they didn't want to give us the share until we went asking for it. And finally if the correct sales report was shared, the payment was not released on time.

But not all was bad. There were good things too. Sid's designs which until now were published internationally, got published in India too.

Sometimes the magazines informed us when they published and also sent us a copy of it. At times we came to know of the publication from designer friends in the industry. And Sid also regularly checked for the magazines at a bookstore near our house when we visited Mother Dairy.

Sometimes there were calls from the stores where we retailed whenever a model or a television celebrity or a journalist wanted to wear our outfits for media events. The deal was that when these people would get published in the page 3 parties, the designer was also mentioned.

We continued working on the orders and consignments and over the months, when the business started growing at a steady rate, we wanted to do more. Reach out further. Be known more. The new desire was to meet our customers, have our flagship store and see the customers carry our brand bags.

Our dreams were big and had no affinity for money. We also scored a ten on ten on the following traits. These are the traits of a creative person that I found on internet:

• Easily bored • Risk takers • Colour outside the lines • Think with their heart • Make lots of mistakes • Hate the rules • Work independently • Change their mind a lot • Have a reputation of eccentricity • Dream big •

Check if you have these. If yes, start right away before it is too late.

> **One day you will wake up and there won't be any more time to do the things you have always wanted. Do it now.**
>
> **—Paulo Coelho, *The Winner Stands Alone***

I was happy to see Sid not get selected. Was our pact broken?

"What is this?" I asked Sid as I picked up a craft work.

After walking up the stairs to the second floor of our house, the first thing I wanted to do was to keep my laptop down. But the place where I usually kept my laptop had a piece of silk cloth. I picked it up to make place for my laptop and noticed it was a beautiful piece of work. Yellow and royal blue silk was finely quilted and it was embellished with pink and yellow coin size origami 3-D patterns.

"Nothing, you come here. I have to show you something," Sid called me to show me something on his laptop.

"No, first you tell me what is this?" I asked still inspecting the piece in my hand.

And it suddenly struck me. "Wait, wait... wait. Don't tell me you are participating in the fashion week again."

He smiled and got up from his chair. I got my answer.

In his quest of creativity, Sid had decided to apply to the fashion week again. But I didn't want him to participate so early. We already had enough buyers. Participating in the fashion week could get us few more buyers but who knew how much these new buyers would contribute.

Also, participating in the fashion week meant expenditure. The existing business would also suffer as Sid would have to focus on the show.

I thought completely in business terms. It had taken us four months to break even and that too because we started humble and had saved every single penny by doing things on our own. Also, thanks to the order from Mexico and excellent sales in the designer stores.

However, Sid didn't listen and sent his entry. Seeing his effort and conviction, I too prayed that he gets selected.

After a month, the results were out. He had not been selected and was upset. Being in this business and having done the show earlier, I knew that the design he submitted deserved to be selected. But the selection is governed by many other factors too.

"Good that it didn't happen," I blurted out after a long silence in the house. I didn't mean it literally. I wanted to say something else but I ended up saying this because I could not see him sad after having achieved so much.

Before he took me wrong, I explained my point of view, "Don't travel on two boats. You want to be a brand, not a label. We talk about UCB and Armani. Tell me who was dependent on a fashion show?"

"You are absolutely correct," he bounced back as if he was waiting for me to reason out the failure.

"I'm not saying that you should not do fashion shows at all. I am just saying that when you have earned enough from your business then we can fund your fashion show from that money."

"Okay. Yes, I understand. I got carried away a little," he said and I could understand that a creative person has his own set of private emotions.

To confirm that I was able to motivate him enough, I said, "And do I not read the designer interviews to you that show that apart from a few who are closely associated with Bollywood all the others, even the big names say they are struggling. You want to be one of them or be a brand?"

I reminded him of a few other important things. "It is just a few months back that your green fashion DPOL work was published on the Tree Hugger website. You think it is a small thing? Tree Hugger is a Discovery website. And a month back, your interview was published in the FTV website. I can go on about the numerous other publications. You know them better than me."

Sid had set up a Google alert to track where his articles were being published. He was aware of the articles that were published about his work.

I went a little overboard in my attempt to motivate him and heard myself speaking, "Why don't you just pack your bags and go to the US. Live there and explore the opportunities. So many people from the US send you queries to buy your designs. You can focus on them at the moment. And then maybe do an international fashion show?" I added.

"Yes, you are right," he said and sat straight up. "The Portland fashion week manager has also liked my work and has been asking me to come and do a show there for the past two years."

"See, then why waste time here?"

The coming days saw Sid busy in the factory. In the evenings he saw to the finishing of clothes. Weekends were spent sourcing the fabrics. Late night hours he spent responding to the magazines. He reconnected with his journalist friends to proliferate the benefits of green fashion. He was also the guide to many international students on their research work, developed Go-green community and conducted workshops in colleges.

Fast forward to two months, Sid said to me. "I have invitations from the Paris Ethical Fashion Week. What do you say? Shall we do it?"

Knowing that I wasn't keen on fashion shows, he immediately added, "We can go to the Paris Ethical Fashion Show only as invitees. Since the DPOL garment is on exhibition in the London Science Museum and there are publications on Tree Hugger about it, we have received the invitation."

"Great!" I was happy but didn't show the kind of excitement I usually would.

Sid noticed it. I was caught up in a myriad of thoughts. I was thinking of doing this show from the perspective of the money involved in the process. We could do it later, but at the same time I didn't want to disappoint Sid.

"I know what you are thinking," Sid said. "The cost of doing this show will be much less than any Indian fashion week because we have earned the invitation. And we are not going immediately. We will go after six months."

He continued, "We do not have to even create a collection. We have the brand new DPOL collection. So, no cost of creating a collection. And anyway, we have seen the Indian fashion weeks didn't let us present the DPOL. So let's go where it will be valued."

"So, Paris it is!" I finally exclaimed with my usual enthusiasm as Sid looked at me enjoying the moment.

8

Paris – 2011

"It is so cold," I said squeezing and pulling my hands in my sweater.

It was six in the morning and we had arrived at the Charles de Gaulle Airport of Paris to attend the Paris Ethical Fashion Week.

"But weather forecast predicted that two layers of clothing would suffice," Sid said.

"They can do with two layers because they are used to it."

We discussed the temperature as we waited for our luggage to arrive. It contained the collection we were going to present at the fashion show. The dresses which the models were wearing on the ramp were already sent for fitting but the other dresses to be displayed at the stall were in our two check-in bags.

"Come," Sid called me. Our bags had arrived.

It was pretty quick. Europe's busiest airport in terms of aircraft movement was very efficiently managed. Seeing the humble aesthetics, the patriot in me had doubted its services too.

Looking around to make our way from the arrivals, Sid grabbed a free map of the city from a self-service panel.

"Taxi or train?" Sid asked me after reading the map. There wasn't any direct train to our destination.

"Train," I said without giving it a thought.

I wasn't ready to shell out a fortune at the outset itself. And I was confident we could take the train. The basis of my confidence was my everyday train ride to office in Sydney for more than a year.

"Two tickets for this destination please," Pointing my map, I said to the tall and robust lady at the counter.

I didn't want to say the French name of the place with the incorrect pronunciation. I tried to show it to her on the map.

"English," the lady said loudly and then used her hands to tell me that she didn't understand English.

She returned the map to me and said something which I could not follow. She was definitely speaking in French.

I looked at her to prepare myself to explain to her once again. But before I could do so, she made the similar sounds again. It was clear she was losing patience.

"Yes, I am saying two tickets to this place... this place please," I said.

Again I used the map to the best of my ability to explain to her. But she neither looked at me nor my map. Instead she looked beyond me. She showed me the queue behind me. She wanted me to step aside and let her serve the others.

There were only three people standing behind me. This by their standards was a long queue. I stepped aside. But Sid didn't step aside. He was standing beside me.

Sid passed four euros underneath the window cut out and said, "Two tickets."

Sid was observant during my failed attempts.

I failed to do what Sid did in a few seconds. One of the reasons for this was that I was overloaded with my past experience and wasn't ready to face this unexpected language issue.

Sometimes when we approach a situation with the knowledge we already possess, we make even simple things very complicated.

"Which terminal should we take with this ticket?" Sid asked a person.

We were standing near the airport exit leading to train terminals. After swiping our ticket we had to exit the airport and enter the railway station. But we didn't know the terminal.

"No English," the man said on the move.

We had received the same response from almost six people before him. The one or two who stopped to help us didn't know the place.

We were hopeful of the fact that people communicated even when there was no language. All we wanted was a kind heart who could look beyond the language barrier and spend time to understand our request. But one thing was clear that language was going to be a problem during our stay here.

"I know English but I don't know the route. My mom knows the route but she is there. Can you see?"

We saw Rojer's dad, mom, two brothers and one sister on the other side. "You will have to come with me to that side."

"But if I cross, I can't come back and am not sure if this is the right terminal," Sid said.

In the meantime Rojer's family called him. Their train had arrived.

"Come, come..." Rojer said to us as he ran to swipe his ticket.

It was a rush. Wondering when we would find another English speaking person and one who knew the train routes, we swiped our tickets too.

Next moment we found ourselves standing inside the train with our luggage.

In a broken English, Rojer's mom said, "The route not simple. Time being stay on train. I tell you when you get down," she said after looking at our map. And the doors closed.

"I thought it is a landmark in the city but why does no one know about it?" I said to Sid.

"It is the Louvre. It is a landmark. But I am also wondering why people don't know how to go there and it is more surprising that there are no direct trains to the place," Sid said.

I had few questions for Rojer's mother but before I could ask, I saw the family getting up. They gathered their luggage to get down.

We felt weird and abandoned. I continuously looked at her. I wanted her to say something to us. Thinking that she may have forgotten us, I got up from my seat and walked to her. Just then the train stopped and while getting down, she said, "Six stops from here. Get down."

What if I would have not walked to her to ask? I wondered. And still, we didn't have complete information. I wanted to ask, sixth stop from here or after the sixth stop from here?

Sid and I moved to a corner seat to sit together. Office goers boarded and disembarked the train frequently. We were nearing the city centre.

"Are you guys from India?" A boy asked us.

He spoke perfect English. He sat on the corner seats adjacent to us. In front of him sat a girl. Both of them looked at us with friendly smiles.

"Yes, from India," I replied. Sid joined me by flashing a smile.

For the cold weather, they were strangely dressed. They were loaded with clothes on upper part of the body but the girl wore a pair of knee-length black shorts and the boy wore a loose pair of cotton pants. Both constantly rubbed palms to keep warm.

"Great country. We are coming from there," the boy said.

"Yeah, true. He's been visiting India every alternate year for the past six years and I have heard so much about it from him that this time I also visited," the girl said.

"Nice. So where did you go?" I asked.

"This time, mostly the northern part of India," the girl replied looking at me and then turned her head towards the boy to say. "Though we wanted to stay and cover south India too."

"Don't worry, honey. We will be going back again soon and this time all equipped to stay longer."

"Equipped?" I asked.

"This happened." The girl pointed to her right leg below the knee.

"O' lord, how did this happen? Must be terribly painful?" I said. She had a fresh wound. It was quite deep too.

"It is much better now. It had developed maggots inside it," she laughed and showed the yellow spots made by the maggots.

"How did you get this?" I asked.

"It started with an insect bite in a village in Uttar Pradesh. We stayed there for one month to teach village students."

They both were the students of Stanford University, USA. They had combined their India trip with the social welfare activity they had to undertake in a developing country as part of their curriculum.

She also explained that it was for the wound that she was wearing shorts in this cold weather and to give her company her friend was also wearing slippers and cotton pants. Love doesn't need words. It shows.

We got down at the sixth station. It was a junction. It had multiple escalators, underground pathways, shops selling magazines, fast food stalls. People ran in all directions. Amidst this, we stood again, reading our map.

'No English' was again a challenge that we faced, but this time help arrived early. A beautiful lady herself walked up to us on seeing that we were being turned down by the busy commuters.

Linda must have been in her late thirties. Extraordinarily thin like a model, dressed in black trousers and coat on a white shirt, she looked drop dead gorgeous with a bright smile she wore on her red lips.

Looking at our map, she asked us to follow her. She was going exactly where we were headed. We took our next train with her. It was a short ride. We parked ourselves near the train's door.

Getting down from the train, we boarded the longest escalator I had ever seen. As I looked down the escalator, a sense of achievement prevailed realising how far we had come for our dreams.

We were tired but Sid matched up with Linda's speed. He signalled me that I need not walk fast.

Having walked for ten minutes, we stopped to cross a road. After this brief pause, when I recollected the strength to walk again, a cold drop of rain fell on my nose. I looked up to see the overcast sky. The cold breeze brushed my face. It was about to rain. It felt the city was welcoming us.

A little ahead, the fragrance of fresh flowers literally gushed into me. We were passing by a garden. The shrubs and trees were overloaded with colourful flowers, mostly yellow and magenta. Whatever leaves were visible were glistening.

"Paris is beautiful," I said to Sid as we stopped again for a minute to catch our breath. I hate walking long distances, but outside India, I have never been able to escape the walks.

Sid too looked at the garden and smiled, "Yes it is. We'll come here later."

"It is the best weather of Europe," Linda said with a smile.

We walked past the road side cafes, which were beginning to open. The aroma of freshly brewed coffee and pizza cheese filled my nose. I marked the places in my mind to come back later.

Walking with the luggage was difficult. However, it felt proud to feel how with each step we were coming closer to our dream.

"This is your place. Good day." With a smile, Linda left us in front of a big royal building.

It was a narrow lane with similar buildings on both sides of it. A narrow lane in Europe could also be beautiful. All the windows had terrace pots with red flowers in them.

"We have a booking here from today," Sid said to the receptionist. She was a beautiful Chinese girl.

Sid had made arrangements for our stay in a city backpacker. We were close to the venue where our fashion week was to happen. Staying in a backpacker was one of our many ideas to make a show in Paris economical for us.

Staying here was not only going to save us money on the stay, but save huge on daily travels too.

"We don't take bookings. We give rooms to those who show up," the receptionist said.

Suddenly, I didn't find her beautiful anymore. Even her canary yellow top that she had paired up with cream coloured trousers didn't help.

"But I have a confirmation email from your admin team," Sid pulled out a print out from his bag.

She turned mellow after reading it and opened her booking register, "Yes, your name is there."

She made no eye contact. It felt like a victory. Few minutes later, keeping her register aside, she said. "But you see, last night a cycling group came from the mountains. So to accommodate this large group, we used your room."

Were we facing the Indo-China animosity? First she had lied that they didn't take advance bookings and now she said our rooms were occupied.

"Okay, I understand but is there anything else available at the moment?" Sid asked her.

"Yes, two beds are available. But they are in the dorms. You can move there if you want."

"But we asked for a private room with two beds. When can we get that?"

"Yes, I know, but for that you will have to wait until three. It will be vacated by noon. I will get it cleaned. So you can take the keys at three."

"Three hours for cleaning?" I asked. Extremely tired, I wanted rest. But I also doubted her intentions; she seemed to be troubling us just for the heck of it.

"Yes, we have to clean more than hundred rooms in this six-storey building," she said indifferently.

She said we could roam around the city after leaving our bags in the cloak room. She signalled us to reach the cloak room.

Very less space to move around, the cloak room had bunches of bags huddled together. There were cycles, skates, compasses, ropes, gloves, sleeping bags and tents. The walls were covered with maps. There were also collages with pictures of smiling faces taken at famous places of the world.

We kept our bags in the room and returned to the reception to find a place to sit. We entered a veranda. Being the centre of the building, everyone crossed it to move around the building. With the reception on one side of it, the opposite side had the cafeteria. The other two sides were the cloak room and a broad staircase leading to the dorms.

The veranda was open to the sky and on the sixth floor it was covered with glass for natural day light .

It was packed with boys and girls, mostly Europeans. They were busy browsing the internet, reading maps, packing and unpacking their oversized trekking bags. We sat there briefly and prepared to take a walk outside.

We put our laptops, passports and tickets in Sid's shoulder bag. It was eight in the morning. The girl's shift at the reception was also over. A boy had replaced her. He was friendly and we asked his help to mark important places for us on the map.

"Let's go around see these places," Sid said to me looking at the map.

"It is breakfast time. It is complimentary. Have it before you leave," the boy at the reception said. He was looking at a noisy group of backpackers who had descended the broad stairway and made their way to the cafeteria.

We were the only Asians in the busy cafeteria. We helped ourselves to a big bowl of cold milk with cornflakes floating, jam and butter cubes, a small tub of curd – I wondered if that would be sufficient.

Just then, a baguette caught my attention. Sid got a basket for us. A lady broke the long bread into small pieces in the baskets.

"I am still hungry. Let's find some places to eat," I said. The bread was too hard and the cold milk with cornflakes in the chilling cold weather sent shivers through my body.

"I liked it. Breakfast should be like this. No oil and no cooking!" Sid said.

"I am not done unless I get some toast with Bournvita milk or a paratha with lassi!" I said.

"I knew it," Sid grinned.

"Let's see for how many days you can eat this. Huh!"

"I enjoyed it. The only thing I missed was salt. Some salt should have been there."

"Some salt?" I laughed aloud, "That is your craving for an Indian breakfast. But I know, you won't agree."

We went directly to Mc Donalds. It was jam-packed. We were hopeful to find a salad burger but we didn't find any vegetarian option. The only option was fries but it made no sense to stand for an hour for a pack of fries.

We wandered around on the streets looking for food.

"Wow, let's have a dosa," Sid said.

An Indian boy who must have been a student was making dosas in a stall. He had placed a big tilted pan with fire burning under it on a metallic table. He was standing outside a juice shop. People had queued up for his dosas.

"Dosa and here! Wow!" I said as we approached the boy.

But the feeling of respite didn't last long. He put some chocolate and peanut spread over it, rolled it in butter paper in the form of a cone and filled it with round slices of a banana.

"Your crepe, sir," he said as he served a customer.

A sweet dosa would not do! We walked around to find other warm and salty vegetarian options.

Finally, we packed muffins, croissants and juice from a bakery. They would have to do for dinner as well.

First the language and then the food; they were certainly going to be a problem.

The two extremes – backpacking and fashion show

The luggage was heavy and our room was on the fourth floor with no lifts in the building. We decided to keep our luggage in the cloak room on the ground floor. We could directly take the bags from there and go to the show. But this also meant that we would have to walk down the stairs for every single thing we required.

A small room on the fourth floor, with shared toilets (douches) and bathroom, the breakfast time ending at 9:00 am and extremely cold weather to battle – life at backpacker wasn't easy at all. But all the hardships were worth the satisfaction. In this expensive city, we were able to live with the everyday expense for the two of us not going beyond sixty Euros. It included our stay, three meals, fruits and snacks.

It was tourist season. The streets and gardens were full of tourists from around the world. Paris is very beautiful and planned. One can cover most of the places walking. We also walked around and in two days covered the Eiffel tower, the zoo and a couple of historical places and gardens.

Out of all the places, the Louvre turned out to be our favourite. For a change, we unanimously liked the Louvre more than Eiffel. For its pyramid shape, serene waters and the beautiful gardens, we found ourselves sitting around it for hours.

We had covered many places but finding the venue of our show turned out to be tricky. Each time we searched for the address, we reached the Louvre. There wasn't any place where the show could be held at Louvre so disqualifying the option we looked for places around it. How could the organizers make a mistake of giving us the wrong address, I wondered.

The afternoon of the second day, we sat feeling helpless. After sometime, we noticed a boy at a distance. He wore a body fit blue checked shirt and slender khaki coloured pants. His swanky hairstyle caught our attention.

He repeatedly tip-toed and walked, and bowed too. At first, I thought he was on drugs and was doing things to amuse himself but when I saw a girl and cameraman appear from behind a pillar, I realised that he was most probably a model practising his routine.

"I am sure, this is the venue," I said.

"The address too says so but where exactly? It is all open here," Sid said. "Shall we see what is underneath? We may find a clue."

It is the Louvre museum underneath the Pyramid and houses the original Mona Lisa painting by the Italian artist Leonardo Da Vinci. We had not been there so far and had reserved it for a visit later.

And what we found underground amazed us. We discovered a complete city. We walked past the museum to explore other places and we had not gone far when we saw something, beyond which we could not move. It was splendid and unbelievable.

It was exactly the similar pyramid that stood tall above the ground. But it was inverted. Such a colossal, sharp and bright structure hanging upside down was a breathtaking sight. In the meantime, Sid noticed the arrows leading to an auditorium. We had found our venue.

Our problem had been solved so we explored the place that was lit up. The first thing to catch our attention was the Virgin Records music store. Anything is possible! The thought struck me as I entered the store. I recalled Richard Branson's first venture that was a magazine called *The Student*. Did he ever think in the formative years that one day he would hold the store at such a prominent place? After inspiration and motivation, it was time for some fun. The two of us fancy toys and it was a bonanza to discover the Pylones store.

The next morning we reached the auditorium. We rolled our bags on the wheels from the backpacker to the auditorium. The streets had adequate slopes and the traffic stopped for pedestrians.

The experience at the fashion week was also smooth. There was a standard process to do everything, be it the setting up of the stall, using the fixtures or communicating with the buyers.

We unpacked our bags and the stall was set up in no time. The dresses that had to go on ramp had already been sent a month ago to customize them for the models. So dress rehearsals were not a concern. But everything has a merit and demerit. The fashion week lacked the personal touch.

The merit of the show was that all the designers and exhibitors had a default invitation to attend all the shows. It was unlike in India where the New Gen designers didn't have the invite to attend the shows of the established designers.

If the fashion week in India was about team work, bonding and personal touch, here it was more about professionalism and the opportunity to learn.

"It is very expensive to stay in the city. I am living in a suburb where I can save some money. But then taxis are also expensive. Coming here daily costs around sixty Euros. Plus there is daily expenses like food," Sharad mentioned.

Sharad was an exhibitor at the show. He was representing an Indian NGO and was showcasing jute and silk fabrics in their stall.

"You must first get a place in the city to live and then we will talk about expenses," said Runul. He was also an exhibitor at the show.

It being the tourist season, the hotels in city were overbooked.

Listening to the innumerable concerns of the group, I was happy at Sid's idea of staying at a backpacker. Our combined living expense was also less than the taxi fares others paid every day.

What if we slept on bunker beds in our tiny room, and what if the shower worked only until we pressed the shower button with one hand and took bath with only one hand. What if we ran up and down the stairs early in the morning, and what if he had cold breakfast – it was a lifetime experience and the outcome was brilliant too!

To learn the maximum in a lifespan – travel.

In two days, we had become accustomed to living the life of a backpacker. We spent the whole of the day at the show so it didn't matter where we returned to sleep.

For the days, which Sid had defined as "I need some salt" day, we splurged our savings on an elaborate lunch at a Pakistani restaurant. Sid could not eat the English breakfast beyond two days. Lunch and dinner obviously had to have salt. So eventually every alternate day was an "I need some salt day".

Backpacking and the fashion show were the two extremes, and Paris brought them together for us.

Where will I live? What will I eat? Who will help me, if I need help at an unknown place? – These questions will only deter one from pursuing the dreams. The only focus must be your dreams. Rest all falls into place.

The show day

The runway looked straight out of a Fashion TV show. Around the ramp, guests from the fashion industry were seated. Everywhere else, the audience was standing and cheering.

Watching the creatively dressed audience was equally delightful as was watching the models on the ramp. Amidst this, it was a proud moment to watch the audience cheer when the models walked the ramp wearing Sid's outfits.

"Go slow. Go slow," I heard someone say this aloud when I stood in front of our stall waiting for the hanger stand loaded with dresses to arrive.

I looked around but didn't find anyone. I ignored the voice.

"Which one is yours?" The women coordinator who brought the hanger to me said and started looking for the dresses with our participation code.

I searched and found one. But when I tried to take off the hanger, it didn't move.

"Is it pinned up somewhere?" I asked the coordinator who was busy looking for the other dresses.

This time she pulled it. Again the hanger didn't come off but someone spoke from the other side, "It's me. Don't pull."

The voice was similar to the voice I had heard a few minutes back. I sat down to see who it was. I saw a pair of feet in black bellies on the other side of the hanger stand.

Within seconds, a beautiful old lady with golden curly hair, dressed elegantly in a pink top, grey skirt and a pair of pointed black bellies walked on to our side.

I looked at her with a smile and waited for her to explain herself.

Catching her breath she said. "You know, I have been running after this dress from the backstage."

She spoke French and I of course could not make much sense of it until the coordinator translated it to me.

"But why, what happened?" I asked the coordinator to ask her.

She understood English in bits and pieces. So before the coordinator could translate my English to French for her, she replied, "I am in love with this one. Look at the gorgeous colour combination," she said showing me the dress, which she was now holding in her hand.

"Thank you," I smiled and waited for her to give the dress to me. But she didn't give the dress to me. Instead, she looked around. She was looking for someone.

When she could not find whoever she was looking for, she smiled looking at me. She was apologetic in her smile for making me wait and then she said something.

It was French again. This time I didn't understand a word. The coordinator had also left.

Seeing me struggle, Tulip's mother stepped in. Tulip was Sid's friend. She was a model and a TV actor in Paris. While Sid was doing the photo shoot with Tulip in the studio, Tulip's mother, Daniele who looked more like her elder sister stayed with me. She too didn't speak good English but she was better than the others around.

"Sussan loves the dress and she wants to buy it," Daniele told me excitedly.

I looked at Sussan and smiled. She was anxiously waiting for my reply but I had only a smile to return. I didn't know if we wanted to sell it. I had to talk to Sid about it.

Sussan walked inside the stall and looked around for a changing room. There wasn't any. She held the dress close to her to check the length and fitting. She looked gorgeous.

The dress had Peter Pan collar. To check if it would fit her neck, she slipped the dress till her neck. And she had hardly popped out her head when she exclaimed seeing her friend who was running towards us.

Martha hugged Sussan. The hug was exchanged with the dress still hanging around Sussan's neck. I was worried about the dress. But the expression of joy on their faces made me forget my worry.

It is heartening to become a reason of happiness for people.

Daniele was equally elated. She looked back and forth at both of them as they spoke.

"What are they discussing?" I asked Daniele.

Daniele translated their conversation for me, "They both like the same dress. They liked it from the moment they saw it on the ramp. They decided whoever would reach the dress first would get to buy it. Sussan chose to tag along the hanger stand and reached here before Martha. So Sussan is taking this dress but she wants Martha to take the other dress of yours."

Daniele had not even finished translating the situation to me that Martha took off the outer layer of the top that she was wearing and slipped into the second dress.

Extremely elated to see each other dressed in their favourite dresses, they jumped like kids.

Sussan wore the dress they had competed for. It was a multi-coloured vertical strip dress with Peter Pan collar. It had yellow, orange, red and green stripes. Martha wore a white dress that had the collar of a coat and on the sides it had a navy blue and crimson red thin ribbon pattern.

I could not wait any longer for Sid to return. I ran up to him where he was shooting with Tulip. The fashion week had arranged for the official photo shoot for their news bulletin.

Sid's photo shoot was over but he was shooting with Tulip for the pictures he had to share with his journalist friends.

Seeing him in a hurry to give back the place to the photographer, I quickly narrated the situation to him. He said. "Ok sell them. Any price you decide would be fine."

"So less?" Daniele was startled, "this is worth so much more."

"How much do you think it should be?"

Daniele went to Sussan and Martha and quoted double the price, And I instantly knew that if this deal failed, it would only be for the high price.

And I was correct as after the price was told to Sussan and Martha, they looked worried.

I asked Tulip's mother, "What's the matter? The price you quoted is too high, right?"

"No, no, they are happy to buy them. It is just that it struck them now that they do not have enough cash. They have directly come here from the hospital. They both are nurses. They have their cards though. Can we look around for a machine where we can swipe their cards?"

I could not find any machine and came to know that Martha had left to arrange for cash. Daniele was talking to Sussan who stood there, still holding her favourite dresses.

I attended to the customers. In no time, my hands were full. Two college students had tried a dress earlier but had gone away. They had returned now to buy it. Then there were women who asked for the dresses which were already taken by Sussan and Martha.

Sid was still not back. I was tired. Giving the charge of the stall to Daniele I stepped aside to look for him. I saw Sid was winding up things. I could also see Martha walk towards me with cash in her hand.

"Oh, what is this?" Sussan pointed towards a mark on the collar of her dress. It was faded but it was visible.

"It looks fresh," Daniele said taking the dress in her hand. She smelled it. "It is a lipstick mark. The model must have rubbed against it in hurry when changing backstage."

Sid suggested Sussan could take another dress.

But Sussan wanted the same dress. She asked Sid, if the mark would go away with a wash. The moment Sid said yes, Sussan asked me to pack the dress.

Sid was hesitant to give her the stained dress. He tried to persuade her to take another dress but Sussan insisted she would take the one she liked. At last, they reached an agreement. Sid said he would not charge for the dress until he cleaned the collar and would give the dress to Tulip the next day. Sussan coincidentally lived close to Tulip's house.

"I like it. Can I have it?" a boy asked.

His arms were covered in tattoos. He showed them off wearing a white t-shirt. He seemed restless. He was changing weight from one leg to the other frequently. He sure must have been part of a rock music band. His demand also gave me a reason to believe so.

He wanted to buy the Michael Jackson white coloured t-shirt with Michael Jackson's face made on it using black shimmering sequins. Sid had sketched the legend on the t-shirt and it was hand worked by a group of underprivileged women. This brilliant art work never missed to attract anyone who caught even a slightest glimpse of it.

We had many t-shirts with faces of Elvis Presley and the likes. But the Michael Jackson one, I was sure we did not want to sell.

"Can you please wait for a minute? I need to confirm with the designer if I can sell it."

It didn't feel good to turn him down outright. Also, it was my attempt to buy some time. All I wanted was that he spent some time looking at other t-shirts and pick one of them.

I was sure Sid would not want to sell it. He had always been in love with his creations more than the love for money.

I asked Sid if I could sell the t-shirt. As expected, I heard a typical Sid's answer. He left it on me to decide.

We didn't sell the t-shirt. That's the conflict between an artist and a businessman.

The love for art is beyond the love for money.

Making a wish with a nose pad

It was a priceless feeling to meet our customers, see them appreciate the value of art and the effort behind it. Beyond this, there was another overwhelming emotion which Sid and I shared privately. It was the first time when we were engaged in direct sales. It was here where we clocked our highest direct sales and that too in Euros, abundant Euros.

The days at the fashion week were very tiring. It wasn't like in India where our friends were around to help us. But despite being tired, Sid made sure that we slept only as much as required. He said we had not come this far to sleep. So every evening we celebrated the day sitting by our favourite place – the Louvre Pyramid. We left after watching the Eiffel tower shimmer in the night.

The Pyramid of Louvre turns even more magnificent at dusk. Thousands of lights shimmer in the waters of the Louvre and the wandering tourists settle down to dine in the open air restaurants. Sid and I too spent hours lying by the waters of Louvre discussing our journey so far in endless conversations.

When we decided to do the show in Paris, we just knew that we wanted to do it but we had no idea how we were going to do it. But today, a task which had appeared daunting was achieved.

Doing the show wasn't as difficult as it was to take a decision to do it. At the beginning, it felt like setting out on an adventure fraught with unknown challenges. But for the love of chasing our cherished dream, we took the leap beholding the faith that challenges don't last forever.

Things aren't as difficult as they appear. Have the courage to take the first leap.

The vast expanse of water around the Louvre Pyramid is considered to be a wishing pool. Thousands of people fling coins into it and make wishes. One evening when we were there, the nose pad of Sid's spectacles dropped in the water. After several attempts we could not find it.

And then Sid said to me. "You know what? The wishing pond has taken my wish. My coin was the nose pad of my spectacles. It is a sign. We will one day come back here again and retail from Paris."

We had accomplished our dream to do the fashion show in the city of fashion and a new dream was born for us.

'Where will we stay? What will we eat? How we will do?'

These are some of the dangerous questions we ask ourselves. These are detrimental to success. I thank the almighty that we did not think about any of these questions. This is the only reason how we with just two check-in bags and two hand bags represented India in the ethical fashion week in the fashion capital of the world.

An international show, the discovery of a new dream with Sid's wish in the waters of Louvre, thirty percent of expenditures refunded on filing the taxes, great sales, spending well under the budget – we couldn't have asked for more.

The danger of an adventure is worth a thousand days of ease and comfort.

—Paulo Coelho, *Veronika Decides to Die*

9

Fancies of a Fleeting Mind

On our return from Paris, we wanted to set up an internet marketplace to reach out to our global customers. We decided to develop our website. Who could do it better than our friends who ran their IT company. We bought the domain name www.pretcastle.com. In November 2011, Pret Castle was born.

We decided to retail August, AIGHT and other future brands that we wanted to start under the brand name Pret Castle.

While Sid worked on the website, I moved to New Zealand. Sapan and I had gotten married in February 2011. He worked with an IT company in New Zealand. When I got a job in New Zealand, I joined him. There was an option of Sapan coming back to India but Sid and I wanted to make a little more money to set up the physical flagship store of Pret Castle. So Sapan stayed back in New Zealand and I joined him.

The plan was in line with the pact, which Sid and I had entered in in 2008. Sid was continuing to grow the business while I had to earn.

Dad offered help but we wanted to do it ourselves. He was very happy and extremely proud of us. We had come a long way and were close to our goal. But just at this time, the chain of events which took place in our life changed the entire course of our life.

Just after two months of me leaving for New Zealand, we lost our father in April 2012. With this we also lost the direction of our life. This was accompanied by unforeseen challenges. Under the circumstances, after setting the basic things right, we all went to New Zealand for a while.

One day Sid decided to visit the Massey University. The head of the department was impressed with Sid's work. Sid expressed his desire to conduct a workshop for the students. It was vacation time but she still agreed to put up a notice though she feared there would be very few in attendance.

However, the response was overwhelming. Most surprising was that there were students here who were already following Sid's work. They had even written to him showing their interest to do an internship under him.

If you are passionate about work, you will find an opportunity to work wherever you are.

Sid's workshop was attended by both students and the faculty. They wanted Sid to conduct more workshops. Sid could foresee joining the university for research and for a special reason too. Dad wanted to work with Massey but for his love for India, he had decided not to settle outside the country.

We were kind of settled in NZ, and felt life would go on the same way until one evening when Mom said, "Your father was the happiest to see you living your dreams. And if you want him to be happy always, let's get back to work."

Mom was right. Dad would have been hurt to see us like this.

He had always said no matter what, don't stop working on your dreams. I recalled how much he wanted us to set up our business house. How he had been prepared for it by collecting extra chairs and coolers. He always spoke of growth, expansion, looking forward and we were doing just the opposite.

He had always said that seeing difficulties ahead don't change the goal. Everything takes time. Remain focussed. Don't have a fleeting mind. Life isn't long to accommodate the fancies of a fleeting mind.

And what were we doing? Seeing the changing circumstances, we were redefining the dreams. Redefining them when we were almost there. And redefining that very special dream whose journey Dad had been a part of.

We returned to India.

> **The pain of yesterday is the strength of today.**
>
> **—Paulo Coelho**

10

The Deal

Bata came for help

As soon as we got back, we decided to open a store for our brands. We met the property dealers in our area. They suggested properties in many commercial centres in Greater Noida. Not that we didn't want to explore Noida, Delhi and Gurgaon, but Greater Noida was the best option as we lived there.

We searched for days but we couldn't find any suitable place. But this didn't dent our progress. We were not alone in our search. We had the property dealers who were much more interested in getting us a place to the extent that they flooded our mail box and our phones. But it worked as a blessing in disguise. They were the ones who literally chased us to take a decision.

> **Introduce elements in your life that are capable to chase you and take you closer to your dreams.**

"As per your requirements, I think you should consider the property in a mall," said a property dealer during a discussion.

We had told him that we wanted to open our flagship store which required visibility and footfall from day one.

He sat on an off-white sofa in his plush office. I was not too impressed when we met him but he turned out to be the first sane property dealer we met who was interested in understanding our requirement rather than just pushing us to buy what he had.

"This budget can get you two or three properties in commercial centres which will earn rent from the first day. But in a mall you will be able to buy only one property and it comes with a warning .

The warning was about the monthly expense that the shop owners of the malls pay for the maintenance of the mall. It is like a monthly rent paid to the mall.

He suggested we go to the two malls in Greater Noida and he would help us in the deal.

"Gurgaon malls will have a good footfall but Gurgaon is far from where we live," I said. We were revisiting our location options. It was time to knock off the options to clearly arrive at a final decision.

"Right! So it can either be in Delhi, or Noida and Greater Noida," Sid said.

"Delhi and Noida – the prices are exuberantly high. Would it be worth it to stretch our budget?" I asked Sid. We wanted to buy without incurring liabilities.

"I think Greater Noida would suit us. The disadvantage of not having a high footfall would definitely give us the benefit of low property prices," Sid suggested.

The footfall in both the Greater Noida malls was not good enough but Myers Plaza Mall was better in approachability so we began our search from it.

The property dealers quoted their favourite rates. We dropped the idea until a week later when we worked out an average of the prices quoted by them and arrived at an approximate rate of per square metre.

We then evaluated the performance of the mall as we didn't want to block our money in a wrong investment. We spent hours in the mall to do our research on the profile of customers, and the footfalls on weekdays and weekends.

Five years ago people only came in to get respite from the heat wave. But the mall had picked up and had finally started enjoying the benefit of its location.

The place had three kinds of inhabitants: Students from all parts of the country; software professionals – the city offers vast expanse of land to the software companies to set up their campus; and farmers. They once owned acres of land and now own truckloads of money that they had earned by selling their land to the builders.

Next we spoke to the shop owners. There were two types of shops – the brand stores and individual shops. While the employees at the brand stores extended all possible help, the individual shopkeepers would just not talk to us. They saw competition in us. They thought a new business would eat up their footfall. But does more business around not translate into more footfall in the mall? And does that not eventually increase individual shop footfall?

Those who hesitantly agreed to talk dissuaded us from investing in the mall. Their two concerns were weak footfall and the students who comprised a large part of the footfall but didn't convert into customers. The mall is surrounded by more than fifty colleges.

A few suggested that we consider another big mall coming up. We already knew about it and we had dismissed the idea. The new mall was going to take some time to be operational. Also, they were only leasing out the property and not selling it.

Finally, we had enough reasons to make the decision.

The **first reason** – Lakshmi Mittal became what he is because he took over sick mills and turned them around. He bought sick units. They were priced low and no one was interested in them. He worked on them and made them functional. We could draw a parallel. Agreed the mall wasn't doing very well and the footfall was low, but we were getting the benefit in terms of cost.

The **second reason** – The major footfall was of the students. We saw an opportunity in this. Here we applied the Bata story. Two salesmen were sent to Africa to set up the first Bata store. One returned saying that there was no scope to sell shoes in Africa as people didn't even know what a shoe was, but the second salesman said that the whole market is open for us. We can sell shoes to everyone. So it is just the perspective! We were confident to make a place for us.

The **third reason** – It was a growing city and people were moving in. We were going to be one of a kind of store here and in years to come we would be able to reap the first mover advantage.

Listen to all but finally decide what you want to do.

"There isn't anything left in the centre dome," I said after taking a look at the shops in the centre dome. I was disappointed. We wanted a high visibility shop so the centre dome was our first preference.

"That's the only one left," Sid looked closely and could find the only one available shop behind an ice cream outlet, "But how do we go about it?"

"You remember when we were talking to the shopkeepers? The jewellery shop guy said he knows a lot of shop owners."

The moment we expressed our interest in the shop, we saw a change in attitude of the usually friendly jewellery shopkeeper. He donned the cap of a property dealer and said he was the property dealer for that shop. To gain our confidence he also shared the details of the shop owner.

"So you mean to say you are the property dealer?" I had my doubts.

"Yes," he said rolling his eyes at the boys who were assisting him in his shop so that they did not give away any surprised expressions.

The two boys who were arranging bangles and earrings in the glass closets could not control themselves. They hung their heads down and tried to suppress their laughter.

"What all you will do as a property dealer?" I asked. I knew he was lying.

"I will coordinate the meetings between you and the owner of the shop."

"And...?"

"That's it...." he shrugged his shoulders.

"Who will help in negotiations and preparing the deal papers and so many other things, which we know nothing of as this is our first time with a commercial property."

He dismissed my question with a laugh and said, "It is very simple. You are thinking too much. There is no need for any negotiation. The price they are quoting is already very low. And regarding the papers, don't bother, you hire a lawyer and he will prepare it all for you. You have to just go to the court and it will be done."

"If I have to do all this by myself, why do I pay you?" I said.

"To arrange the meetings," he retorted.

"If your role as a property dealer is just to coordinate the meetings, then I can talk to the owner myself," I said and we left.

From fashion world to the world of goons

The same day in the evening, we met Sandeep bhaiya. He had studied M.Tech at campus when we were in school. He was now a director in an engineering college.

"It is in Myers Plaza," Sid told him when he asked if we could find anything.

"If it is in Myers Plaza, let me talk to Anuj."

Anuj bhaiya was Sandeep bhaiya's colleague in college.

He continued to talk to us as he dialled the number, "Anuj can help. He is from Meerut and he once told me he knows a neta ji who has a property in Myers Plaza. That neta ji can become our reference when we talk to those whose properties interest us."

Anuj bhaiya confirmed that he knew a local neta ji from Bulandshahr very closely and he could tell him about us.

"Anuj has spoken to the neta ji. You can talk to neta ji directly. Give Anuj's reference. Take down the number," Sandeep bhaiya called us the next morning.

He continued, "Anuj was also saying neta ji wants to sell his own shop. The shop is in the central dome and the number is 79. Check if you like it."

It was the same shop that we had liked. No confusion there because it was the only one left unsold in the centre dome.

"I suggest that we do not talk to neta ji on the phone. Let Anuj bhaiya tell him we are interested in his shop and arrange a face to face meeting for us. It will help us know what kind of person he is."

After our experience with property dealers, we were cautious about every step.

Neta ji was busy so Anuj bhaiya could not arrange our meeting. But finally, one afternoon, Anuj bhaiya called up to inform us that neta ji was passing by with his troop and had come to his office. He asked us to come too. We were out for some work and by the time we reached, neta ji had left.

"Neta ji was in hurry," Anuj bhaiya said. "But he will meet you soon and he has said to consider the shop to be yours. He will not give it to anyone."

Anuj bhaiya also told us the price which neta ji had quoted. It was higher than the market rate but we were hopeful we could arrive at something in between after our meeting.

Sandeep and Anuj bhaiya joined us to go to the mall to have a look at the store once again. It felt like it belonged to us. After all, neta ji had said so and Anuj bhaiya ensured he was on good terms with him.

"Anuj bhiaya, please arrange a meeting at the earliest," I said as we were about to see off Sandeep and Anuj bhaiya.

Just then Anuj bhaiya remembered something and handed me a chit and said, "Okay, I will. And I forgot about it, Neta ji has given this for you."

I looked at it. It was a crumbled piece of paper. Uneven edges, it was clear that someone had carelessly torn it from the corner of a newspaper in hurry.

"1234567 a.c no. 3 lakhs + 20 thousand Vijay."

I read out the chit with great difficulty as the handwriting was illegible and looked at Anuj bhaiya.

He smiled, "This is how it works."

"But first tell me, what is this? And why are you giving it to me?" I folded the paper and returned to him.

Sid and I exchanged a look. We kind of understood what it was. However, we didn't want to assume and we wanted to hear the demand clearly.

"If you are interested in the property, just transfer this amount in the bank and give twenty thousand to this boy in the mall. We will figure out who he is. That should not be a problem."

"And what about the meeting?"

"That will happen whenever neta ji finds time."

"But shouldn't there be a meeting first? Ideally, the amount he is asking us to transfer should also be recorded, like what amount of money, given to whom and for what purpose. Anything on a stamp paper," I said.

Sid and I both felt something was wrong.

"And Vijay? Who is Vijay?" Sid asked.

"Vijay is the property dealer,"Anuj bhaiya said. "He runs an artificial jewellery shop. He has told neta ji that you are his clients. So neta ji has promised him that he will be the property dealer for this deal."

"What does this neta ji think of himself?" I grumbled. "The guy doesn't know anything about property and we are not his clients."

Anuj bhaiya saw me angry for the first time but I could not control my anger .

"If neta ji wants to do charity, let him do it on his own, we are not doing," I went on non-stop "And if he says we are like his relatives and hence no need of meeting before the deal, then why has he over-priced the property?"

Furious, we left the place. The next day was the deadline for the amount to be transferred.

"I really like the space," Sid said to me.

"So shall we transfer the amount?" I asked Sid.

"No, that is not correct. We need to negotiate the price first. For now neta ji is saying we will see later but what if he denies any negotiation?"

Anuj bhaiya conveyed our apprehensions to neta ji. Neta ji got furious and said that in big deals, four or five lakhs were nothing. If we were so hesitant, then we must not buy. However, on persuasion, he agreed to document the initial transfer. Though he conveyed that price wouldn't change, he would wait only for one week to let us decide and he demanded eighty percent payment in black."

"Isn't there something fishy?" I said imagining Bollywood scenes where deals in black money were done using black briefcases.

"Yes, it is fishy! And what if they send men to rob us when we are on our way to give them the money? Black money means cash. No draft or cheque," Sid was thinking exactly what I was. A little more carried away by Bollywood, he said. "Also, so much money will take many bags."

We felt threatened. Another worry was that we had all white money. Tax paid on every single penny.

"I think we should drop the idea of buying property in this part of the country," I said. It was the second time we were thinking about dropping the idea.

But fear could not hold us back, not even for a week and Sid said to me, "To grow, calculated risk is a must. Looks like this is the required calculated risk we must take."

We decided to increase our budget and assumed neta ji would agree to let go of his demand of black money.

"Can you please inform Anuj bhaiya that we are ready to go ahead with the deal," Sid said to Sandeep bhaiya.

"The shop has been sold," Sandeep bhaiya called us back within few minutes.

Out of one trap to enter another

"There must be something good hidden in this. You will know later," Mom said.

It is a standard statement from elders in such situations. It is wisdom. I used to be angry when I heard it as a child, but had recently started using the phrase myself. I had learnt to connect the dots.

We were standing in front of the shop that once felt so much like ours. But as they say, there's many a slip between the cup and lip.

"Hmm... yes. And anyway, I didn't like it much. I told you the front face of this property is small. Didn't I?" I said

"Hmm... and it was over-priced too," Sid said.

Sid and I individually felt guilty about not taking a timely decision, but we didn't bring it up so that the other didn't feel bad. We actually hadn't taken long in taking the decision; we were just being cautious.

The decisions we took in the past may feel wrong today. It happens because we evaluate the decisions of the past in the context of the present situations. So we must not evaluate past decisions, and if we do so, we must evaluate them in the context of the past only. And do not forget that the decision was the best under the circumstances you faced in the past.

We walked away, but Sid was still looking back. To distract him, I said, "If the location is good, does that mean they can charge anything they feel like?"

"But you see, it has two doors," Sid said.

"Yes, I know. But do you think the mall allows you to use both the doors?" I retorted. I didn't want him to be sad for something that could not be ours.

Finally, he smiled and said, "Okay, enough! Accept it that it was nice and we didn't get it. But that doesn't mean there is no other place for us. There is definitely something better stored for us."

"True, so let's forget this and why not watch a movie," I proposed.

We saw *Matroo ki Bijli ka Mandola.* But neither the pink cow nor the head over heels dance of the African troop could take the shop out of our minds.

Coming back home after the late night show, Sid as usual settled on the study table with his laptop.

I woke up at four in the morning to see Sid still working. I went back to sleep. I then woke up at eight to find Sid sleeping between me and mom.

As I got ready to leave for office, Sandeep bhaiya came home. He had spoken with his engineering college friend Yogi to help us. Yogi was a political leader and a property dealer as well. A very obvious career for high profile political leaders in India.

"Call him," Sandeep bhaiya said handing over a visiting card to Sid.

Yogi recognized Sid. "Hi Sid, yes Sandeep told me. We are very good friends. Treat me like your elder brother."

"I am looking for property..." Sid could not even complete his specifications that Yogi interrupted. "Okay, if you have made up your mind to buy... (thinking)... do one thing, come this afternoon and deposit ten lakhs in my office," he said.

"Ok, thank you. Where is your office?" Sid asked.

"Call my secretary and she will give you the address. And now you don't worry. Once you have deposited the amount, I will definitely get you a place of your choice," he said.

"I will take a couple of days to get back to you."

"No problem and don't worry, if you are hesitant to deposit the complete amount, you can put in half today and the rest in two or three days. After all, you are related to me now," Yogi said.

After keeping the phone down, Sid laughed aloud.

"What happened, why are you laughing?" Sandeep bhaiya asked.

Sid blurted out what Yogi said and laughed along, "What the hell? Everyone is asking for money. I mean isn't there any procedure or is ten lakhs just an amount? First that neta ji demanded three lakhs and now this other neta ji wants ten lakhs."

Sandeep bhaiya called Yogi. "Hi Yogi, Sid told me that you have asked for ten lakhs deposit."

"Yes, I did. Have included your cut too," Yogi said casually. Sandeep bhaiya had put his phone on loud speaker.

"My cut?" Sandeep bhaiya asked surprised.

"Yes, you have got me this party, so one lakh is for you."

"No, no, you are getting it all wrong. Sid is like my family. Please think you are helping me."

"Oh okay, but if cow befriends the fodder, what will it eat? Anyway, if you say so, I will not insist on taking the money in advance," he said.

So that Yogi does not lose interest in helping us, Sandeep bhaiya told him that we would pay for his help as a property dealer, but he must first get us a suitable deal.

Yogi agreed and asked us if we liked shop number 76. It wasn't in the centre dome but it was close to the one we had missed. With no other option, we agreed to consider it.

The next day, Yogi confirmed our meeting with the owner of the shop in his office.

"Is there any way I can look at least five years older than my age?" Sid asked me as he combed his hair. We were getting ready for the meeting.

He looked dapper in his black coat that he wore over a crisp white shirt. His deep grey coloured slender fit trousers and black shoes added to the professional look. I liked to see him well dressed. He had started to look like dad who had always been known for his style and charisma.

I smiled, "People want to look young and you want to look old?"

"When people realise our ages, they want to take us for a ride," he said. "So I have grown my hair. You also do something. You look even younger to me," he jibed.

Yogi's office was in a residential colony of Greater Noida. It was a three storey building with a sprawling garden where the helpers were arranging white garden chairs for a garden meeting under the afternoon sun on the winter day.

One helper escorted us to Yogi's office. The door was closed. He knocked for us.

It was a compact room with modern interiors. In the centre, it had a bigger version of a dining table. Yogi sat on the longer side of it. To his left a man was seated with whom he was already having a meeting. After a brief exchange of greetings, we sat on the black chairs in front of Yogi.

For a neta, Yogi was very polished. He wore a fine round-collared black blazer with a broad watch and a good perfume. His furniture was classy. He was stylish in his taste that reflected in the big lamp that focussed from top as a spot light on his table. Taller than him, this huge stainless steel lamp with soft white light was magnificent. Sid later told me that he had seen these kinds of lamps only in Hollywood movies.

"I didn't expect you guys to be so young. I must say you are early starters. Your age is to party and have fun. I am impressed seeing you here for these kinds of deals," he said.

"Same goes for you. We also didn't expect a political leader to be young and stylish as you," Sid said.

Truth unveiled

After the mutual admiration and talking a few common things about Sandeep bhaiya, we got to the point.

"So let us now talk about your work," Yogi said and turned towards the guy to his left.

All this while, this guy had been listening to our conversation. He sometimes smiled and sometimes fiddled with his mobile.

It was clear that he was bored. Guess Yogi also realised this and finally introduced him. "He is Mr Shekhar. He will talk with you about shop number 76. He is a good friend. So if the deal is done at home, it is good."

Mr. Shekhar looked very kind and was well dressed.

"So, you like the shop?" Shekhar said.

"Yes... out of all the available options now," Sid said.

"Available options 'now'?" Shekhar smiled questioningly.

"Yes, actually our first choice was shop number 79."

"Oh, that centre dome shop? It was sold a few days back. That shop was on sale for years now."

It felt even sadder knowing it was on sale for years and we still missed it.

"So I must tell you Sid that it is good that you didn't take it."

"Why, what's wrong with it?" Sid asked him but looked at me. All these days, we had wanted someone to give us one good reason to help us stop lamenting on our loss.

Shekhar smiled looking at Yogi. I could not wait for him to answer, "Such good location! Why was it not getting sold?" I impatiently prompted him to share the secret he was holding.

"There are two big reasons for which it took so long to be sold. Firstly, it is disputed."

"Disputed? No one told us about that. We were very close to taking it," Sid said.

"No one tells you these things, sir. You have to find out yourself."

"What was the dispute?" I asked.

"I heard this shop does not exist in the original floor plan of the mall. The approval was taken on a map, which does not include this shop. The builders usually keep space to create such shops later. And it becomes disputed because you cannot register the place as it does not exist."

"Ah... okay . And what is the second reason?" I asked.

"The Bulandshahr neta ji you mentioned, he is just one party to the deal. The property belongs to four people together. They collected money and bought it at a throwaway price ten years back."

"So what is the problem? Property can be owned by more than one person," Sid said.

"True, but at no point of time did all the four agree to sell it. And in past when three agreed to sell, the fourth person would go and threaten the buyer. So why risk your life?"

"Oh! So who bought it now?" Sid asked.

"Goons work with goons. It has been bought by another party of goons," he smiled.

Shekhar won our confidence and freed us from the guilt of not taking a timely decision. He appeared to be genuine and also someone we could trust.

"Whatever happens, happens for the good. We should never hurry in property matters," Yogi said.

He contradicted himself. Just a day before he was hurrying us to deposit ten lakhs in his office.

"Yes agreed," Sid said repositioning himself upright on the chair. He asked Shekhar, "Can you also tell us when you bought it? What is the area and how will you accept the payment?"

By now we had learnt the set of relevant questions to be asked during such deals.

"It is a furnished shop located on the ground floor. It is 519 sq feet. For the payment, it can be thirty percent black and rest you can do in white."

He also told us the price of the property, but he had missed telling us when he had bought it. Before I could ask him again, the price he quoted swept away the discussion.

"Aren't you quoting a tad too high a price?" Sid quipped. "It is unreasonable. The centre dome where they charge for the location is not as much."

"The location is not that bad. It is on the ground floor," Shekhar said.

"There are only two things with the location – it is either good or bad. And I agree it is on ground floor but it will be visible only to those who will take the lifts. And these three lifts run full all the time. People have started using the escalators now."

Shekhar was speechless. With hope in his eyes, Yogi looked at him to give another point in favour of the shop. We also waited. Silence prevailed for a few seconds until Shekhar spoke up.

"Okay, so you see that it is A-1 class furnished and the interiors are all done," he fumbled to complete the sentence. "It has first class lighting, big mirrors and wall fixtures too."

"What are you saying, Shekhar?" Sid smiled sarcastically, "The interiors would not cost more than three lakhs."

Sid's confidence shook Shekhar and Yogi. They didn't expect Sid to estimate the value of the interiors so accurately.

Sid was irritated when Dad had left him to manage the planning and finance for the makeover of our house but now he started realising the importance of the experience.

The discussion almost came to a halt.

To ease the tension, I interrupted with the question that Shekhar had not replied to. "When did you buy this, Shekhar? Are you the first owner?"

In a normal situation, seeing him skip the question earlier, I would have thought that he was trying to hide something. But now that he had our trust, my intention of asking this question again was just to get the conversation going.

Shekhar looked at Yogi and there was silence again.

"Actually, he is not the owner," Yogi said.

"But you said we will meet with the owner of the shop and we have been talking so far thinking that he is the owner."

"I am the property dealer. This property belongs to Mr Gupta. He could not come because he is very old and not keeping well," Shekhar said.

The trust that was built so far with the two men shattered. Suddenly, they felt like strangers.

"Hmm...so do you know when was this bought? How many owners have been changed?" Sid turned to the interrogative mode. We were now a little defensive.

"Mr Gupta is the first owner and he got this in the initial allotment ten years back," Shekhar replied.

"First owner... bought this shop ten years back... it means Mr Gupta is earning a good return as per the present market rate. But tell me, then why are you quoting an unrealistically high price?"

"Sir, you try to understand, this is the market rate," Shekhar said.

"No, it isn't. Tell me what is the final price?" Sid asked Shekhar.

"Sir, Mr Gupta is in dire need of money. After getting the money from this deal, he has to put it into another construction project that is going on. And he said there is no scope for negotiation," Shekhar said sounding innocent and genuine.

"Then there's no point of discussing anything further. But let me know if you can give me a reasonable price," Sid said.

"No, I can't," Shekhar said.

"Then... let it be. I think we are done," Sid said and we were ready to leave. But seeing both the parties give up, Yogi quickly intervened.

"Some flexibility is required from both sides. I think we can arrive at a mid point," saying this he gestured to Shekhar to go with him outside.

"Sid, if you don't mind, can Shekhar and I step out for a minute? You guys also discuss what maximum amount you can stretch to."

"What do you think? Will Shekhar reduce the price?" Sid asked me.

"Yes, of course he will. They are talking outside to reduce their cuts. If they reduce their cuts, the price will drastically come down," I said.

"Their cuts?" Sid asked.

"Yes, Yogi is getting a huge cut to finalise this deal. Shekhar is also a property dealer so he is also getting his cut. Basically two property dealers in one deal is resulting in the over price of this shop. And both the dealers are high flying too, so obviously it translates into heavy cuts."

They returned after some time. Yogi spoke to us as Shekhar looked down, "Just because we are related, Shekhar has agreed to reduce the price, but it cannot be as much as you want."

"No, this is not done," I said.

"Okay. For your happiness, let's reduce it further..." Yogi said.

We still didn't agree. A few more rounds of offers and rejections happened until finally Yogi gave the final price after punching hard on his calculator.

"Now this is the maximum I can do."

He turned the calculator towards us to show the amount and said, "So deal done? Happy now?"

Shekhar who was also looking at the calculator tried to stop Yogi from making the offer. Not sure though whether he was pretending or did he really want to stop him, we didn't bother as we were happy with the offer.

Yogi looked at us waiting for a 'yes'.

In the meantime Shekhar interrupted, "The price has taken a dive so if Gupta ji agrees, I will tell you the payment schedule and if he does not, I will return your booking amount."

"He will agree. It is a good deal for him. After all, who makes the complete payment within fifteen days. You think of the interest on this amount also," Yogi said to Shekhar.

Yogi then looked at Sid and said, "Sir, now smile, deal is done."

Yogi appeared excited at the final price too. I wondered about the margin they had reserved for themselves.

"Sounds good!" I said, "So we pay the booking amount?"

Yogi quickly whispered something to Shekhar and calculated the booking amount and told us.

"This amount won't be possible to arrange today in cash," I said.

"Why are you embarrassing me? We can seal the deal with one rupee also, or if you want I can pay on your behalf," Yogi said.

The sudden hurry and kindness was a little worrying but I ignored it to keep things going and proposed a minimal amount of a few thousands to be considered as the booking amount.

Yogi's office boy followed us in his car to the ATM in the mall. We gave him the booking amount and then went to see shop number 76.

I peeped through the glass door, "Nice shop, looks bigger too... may be because there are mirrors on the walls and the interiors have been done. Now this sure looks like ours!"

"A few days back 79 felt like ours and today 76. Let's wait to see what Mr Gupta has to say." Sid laughed.

Was the risk worth it?

"How are you feeling?" Sid asked me.

I wasn't well and had just got back from office. I drove from Greater Noida to Noida every day. I had taken a transfer from my New Zealand office to the India office.

"I am fine. What is it?" I knew he wanted to talk to me.

"Can you come with me to the mall around six just for fifteen minutes?"

"In the evening? Why? It is already dark and there's dense fog outside," I said.

"There is a boy. He wants to show us a property."

"What are you saying? We have paid the booking amount for what we have finalised to buy, then what is the point of seeing a new one," I was surprised.

"Yes, I know but he is really a nice boy. He has been working for me for the past one week."

"But you can tell him that the deal has been finalised," I said.

"I want to respect the fact that he worked on my request with urgency. He can help us for future deals too."

"I am not coming. And you also don't need to go. He can tell us the number of the shop and we will have a look later."

"I am going and you are also coming with me," Sid said stubbornly.

"We can go some other day," I proposed.

"We are going today and don't forget that there have been instances when people have denied meeting us. And it is you who has always taught me that we should never turn down anyone who wants to meet us. I have learnt it from you and you are not following it."

Never turn down anyone who is trying to grow by hard work. What may not matter to you may be a big stepping stone towards success for another.

We were on our way to the mall fighting the dense fog when I asked Sid. "When we had already finalised a shop, why did you start talking with him?"

"You remember a week back when we came to know that shop 79

was sold, and we had gone to watch a movie?" Sid asked me.

"Yes, *Matroo ki Bijli ka Mandola*," I said. It instantly reminded me of the pink cow and Anushka Sharma dancing away in her black knit top and aqua blue skirts on the song *O boy, o boy Charlie.*

"I could not sleep the whole night after we returned," Sid said.

"I thought you were working on your book," I said. Sid was in process of publishing his book on sustainable design ideas.

"No. That day I promised myself that I have to find one property for myself within a week. So I registered myself on www.magicbricks.com and it is there that I found this young boy."

"Oh okay, so this happened even before Sandeep bhaiya introduced us to Yogi," I said after connecting the dots of the incidents that had taken place over the past week.

"Yes," Sid said.

"Call him and tell that we are standing in the centre dome," I said.

After speaking to him, Sid told me. "He will be here in five minutes. Keep an eye. He said he is wearing a black jacket and jeans."

I looked around. Most of the boys I could see were wearing black jackets and jeans – common clothes in winters.

Seeing this, I asked Sid, "Did you tell him what you are wearing?"

"Yes, I have told him."

"Hello Sir. Hello Ma'am," a young boy said from behind us. We turned to look at him. He seemed too gentle and soft-spoken to be identified as a property dealer.

We followed him to the left dome. The mall had three domes.

"Where is he taking us?" I asked Sid showing disappointment. We never considered looking towards the side where he was taking us.

"Let him show us at least," Sid murmured.

Prateek took us to the first floor and stopped at the end of the Reliance Footprints store.

"Sir, see this," Prateek pointed to a huge Dell store. With glass walls on four sides, this big store sat alone on the railing like a solitaire on hooks.

"Wow!" I could not hold back appreciating it. Sid was also happy.

"Sir, so you like it?" Prateek asked excitedly.

"Yes, but we will not be able to take it Prateek," Sid said.

"Why, sir?" He asked.

"I have finalised a deal just two days back," Sid replied.

Also, the Dell shop was double the size what we had finalised and it was definitely going to cost a lot. So while we liked it, we were not sad to come to know of it this late.

"Sir, you must have only given the booking amount. If you can forgo it, I can get you a good deal on this one," he insisted. "Sir, for one year I have been working hard but not able to crack any deal. Sir, please take it."

"Hmm... what is the price?" Sid asked.

I looked at Sid. He really wanted to help Prateek but it was not a mutual fund or insurance policy he was persuading us to buy.

Prateek gave us the price. It was the first time anyone had quoted this big a price to us. It felt good. I wondered if we were really capable to work out this big a deal on our own.

"Prateek, it is completely out of our budget. I am not saying that it is overpriced. It is worth the price. I would love to take it. But I can't," Sid said.

"Sir, if it was not this high price, then if I ask you to cancel the booking that you have done and book this one, will you do that?"

"Yes, I could have done that," Sid said to him but looked at me for consensus.

"Ok sir, tell me what range are you looking at?"

"Exactly the same price that I am paying for the one I have paid the booking amount for. But it will be complete injustice. How can I desire for two for the price of one?" Sid said.

Sid quoted a price by adding a decent amount to it.

"Sir, it is very less..."Prateek replied looking embarrassed.

"I understand Prateek," Sid always found difficult turning down someone so he was trying to do it as gently as possible. "But I promise, next time we are working with you," Sid assured Prateek.

We came back to the car.

"What are you thinking?" I asked Sid.

"I am thinking exactly what you are thinking..."

"The shop is amazing, right?" I said.

"Lol, yeah! I knew you would be thinking about it too. So what do you say?" Sid said.

"Call him and say that we are ready," I said.

"But we will have to change our other plans to accommodate the price. And what about the money we have already paid to Shekhar? He won't return it and it is no less an amount," Sid said.

"You bet the seller will not agree to our offer. And if he agrees, it would definitely be a good deal for us, though we would have to work it out. But I am sure he will not agree. So relax, let's have some fun," I said.

Meeting the sugar baron of Noida

The next morning, as I prepared to leave for work, Sid asked me. "What do I say to Prateek if he calls up to say that the seller has agreed?"

"If he calls you in the morning then it will be to say 'no' because no one would say 'yes' in haste to let go this big a place at a price we have quoted."

I reached office. I hadn't even set up my laptop, and my phone rang.

"Prateek called. The seller has agreed to our price and wants to meet us today evening," Sid told me.

I wasn't prepared for this. "Lol! I hope you didn't show any surprise to Prateek."

"No, no, I didn't," he laughed. "But tell me what do we do now? I need to confirm with Prateek if are ready for the meeting this evening."

"See, there are two options with us. First option is that we tell Prateek our plan has changed and we don't want to take it anymore. The second option is that we go for the meeting."

"Go for the meeting? What are you saying?" Sid said.

"Yes, no harm in having a meeting. And I am curious to see the owner. I mean who would decide so quickly to give away such a nice place at this price?"

We confirmed the meeting at 6:00 pm at the property dealer's office.

"I hope Yogi did not call you today to confirm the deal!" I laughingly took a dig at Sid who appeared a little worried already.

"No, no... we just have this mess to clean up for today," he said. "The seller will come from Noida. He will be disappointed if we do not buy his property. I'm feeling guilty for wasting everyone's time."

"Come on, at least we are not like those fashion week buyers who only look for the show passes. We are not looking for any favour from the seller. And who knows, we may buy it!"

"Buy it? Are you crazy?" Sid said.

We reached near Prateek's office. To find the place, we asked a man who was selling eggs. His face was hidden behind the steam from the aluminium vessel filled with eggs. He was chopping onions and green chillies to garnish the golden yellow eggs placed half cut in the plates.

With a knife in one hand, he pointed us to a shopping complex.

Such is the warmth and hospitality in India that people help each other in finding places. Even if they are on a moving vehicle, they can stop and help you find your directions.

"I don't think it would be that one because that complex belongs to the biggest property dealer of the area. They do not deal in small property matters," Sid said.

I called up Prateek. "We are close to your office. Can you come out so that we can see you?"

Prateek was standing exactly where we didn't expect him to be. It was the same complex Sid was talking about. Prateek opened the door of a cabin for us to sit in and went to get his boss. The sellers had not arrived yet.

"What are we doing?" Sid smiled and asked me.

"Relax. Things will unfold soon," I said returning the smile though I was nervous too.

The room was done up in black and red. In fact black mostly because the only two red things were a big red chair and the red coloured Feng Shui bells on the black glass table top.

"Sir, meet my boss," Prateek said as he entered the room in hurry and held the door to usher his boss.

He was a young boy, and must be our age. To look older than his age, he had grown a French beard. It clearly didn't suit his face. I controlled my urge to laugh, and reserved my comments for Sid and my discussion later.

He sat on the big red chair and Prateek stood next to him as we waited for the sellers to arrive.

"Get some coffee, Prateek," the boss ordered Prateek and looked at us smiling.

"No, thank you please. We don't drink coffee or tea," I said.

In the meantime, another person entered the room. Seeing him, Prateek's boss literally sprung up from the red chair and stood next to Prateek. And now this person sat on the red chair. He was definitely elder to Prateek and the French cut.

"Sir, he is our CEO," Prateek introduced him.

After a few minutes, two more men entered the room.

"Hello, sir," Prateek greeted and ushered them to the two chairs next to us.

Who were they? Were they the sellers or another party to buy the same property? As I wondered, there entered another man. Seeing him, the CEO left this red chair and stood next to Prateek and the French cut. Now this fourth man sat on the most coveted red chair.

"He is our Managing Director," Prateek said, looking at us.

The Managing Director was the eldest of them all, but we had no expression left to return. In past ten minutes, we had met a boss, a CEO and a Managing Director and all of them were equally fond of the big red chair. I hoped the game of musical chairs would get over soon.

Finally the Managing Director who was currently seated on the most coveted red chair quickly touched a few things on his table. It was probably a ritual he followed and said, "Mittal ji, this is Sid ji. Sid ji is interested in your property. Sid ji this is..."

Mittal ji interrupted the Managing Director and did the honours for himself on his own.

"I am Mittal. I am the sugar baron of Noida. You take my name and everyone knows me," he said pulling both sides of his coat to button it up. Shoulders raised and tight, his body language was boastful.

"And he is my son."

Mittal ji had scanty hair and a generous beer belly. He was carefree whereas his son sat beside him, attentive like an obedient boy with a bundle of files that he had placed in front of him on the table.

He continued. "Prateek told us you like our shop."

"Yes, it is a nice shop," Sid said.

"Yes, it is and it was used as a Dell showroom until last month," Mittal ji said.

"Okay," Sid said. "Can you please tell a few more details about the shop? Also, is there any loan on the property?"

"Yes, there is a loan on the property but we will clear it and give it to you," Mittal ji said.

He also shared the details we wanted to know. It was our turn to speak. Sid looked at me. I gave a silent nod with my head. It was satisfying to know that this time we were dealing with the owner and not another property dealer.

Sid asked Prateek, "Prateek, I hope you have conveyed our agreed price to everyone?"

Mr Mittal turned his head towards Prateek in surprise and said "What price?" and then turning towards us he quoted the price that he was expecting.

Sid asked Prateek again, "Prateek, did you not convey the price we agreed upon?"

We were more surprised than Mr Mittal because when Prateek called us in the morning, he had said that Mr Mittal had agreed to our price.

Prateek stood there with a baffled expression on his face. What I could read was that Mr Mittal was acting smart. He must have agreed to our price when Prateek asked him, but now he was quoting his favourite price. This surprised Prateek too, but he could not contradict Mr Mittal in front of his three bosses who were constantly staring Prateek down.

Still, he tried looking at Mr Mittal, "Sir, but I told you..."

Turning a deaf ear towards Prateek, Mr Mittal said looking at us, "We can talk now..."

I was already furious. So was Sid. We kind of withdrew from the discussion.

"What is your price?" Mr Mittal asked making an attempt to strike a conversation again.

"It is nowhere close to what you are expecting, so there is no point in discussing it also. There seems to be some misunderstanding," I said cutting the conversation short because I had sensed what

Mr Mittal was trying to do.

"Hmm... still there would be a price," Mr Mittal asked again.

To see Mr Mittal's reaction, I quoted our price.

Mr Mittal instantly said, "No, no...this is not possible."

He wasn't surprised to hear our price even when it was considerably less to what he was quoting. It proved that he was aware of our price before the meeting.

He continued, "You see the property can't be sold for this amount."

"Yes, Mr Mittal that is what I am saying. Your property is very nice. And the price I mentioned is very less for it. I again say that there is some misunderstanding. I think we must leave," I said.

Seeing the conversation coming to an end, the Managing Director interfered and said to Sid, "Sir, you increase a little and Mittal ji will decrease a little and we will arrive at a good deal."

"Agreed, but the price we have quoted is the maximum. After that, we don't have money for this investment," I said.

Mr Mittal also responded in a flow, "We too have nothing to reduce. You must see the shop and then talk. Few days back also I got a buyer for the price close to what I have quoted. I have him waiting till date."

"That's what we are telling you, Mittal ji. You deserve a very good price for your very special shop. And we are here through some misunderstanding. I think we shall leave. Please excuse us," I said and picked up my wallet and phone from the table to leave. Sid and Mummy also rose up to leave.

"Wait wait wait... Mittal ji and Tarun ji, can you please come out with me for two minutes?" said the Managing Director as he got up from his chair in a hurry and signalled Sid to excuse them.

They returned in a few minutes. Mr Mittal was mellow this time.

"Sir, now can you guys please come out for a moment?" the Managing Director said looking at us.

He told us that Mr Mittal had agreed to our price. Now, for the sake of respect, he wanted us to also to increase the budget a little and agree to the deal. He said the deal was too good to be true.

"We don't have the money," I said. "The price we have quoted is the maximum we have for it. Please understand, it is not the only agenda in life. There are many other things to be done."

"I understand, but please take this one. If you want I will give the money," he said. Imagine a situation where the property dealer was ready to pay on your behalf. We laughed after he left us to take the final decision.

"Mr Mittal, all the best to you. Please find another buyer. We will not be able to buy it," Sid said to Mr Mittal after we came back into the meeting room.

"Can you make the payment in all white?" Mr Mittal said. We had almost stepped out of the cabin.

"Yes, all white and payment can be done in fifteen days," Sid said.

Mr Mittal agreed to our price. "Tell me what you want from us?" Mr Mittal said.

I could not believe my ears. All this while, we were just playing around, confident that this deal was not going to take place. We absolutely had no plans of arranging the payment in fifteen days.

Sid waited for me to respond.

"But why do you want to sell at this less a price when you already have a buyer," I questioned Mr Mittal.

Mr Mittal who was desperately expecting a 'yes' looked at me in frustration but immediately posed a smile and said, "We want to help you. It is nice to see the young generation doing business."

"Only for our benefit?" I asked in surprise.

"Yes, you are young and you are working for your own business. That is why. Had you been taking it as an investment, we would have not given to you at this price."

"You are kind..." I could not even finish thanking him when he began speaking about himself again.

"I have many properties. My work is to buy and sell. I have milked this property. I will invest somewhere else now," he went on boasting again and contradicted the impression of kindness he had created just a few minutes back.

Soon the Managing Director on the red chair also began praising him. They both got carried away and digressed to a completely different area. Mr Mittal expressed his desire to sell few more properties while the Managing Director took down notes. They were talking of deals no less than ten crores.

Observing them, Sid and I realised what kind of person Mittal ji was. We smiled at each other.

"We want to see the papers of the property. We wish to show them to our bank. The bank will assess and validate the documents," Sid said.

"You are doubting us! Banks work on our name," Mr Mittal boiled with anger.

The Managing Director supported him, "Yes, I issue cheques without signatures and banks honour them."

"Sir, you are experienced people but we are just beginners. No bank honours our cheques without signatures so please understand that we need to show the papers to the bank before we proceed," I said.

On the Managing Director's persuasion, Mr Mittal agreed that Prateek would accompany us to the bank and show the papers to the bank the next day.

"But if you do not confirm by tomorrow afternoon and I get any buyer, I will sell it," Mittal ji said, still not giving up. He was the one who was desperate to sell it off and at the same time was pressurising us. He didn't know that his empty threats were futile.

He then sarcastically murmured to the Managing Director, "I am sure the bank will take months to check everything. I will get another buyer in that time."

"No problem, you may please go ahead, sir," Sid said as we got up to leave.

"Is there any problem? I mean, why is he so desperate to sell it at this price?" Reaching home, I asked Sid.

"Maybe he needs the money," Sid said.

"I don't think so. Even if we forget about the number of properties he was boasting about, didn't you see the diamonds on his rings? He was wearing an Armani suit and Gucci spectacles. He said he is the sugar baron of Noida, don't forget," I said. "But why are we discussing this?"

"Hmm... but I am thinking that if we get it at this price, nothing like it, though we will have to stretch our budget. And another thing to worry about is that we have also paid for the other deal," Sid said.

"If you are considering taking it, think only about the extra amount we need to arrange. Don't talk about the booking amount we have paid. Forgoing that money will hurt today, but in the long run, we will benefit. This one shop is double the size of the one we have paid for. Likewise, the appreciation will be double too," I said.

With our Excel sheets ready, we settled into bed after a long and chilly day in January for yet another midnight discussion.

We were ready to take the big step. It was difficult to believe but cumulatively the small savings we had started in our student days helped us to a large extent. We lived a life of austerity. We travelled in the ac class only when necessary, didn't buy expensive mobile handsets and didn't splurge in coffees shops.

Saving is not a crime. It is a good practice. Start saving early on your dreams.

It was obviously daunting to invest our emotional savings of student days but we remembered what Dad always said – Only those grow who take calculated risks.

And in our calculated risk, our fall back plan was Sapan. The confidence we derived from Sapan reminded us of a story where a lady derived her confidence from an unknown man.

A lady was sitting in a park and crying. An old man walked up to her and asked her the reason of her sorrow. She said that her business was not going well. She wanted money to revive it. She had a last bit of money left in her bank which she could use to revive her business but she feared that if putting it into the business did not make it better, she would lose everything.

The man took out his cheque book and signed a cheque for double the amount the woman required and said – Don't worry, take this cheque and revive your business. The lady hesitated to take the cheque. The man said – take it for now, return the money once your work is done. You will find me here.

The lady thanked the old man and took the cheque. She deposited the cheque in the bank and took out her own money to invest it in her dying business. Finally, she could not only revive her business, her profits increased manifold too. Few months later, the lady went to return the cheque but she could not find the old man in the park. When she enquired about him and told a man that how an old man had given her money, the man recognized this old man and said – Oh are you talking about the man who distributes cheques? The lady said yes. To this the man said – today he is distributing cheques on the other side of the garden. He is a mad man. He distributes fake cheques to everyone.

Moral of the story: *Confidence is a state of mind. The woman didn't use external help. Her confidence that she had a lot to fall back on helped her achieve the impossible.*

The next morning after our discussion with the bank manager, we were ready to take the next step.

"What is the total cost involved? I mean the entire cost which includes the transfer and registration charges as well," Sid asked Prateek.

Prateek handed Sid a paper which was like a long list, "Sir, I have written each amount in detail. You'll be able to understand. If you don't, I will explain."

He was in a hurry to inform Mr Mittal and his boss, and the CEO and the Managing Director about the first big deal he had cracked.

We scanned the list and could make sense of most of it but one point raised our suspicion.

"What is this 'Miscellaneous'?" I asked Sid who was also staring at this amount.

"Let's meet Prateek in the evening," Sid suggested.

Prateek looked happy and more confident. Amidst the coffee, pastries and spinach corn sandwich, I enquired Prateek about the 'Miscellaneous'.

"What do I say about this amount, ma'am. I can just say that it is the most important amount in this entire list," Prateek said sheepishly, looking at the guy who he had brought along for this meeting.

"Why are you looking at him? Please tell me, I am not able to understand," I said.

"Ma'am, it is for the paper work... you know. I mean, this has to be given unofficially."

"Where does it go? At least give me the details?" I asked him smiling to make him comfortable.

"Ok, if you insist. But please don't let anyone know that I shared the details."

"Don't worry, I won't."

To find a way around the 'Miscellaneous' amount, Sid and I immediately took help from our contacts. It is a blessing to be the children of a professor. More so if he has been a kind one and students' favourite. We have help in every part of the world.

Similarly, we found someone who knew the government official who was the signing authority in our deal and who was also taking the largest chunk of the 'Miscellaneous' share.

Despite the reference, the official made us wait outside his office until Sid, Prateek and I literally barged into his well-guarded office. He got angry and declined to identify our reference also.

As Sid spoke to him, I called up our contact and placed the phone on his ear. He had no time to think. To sound clear and respectful, he sat up straight on the chair. He was baffled at the unexpected move, but very politely he assured our contact that our work would be done.

After keeping the phone down, he grumbled something, though it was not clear what he had said. Nor did we want to know. What we were interested in was that he pulled our file from a bundle of files and started looking into it.

The process we bypassed wasn't easy. It involved many others who had their share in the 'Miscellaneous' amount. They were not happy and it was reflected in unnecessary delays and rudeness of infuriated clerks. It was less than an hour's work, but it took one working day.

"Sir, commercial properties are bought and sold less often. But these give maximum benefit to the officials. That is why everyone seems angry. But I am still surprised at how you got this done without any miscellaneous amount," Prateek said to Sid as we ran with the papers to digitally update our records that was to be done before 5:00 pm.

"Mr Mittal also seems disturbed," Sid said running.

"Yes sir, a little. He wanted you to pay the 'Miscellaneous' amount and not wait whole day," Prateek chuckled.

11

Great Mentors and Doing things by Self

"Hey, did you notice that?" I asked Sid. After the deal, we had come to the store to see it from the inside for the first time.

"What?" Sid asked.

"We are right next to the Reliance store."

Our store was in front of Reliance Footprints store. And it had a special significance to us. In our growing up years, Dhirubhai Ambani was a frequently used example, which our parents quoted to inspire us.

Dhirubhai Ambani's stories were always on our mind but on 6 July 2002, the day when Dhirubhai passed away, I suddenly experienced a hunger to find out more about him. I searched for books on him in all the possible book stores in Noida and Delhi. Finally one day, seeing me come into a bookstore very often in Noida Sector 18, a salesman told me that since he had passed away recently, the kind of content I wanted to read about him would take time to reach the market but he had something, which might interest me.

I wanted to know what Dhirubhai's dreams were and how he started out to accomplish them. The salesman handed me a copy of *Business Maharajas* by Geeta Piramal. The book covered many business houses of India. Dhirubhai's and the Reliance story was a part of the book.

It's been twelve years since I first read the book and each time I read it, I derive new inspiration from Dhirubhai's story. And today, it was a privilege to be standing next to the Reliance store which was an offspring of his dreams.

"Can you help me drag this drawer close to the window?" I asked Sid. I wanted to stand on it and clean the glass walls that were covered with window displays.

Seeing me clear the first window, our carpenter and painter also joined me and the work was completed in no time.

> **Start where you are. Use what you have. Do what you can.**
>
> **—Arthur Ashe**

The next step was to work on the interiors of the store. Hiring a professional meant a few more lakhs so we decided to do it ourselves. Armed with the designs on his tab, Sid called a meeting of our team – a carpenter, an electrician and a blacksmith. With elements from the best of designs across the world, the plan for the interior was soon ready.

The theme was white. The colours had to come only from the garments making them the main focus of the store. Enough space was left for customers to move around. The freshness was to be added by the money plant and other tiny plants in coffee mugs. The changing room made of a metal frame draped in sheer white fabric was going to be the main attraction.

The plan was in place. However, implementing it was not easy because we all were doing the interiors for the first time. But it was nothing compared to the hurdles we had faced to reach there.

Sid designed the first important things – stands and the changing room. The second important thing was designing the lighting for the store. Lights play a very significant role in the visual merchandising of the store. But the lights turned out to pose the biggest challenge. A stage came when we almost gave up and wanted to hire an external expert. But before that, we gave a last shot. We observed the lights being used by the clothing brands, did some research to find out about the various lights and their purpose. With all the knowledge, it took us not more than three hours to design the lighting for our store. All we needed was to get these lights at the most economic rate. We went to the country's most popular market for lights, Bhagirath Palace. Going there for the first time without knowing any specific shop was a difficult situation again. Finally, after spending half a day there, we got a good deal.

The third important thing was the masthead of the store. The aim was to keep it simple, bold and unique. We decided to do it on sun board. We re-used the sun board which we already had. We hired a specialised team on an hourly basis to complete it. Over a clean, black background, PRET CASTLE was written in white.

We decided to bring down the height of its placement a few inches so that we didn't require a spider man. Its height was not going to increase or decrease sales.

Using plants, leaving the ceiling as it is, using a non-electric masthead and doing things by ourselves like the interiors, lighting, the visit to Bhagirath Palace, designing the masthead, standee, bag, tag, and so on saved us many lakhs.

Doing things by oneself does not only save money, it gives an opportunity to reflect upon every fine detail.

We introduced the concept of sitting around the money plant. A set of four chairs were set up around the centre table with money plant for the visitors to sit and relax. Along with this, toffees for children, water and quick snacks for elders made them feel at home. And the self-designed changing room turned out to be a hit.

Most businesses fail not because they are not able to pull sales, but because their expenses are higher than the sales they make.

12

Off to Mars

While the store was being set up, DPOL was also set to become a rocket science.

One day on our way back to home from the mall, Sid told me that he had received an email from COFES – Congress of the Future of Engineering Software. They wanted to know more about DPOL.

COFES is a Silicon Valley conference. It is attended by the nukes of Silicon Valley like Xerox, Nasa, Lockheed Martin, Google's CEOs and promoters. The conference for 2013 was being conducted in collaboration with NASA, Palo Alto, USA.

Reaching home, Sid shared further details, "The email has come from Brad. He is the CEO of Cyon research. He is the one who organises COFES."

"Sounds great!" I said sleepily.

It had been a long day. Certain dimensions of the changing room had been measured incorrectly. But true to his routine, Sid was on dad's study table with his laptop reading out the details to me at 2:00 am.

The next night at 1:00 am India time, Sid had the Skype call with Brad. I was also awake working on an office presentation. An hour later, Sid entered the room looking very happy.

"Brad has been following DPOL for quite some time. He wants DPOL to be part of the COFES this year. He will schedule another Skype call after two days. This time the other board members of COFES will also join him."

In the next two days, Sid read about Brad's company and COFES to prepare for the call.

"White shirt and track pants at 2:00 am, what are you up to?" I asked Sid when I saw him roaming around in this weird combination.

"Going to join Brad's call," Sid said as he slipped out of the half open door of the bedroom.

I had completely forgotten about it. "But why the white shirt?"

"White will make me look fair. White reflects light," he laughed aloud.

He quickly closed the door after stepping out. He was going to the dining room to set up his laptop.

"Don't come outside until I finish my call," he returned to give the special instruction.

Sid walked in after an hour.

"How was your meeting?" I asked putting the television on mute. Mom also placed her books aside to listen to him.

"It was good. It was a senior industry panel. They liked the DPOL and want me to travel to the US to present my work."

After a pause he said, "I was taking it lightly again just like London Museum but it turned out to be a big thing. Life is strange, when I try nothing happens and then suddenly these unbelievable things happen when I least expect them."

Keep your head down and work with faith. Hard work gets rewarded, if not at that moment, but surely when you least expect it.

It was at such short notice and at the moment the priority was Pret Castle. The next day, Sid confirmed he would not be able to attend the conference in person but he would extend all possible support for his work to be presented in the conference.

Brad respected Sid's decision and connected him to Nat. Nat was a scientist at NASA.

Sid and Nat decided to meet every day on Skype at 2:00 am India time to build the presentation, which Nat was going to present on Sid's behalf.

Second day of their call, same instructions applied – do not walk behind me, preferably do not come out of the room. Dressed up formally in a white shirt, trousers and shoes, Sid made his way out of the room with his laptop.

He used his elbow to press the door handle and leg to push the door. His hands were busy. Besides the laptop, today he was also holding a lamp.

"Where are you taking dad's table lamp?"

"I am taking it to the dining room for my Skype with Nat."

"Why do you need a table lamp for a Skype call?"

"I need it. You do your work," he laughed and quickly stepped out of the room. I knew he was up to something.

I followed him out.

"I will stand here and say hello to your Nat unless you tell me why you using the table lamp."

"Go please. It is almost time," he said helplessly. "I need it."

This time he tried to keep a straight face, but I could see the mischief in his eyes.

He circled on his rolling chair and turned his back towards me and started to set up his laptop in hurry.

"Are you tracing your drawings for your call?" I asked.

For a minute I wanted to believe I was unnecessarily doubting him.

"Yes, yes, that only. Now you go," he said instantly and I knew he was lying.

"No, you tell me."

I pulled a chair and parked myself next to him.

He was irritated. There were only five minutes left for the call to start. He wanted me to leave immediately and explained, "A white shirt will make me fair and the lamp will make me bright," he said and grinned. "Happy now?"

"Aah... so you are enhancing your fairness."

"Lol! Yeah," he blushed.

Nat presented Sid's work at the conference. It was greatly appreciated.

Nat was in the core team that developed inflatable entry vehicles to land at different planets, including Mars. He believed that DPOL could be helpful in space research as it allowed manipulation of fabric structural properties in different axis and directions.

13

A Dream Come True

The French Connection

Clad in Indian ethnic wear, these two were our first customers after we inaugurated the store. They were from France and had come to India on a teacher's exchange programme in a nearby college. Their embassy had allowed them to visit India on a condition that they would wear Indian ethnic wear whenever they stepped out.

"Come on tell me, we have so many to try and it's about time we go back," the beautiful lady who was standing inside the changing room asked her friend who was waiting outside the changing room for her turn.

She was confused. However, she made up for the brief silence when she exclaimed, "I want the same one!"

"You liked this one so much? Really?" the lady stepped out of the changing room. She gracefully lifted up her heels and posed in the white flutter sleeve top that she wore over her salwar.

Her friend nodded briskly and turned her head to see if there were other white ones on the rack.

"We have more pieces of these," I said.

After they left, Sid and I exchanged a quick smile. It seems like we had a French connection. After the sales in Paris, the next sales where we were meeting our customers directly was on that day. We were in India but the customers who inaugurated the sales of our store were French.

We picked it up as a good sign from God who was telling us to go on. He can't appear everywhere so he creates events and instils beliefs in us to keep us motivated.

An assumption that was a risk yesterday had turned into a reality of today. The TATA story we based our assumption on came true every day. As expected, college students turned out to be our biggest customers.

It is obvious for students to spot any new business in their vicinity, but just when we were beginning to contemplate the options of advertising to reach beyond students, we saw visitors walking in on their own. Some were curious to look inside the changing room while others were fascinated with the money plants and other plants in the coffee mugs. Whatever reason drew them in, eventually they turned into our customers. Some shopped right away and some returned later. And it was a matter of a month that people started coming by word of mouth. The reasons were enough to not spend on advertisements for the time being.

With the increase in number of customers, we also soon learnt the rules of retail. Start late and call it a day late. It sells maximum on the weekends. On weekdays, maximum sales happen if Bollywood releases a super hit movie. Expect a drop in sales if there is a cricket match. If it is an India-Pakistan match, you might as well consider being closed. A low number of sales on few days should not matter, the weekends and movie weeks could alone lift up the average of the month.

The response was beyond our expectations. It was a great feeling that while living our dream, we became a part of lives of many. Those who sat by the money plant to catch their breath while their family members shopped shared their lives with us when they spoke about happy and sad moments of their lives.

We too longed to meet new people at our store. Each day was a day of a new story. Apart from clothes and fashion, the topics discussed were meditation, women empowerment and festivals.

In India, we celebrate festivals around the year and exchange gifts with friends and relatives. We also get gifts for family and friends when we return from a foreign land. But this giving and receiving of gifts sometimes turn complicated too. One such instance was narrated by Sujoy, my colleague. He went to London at the start of his career. After a year, when he was visiting India for the first time, he decided to take gifts for the relatives. Duty free liquor from the airport was already reserved for friends who had agreed to come to receive him only if he got premium whisky for them. So, for his uncles he bought nice formal shirts. All was fine and everyone was happy when he distributed the gifts. But then, one uncle asked him if he had really brought the gifts from London. The pack of shirts had a tag with 'Made in China' written on it. He tried to convince them, but in vain.

I had almost forgotten this incident but I recalled it when a group of Chinese boys and girls visited our store. They had come to India to attend the International Energy Conference. They have everything, the world knows it. I wondered what they would buy.

Six of them remained concentrated in one corner. They pulled some clothes from the hangers, discussed about them and left. And when I thought it was over, a larger group entered. But it left without buying anything as well. A few minutes later, a girl from the same group entered and asked me if I accepted cash. She wanted to buy a top for her mother. The boy who accompanied her persuaded her not to buy it. I got back to my work. But after sometime, the boy left and the girl bought the top. It felt happy to sell 'Made in India' to China.

Our German friend

We enjoy the vicinity of the colleges and International expo centre. Thus we meet people from all over the world. These exchange programme teachers and industry consultants and delegates come from all over the world.

"Very beautiful! I have not seen anything this creative," said Johann. This man from Germany was buying Christmas gifts for his wife and two daughters.

He was completely amused with the t-shirt that was hand painted by Sid. The t-shirt had two small mice sitting on the two ends of a slice of a watermelon.

Johann wanted to buy it. We had only one of it but we could not say 'no' because it was going to be a Christmas gift. We decided to take a picture of it and let it go.

Johann volunteered to hold the t-shirt for the picture and said, "I can understand your love for your work. Only a few see beyond money and those who do, go a long way."

Johann picked up many clothes for his family. He was in no hurry, but after spending almost an hour, it was time for him to leave. We asked his details for customer records.

"It's confidential. I can't share them," he said. "You see, I am a man on a secret mission," he winked.

The next moment he pulled a card from his wallet and said, "Here is my card. Only for you though. "

I reciprocated his friendliness by asking him,"You don't look like a tourist."

"Yes, I am not a tourist. I am engaged in a contract with an Indian company, so these days I live in India."

"Okay," I said and watched him keeping his bags on the chair. He was not leaving now. He prepared to talk.

"They have booked a room for me in the hotel of this mall for two years. I am going home for Christmas and will be back soon. I would spend twenty days at home then some days in Bangkok."

"Bangkok?" I asked.

"That's the only way I get to enter India else the immigration gets suspicious of me. Seeing me come back in less than a month, they ask a lot of questions so I wait to complete a month by staying in Bangkok for a few days before I come here."

"Explaining your situation to immigration should not be difficult for you. For a German, you speak very good English."

"Yes, I have travelled across the globe and have exhausted six passports."

"And do you not get tired of travelling?"

"I don't get tired because I get to meet interesting people and I visit places which I never thought I would ever visit in my life."

Very comfortable by now, Johann started sharing stories after stories. His excitement could match that of a school boy who is excited to play his X-Box after the exams. He went on.

"You know, once upon a time I went to Moscow. Alex had waited for months to meet me. He took me to a plush corporate office and showed me a long staircase railing. The railing was state of the art and looked extremely beautiful by its grandeur design and the material it was made of. He said it was hollow but he wanted the same thing to be made in solid and installed at his home. I took a closer look and noticed that it was made of stainless steel and what he desired was going to cost him millions. I didn't think of it to be a realistic project that he would wish to pursue after knowing the expenses he would have to incur. So I didn't respond to him until he came back to me the next day. I told him that the entire project would require 1.2 tonnes of stainless steel which meant it was going to cost a fortune. To my surprise, Alex asked me not to worry about the price and wanted me to start the work as soon as possible. A fortune on a railing! Was he kidding? Anyway, I decided to visit his home. It wasn't a fortune for him is what I discovered the next day. He lived three streets away from President Putin. His house was in the shape of a half submarine submerged in water. I was to stay in his home. His home was like an elite luxurious hotel. The house buzzed with theme parties late into the night, and the parties offered anything you could think of under the sun. Food, drinks, girls, music, fun – you name it and you'd have it. But despite the late night parties, Alex was up early in the morning. He read newspapers of different languages and every morning a set of newspapers and magazines were arranged on a table in front of him in the garden. As he strolled in his garden with a newspaper in his hands, he was surrounded by stout gunmen. There were also eight cameras that were visible from my balcony. He was definitely not a common man. I suspected he was a mafia don but I never dared to confirm my suspicion. All I wanted was to finish my work quickly and get out of the place safely. Almost a month later, the stainless steel railing was installed in his home. It looked magnificent. He was happy and it was time for me to leave. On the day I had to leave, he asked me if I had any wish, which he could fulfil. I wanted to see the city of Moscow. He said that the traffic was so bad that it would take around five hours to reach even one place. But he didn't dismiss my request and asked me to wait in the lounge. After ten minutes, a helicopter landed on his private helipad. He said to me, 'Here it is'.

"I boarded the helicopter. And it didn't take me more than two hours to see the city of Moscow."

"So did you finally come to know who he was?" I asked with eyes brimming with curiosity.

"Yes, I did. There were circumstances due to which I came to know of his identity."

Johann continued the story.

"When I was leaving Moscow to go back home, I got late as we started for the airport. But Alex asked me not to worry. The next moment I was fastened to my seat and we were on a twelve-lane motorway. Traffic moved fast and so did we. But to reach the airport on time, we could not go at this speed. I sat with no hope but things changed after a few miles when Alex pulled the car to one side and took out a blue light from the trunk. He threw the light on the top of the car. The light got stuck on the head of the car and blinked in electric blue colour. After this, he immediately changed gears at the lightning speed and we entered a special lane to zoom away. We reached airport just in time. I got ready to get down but Alex didn't stop at the departures. I was amazed but I sat quiet. At high speed,

Alex very confidently entered a restricted zone. Automatic accesses were granted as we crossed the barriers. No manual intervention, just a few lights blinked on his windscreen and we were standing under the aircraft I had to board. It felt great but reality struck me soon. I realised I could not leave the country with no stamps on my passport. I had by-passed security check and immigration. I expressed my concern to Alex. I expected that Alex would arrange for my passport to be sent to the immigration desk for the stamp. But there was more of Alex that I had to see. He took my passport, pressed a few buttons of a secured box that he had near the hand brake, took out his stamps and stamped my passport."

"This sounds like a James Bond movie!" Sid said.

"Yes, very much but it was rather scary too and I wanted to get back home safe and sound," he laughed.

"Who was the man? I asked again. Mafia as you suspected?"

"Aah...no, no. He was a very important man. He was among the top ten of the US President's delegates."

"Wow! Did you meet him again?" I asked.

"No, I didn't meet him. I don't get time. There is another client of mine in Baltimore. He keeps calling me to come and see the helicopters that he has bought recently."

After a brief pause, Johann told us another story. "When I find time, I want to be with my family in my country where I cover 500 kilometeres in four hours in my car. I love my car. It is a two clutch car – one in hand and one automatic. I use automatic usually and prefer driving at night. I also love fishing," he said and pretended to have a fishing rod in his hand.

"What do you do with the fish? Eat them up?" I asked.

"No!"

"Then, sell them?" I asked.

"Exchange it for beer and sumptuous grilled food. There are many beach restaurants in the small towns of Germany. You know about life in the countryside? I love it!"

I nodded my head and gave him time to continue talking. It felt he had not spoken for many days and when he found us he wanted to just talk and talk.

"The water there is full of fish. The fishermen can turn millionaires if they do an organised business. But they don't do it. They are content. There is a very popular story about it. One day a businessman went to a fisherman and said that he had an idea to turn the fisherman into a millionaire. He suggested that the fisherman must preserve and start exporting his fish. After some days, the fisherman would become rich and would be able to buy a boat to do more fishing. By selling more fish, he could earn more money and one day the fisherman could have his own containers in the ships going around the world. Later, the fisherman could buy a resort by the beach and enjoy life with his wife and kids. The businessman's idea was to help the fisherman earn money at a faster pace and then retire early to have a peaceful life. The fisherman patiently listened to the businessman and said that I am already living what you are asking me to dream. Why would I waste my life to get back what I already have?"

"Very thoughtful. These days we find similar stories on social media networks too."

"Okay, yeah internet is good but I just check emails and they are also scanned before they reach me."

"Why are your emails scanned?"

"I work with the world's top most automobile companies. There is a fear of their blueprints getting leaked so they scan my emails. That is why I said earlier that my work is highly confidential."

"Do they scan the emails of all the employees?"

"No. There are just a few who deal with blueprints. I am among the six people across the world who deal in this level of blueprinting in the automobile world."

I could understand emails getting scanned but I was surprised to imagine life without internet and asked him further, "And why do you not use the internet?"

He smiled and answered, "I know what you are thinking, but please don't take me to be an old man. I have thirty years of experience in my profession but I am of the new age. I am just forty-five. I am not on the internet because it is again a part of the confidential contracts I sign."

"That means you started working at the age of fifteen."

"Yes."

"You are among the top six in your field in the automobile industry and you started work at the age of fifteen. Now please tell me what did you study?" I asked.

"I didn't study at all."

"What! Then what do you do that makes you so special? I want to know so that I can also be like you," Sid said.

"You don't have to be. You are already very similar to me, apart from that school thing. I know you went to a good school but otherwise, like you, I also do what I love. I am passionate about what I do," he said and also broke the suspense. "I have been welding since I was fifteen."

"Welding the metal pieces, right?" I asked.

"Yes and today when I weld, people of my age who are highly educated and trained are amazed at my skills. My skills have compensated for the lack of formal education. "

This was our first meeting with Johann. After this, he kept coming back regularly.

Education is just a catalyst. It is your skill, hard work, sincerity and passion that take you far. If you have these basics in place, success will come to you sooner or later.

Today

A month back, Aditya posted an update on his Facebook timeline. He uploaded his picture, receiving an award for his service in welfare activities. Many people had liked and commented on it. As I scrolled down, I saw Sid too had put in a comment.

Sid wrote, "Let me expand Pret Castle and I will fund it all."

With all good intentions, Sid is busy expanding Pret Castle – his dream venture. While he thinks of growth, he also secretly convinces his customers not to buy some things which are very close to him. That's the conflict between an artist and a businessman. He has a rack which has few pieces which he has denied to sell. But he keeps them there to see the admiration in the eyes of art lovers.

One of many Dad's friends who once criticised Sid, visited us recently. He said, "At the time of retirement, everyone is asked to leave, but at this early age you already have an establishment of your own, which you will never have to leave. I keep telling my son to do something like this. Your Dad was a visionary. And I feel sad that when I was chatting with him once, I asked him that being an IITian why did he let his son take up fashion designing when he was ranked 3rd in all India to study at a premiere Architecture and Planning college? But I understood the vision of your father at the time of my retirement." Uncle had tears in his eyes.

Aditya is preparing for his IAS exams and continues to contribute in the social welfare activities. He stays in Delhi and travels to his hometown Patna. He is involved in social activities in

Patna as well. Pawas who is also in Patna now, helps Aditya.

Pawas didn't go to Bollywood, though I still keep telling him to try his luck in Bollywood. After graduating from college, Pawas briefly worked with Mintraz and now he is living in Patna to support his family. He is planning to start a label where he plans to sell his dangerous zardozi ethnic wear. Cured of his OCD to a large extent, he is mostly seen in formal wear.

My business partner Amit AD, is now doing VM (visual merchandising) for an international cosmetics brand and heading a zone. He is happy. I don't think he would return to business. The handicrafts we bought, are sitting in a box. I brought them from Bangalore to Delhi. Sid and I plan to use them someday.

Sapan and I live in New Zealand. But as per the pact, now Sid is earning. I have taken a break from my IT career to pursue my dream of writing and to expand Pret Castle. I wish to complete my incomplete stories and click pictures of people seen around with Pret Castle bags. It was a dream to see people walk in the mall with the Pret Castle bags and today when the dream has come true, our joy knows no bounds.

The twelve dogs in Bangalore have grown up. I once went to meet them when I went to Bangalore for work during the IBMS days. The puppies did not recognize me but their two mothers did. In Greater Noida, we have another set of dogs that live outside our house. Apart from them, we continue to take care of other dogs, cows and birds that need our help. Abhinav continues to love Jazz Billu. The airlines has transferred Abhinav from Mumbai to Delhi to fly a new set of aircrafts, so Jazz Billu has also moved to Delhi.

And how can I forget Mohit and Mehul. They are pursuing their research after earning their Ph.D. One in the US and another in Europe. I am not in touch with them but I am glad we didn't become them.

Mohit Mehul's research reminds me of our new friend. She is the wife of a professor in India's top business school. One day, I drove her from Greater Noida to Noida. I was going to office so I offered to drop her to Noida. On the way, she mentioned that she had returned from the US the previous night. She had gone there to meet her two daughters who were doing their Ph.D in different universities. I asked her about her visit. She gave me a very surprising answer. She said visiting the US was good but she wasn't happy with what her daughters were doing. She said that they didn't know where they were heading. Research they did, so now Ph.D, but they didn't seem to have a vision. She then said that anything will turn out well if it is done with a vision. But people are just following the trend, and they lack vision in this competitive world. And finally before getting down she said that she so wished her children could have also done something like we brother sister had done.

It felt nice to see that we could also inspire someone. But all I wanted to say to her was that let's not compare us or anyone with any other. Everyone is different and has different dreams, goals, skills and circumstances in life.